MARION HALLIGAN is one of Australia's most important writers, with a long list of literary prizes to her credit. She has been shortlisted for the Commonwealth Writers' Prize and the Miles Franklin Literary Award, and has been awarded *The Age* Book of the Year, the ACT Book of the Year (three times), the Nita B. Kibble Award, the Steele Rudd Award, the Braille Book of the Year, the 3M Talking Book of the Year and the Geraldine Pascall Prize for critical writing. She lives in Canberra and has an AM for services to literature.

Goodbye
Sweetheart

Marion
Halligan

ALLEN&UNWIN
SYDNEY · MELBOURNE · AUCKLAND · LONDON

First published in 2015

This project has been assisted by the Australian
Government through the Australia Council for
the Arts, its arts funding and advisory body.

Australian Government

Allen & Unwin
83 Alexander Street
Crows Nest NSW 2065
Australia
Phone: (61 2) 8425 0100
Email: info@allenandunwin.com
Web: www.allenandunwin.com

Cataloguing-in-Publication details are available
from the National Library of Australia
www.trove.nla.gov.au

ISBN 978 1 76011 129 8

Internal design by Sandy Cull, gogoGingko
Set in 13.25/17 pt Perpetua by Midland Typesetters, Australia
Printed and bound in Australia by Griffin Press

10 9 8 7 6 5 4 3 2 1

For John

CONTENTS

'One ray at a time day casts off its boredom,
bursts into flame and spews incomprehensible splendour.'

—*DIVAGATIONS*,
STÉPHANE MALLARMÉ

THIS STORY BEGINS BY WATER

This story begins by water. William remembered reading those words, once, and presumably there had been a story to follow, but what it was he had no recollection. But water always made him think of them. This story begins by water.

Today the pool was empty of swimmers. He'd come in from the gym and there it was, completely still. But soon the whole surface quaked and heaved with his presence. Water slopped through the grilles, plastic imitating wood, that surrounded its edges. He trudged up and down, not in the lap lane, that was for serious swimmers, not walkers, and he'd noticed that a swimmer could do two laps in the time it took him to do one. The water offered a lot of resistance, that was the point. His was not the torpedo body of the swimmer cleaving through, it was a creature out of its element. Sometimes he trailed his arms and that made it harder, sometimes he used them in a finny manner, which didn't make him any faster, but exercised them. Sometimes he skipped, bouncing up and down out of the water. Skipping: he couldn't have done that on dry land to save his life. But the water as well as resisting buoyed him, he could do all sorts of things in the water that would have been impossible on dry land. Paradoxical, it was.

He trudged up and down. The pool was twenty metres long, so if he went along and back fifty times that would be a kilometre. He usually spent half an hour, that was enough. According to the noticeboard the temperature was 29.5 degrees, but it didn't feel particularly warm, and when he skipped and bounced his shoulders got cold. The room that housed the pool was large and lofty. He remembered how nineteenth-century railway stations were called cathedrals of steam, with their towering iron arches intricately formed to support their roofs. Did that mean that for their architects travel was the new religion, not God? He looked at the tall roof. Was this a cathedral of swimming, for the new religion of fitness? A church perhaps, it wasn't so large or grand as a cathedral. Or maybe a chapel. Faith through works. There were no mysteries in its vaulted spaces, unlike the great iron railway stations or the soaring stones of gothic buildings, more beautiful than ever their function required.

There were immense windows on each of the four sides, and from the north the late winter sun shone across the water in huge paned patterns. It was warm in the sun; did that mean that the windows weren't double-glazed? It seemed extravagant with the heating. He confined his movement to a patch of sun, stretching his legs and swimming his arms as he basked in it. He lifted his head to its warmth and closed his eyes so the light broke into glittering iridescence on his eyelashes. He could be a young man, limber and lithe.

This story begins by water. What sort of a story? he wondered. A tale of smugglers and a rowboat with muffled oars, pulling into a dark cavern barely above water level? Of excisemen and torches and blunderbusses and muttered oaths? In that case it would be out of one of the boys' own annuals passed on by older cousins. He felt the delight they'd been in his book-hungry post-war child-hood. Or perhaps some naval yarn, of ships and sailors and one of the wars that provided such excitements, Napoleon and Nelson, or German U-boats, or Japanese submarines. Maybe Conrad and the yearning voice of his narrator summoning up his youth, the unforgettable odour of the East, and man being born to trouble as the sparks fly upwards.

He rested his body in the water, his arms and legs moving ably, gracefully; in the water he was not ungainly. A gainly fellow he is in the water, he said to himself, closing his eyes and rejoicing in the sun.

This story begins by water. The beach, and this gainly fellow standing on the sand, the waves breaking at his feet. A young woman who has been swimming stands up in the shallows and begins to walk to the shore. She is wearing a black bikini and is slender and shapely, her skin is pale brown, her legs long, her waist small, her hips curved out, her breasts lively. She has dark hair in curls that lie close to her head like a sculpture in marble.

A large wave comes crashing up behind her and knocks her over. She is unprepared for it and flounders, is swirled around and takes a minute to find her feet again. Nothing dangerous, nothing that needs a gainly fellow to rush and rescue her. Just an ordinary dumping. She stands up and smooths her no longer sculpted hair out of her eyes, rubs water off her face, and it is only when she lowers her arms, brushing them down across her breasts, that she realises her bikini bra has come off, that she is quite naked down to her hips. She folds her arms across her chest and looks nervously around, maybe for the missing bit of swimsuit, maybe to see who is watching. This is the moment for him; he's given himself a large blue and white striped beach towel and he steps forward and wraps her in it. He could let his arm brush her nipple as he does so but that would not be gallant. She gives him a tremulous smile. The sun shines benignly upon them.

You sit on the sand, he says, I'll see if I can find it. He steps into the sea, which is quite cold. He doesn't think there's much chance of finding a skimpy bit of black bikini washing about in the surf like a piece of seaweed but it is the thing to try. He wants to bring it back to her, to hold the towel up for modesty while she puts it on, and sit on the sand beside her and talk.

The pain was quick and sharp. It came at him from his left arm, that had been making gentle comfortable arabesques in the buoying water. It pierced suddenly, shooting sparking up the arm, surprising him. He thought, what is this? but by that time it was not his arm it was his heart, and he could no longer think, the pain was a spasm through his whole body and there was no part of him that could do anything. There was a brief image of the girl, further up the beach, and the bikini top washing like seaweed in the retreating waves. There was a fragment of light, the warm sun on his body, graceful in the water, and then it was all lost.

Usually he did his exercises by the edge of the pool, holding on to it as he walked sideways, trudging up and down beside it, but today he was in the middle, by the floating barrier that marked out the lap lane, where the sun shone and was broken into a pattern of wavering rainbow lines of light on the blue and white tiled floor. He had pills, but not in the water with him. The pain came again, in a violent kick through his body that thrust him backwards, somersaulting him down into the warm water which was nowhere too deep to stand up in. But he no longer knew that, and nor did his body, it floated down through the water, turning idly, and finally surfaced again, face down.

A heart attack, that was probably what killed him, said a doctor, later. But there was water in the lungs, and that was evidence of drowning, was it not, said the man's wife, who considered suing the hotel for negligence. Somebody should have been there, somebody should have paid attention, he could have been saved.

THE GYM IS BUSY

In the gym the bodies are youthful: lean, tanned, muscular. Though sometimes the faces surprise: toned, taut, but oddly old. Tortoise faces growing out of dolphins.

The bodies in the pool are elderly, pale, plump if not fat, baggy if not plump. Like the woman who went padding carefully from the change room, pushing open the heavy door to the pool space. Straightaway she saw William, and straightaway she saw that something was wrong. His body floating face down just below the surface, his arms loose, the water rocking him in its gentle pumping tide. At her age she thought it was time to expect death, and there death was.

She began to scream and backed out the door and turned and ran. Tried to run. The floor was wet from all the dripping bodies that had traversed it. That floor was never dry, except perhaps in the middle of the night. She slipped and fell and broke her hip. Now she was screaming with pain. A blond guy came running out of the gym, his trainers gripping on the tiles, sure-footed, not slipping. I'm a doctor, he said. The woman stopped screaming on a breathless hiccup and moaned and fainted. People crowded. Is she dead? they asked. The doctor ran into the change room to get his keys out of the locker so he could go to his car and get his bag. Keep back, he said, give her air. Keep the people back, he said to a personal trainer and the receptionist, get some towels and cover her up. Don't move her!

One of the crowding people looked through the glass door into the pool. He stared, and peered, and pushed the door open. My god, he said, some geezer's carked it. My god, he shouted, and other people came. Don't touch him, said the first man. A woman looked down at William's speckled back. What if he's not dead? she asked. Look at him, said the first man. William's body rocked gently in the water. The movement of the water was like breathing, but it seemed clear that William was not. Nevertheless the personal trainer jumped in and turned him over, pulled him up the shallow steps and taking a little rubber protective device from his pocket, began mouth-to-mouth resuscitation.

The doctor's hands were careful on the body of the old woman, still lying unconscious. They knew what they expected to find. An ambulance came and took her away. William had to wait for the police. The doctor pronounced him dead. The manager, who had finally been found, felt pale. It's a risky business, a broken hip at her age, said the doctor. It's a dangerous floor you've got there.

The receptionist searched through the pigeonholes for the plastic cards which would tell him who William and the woman were. It would be the manager's job to inform their families.

A daughter said, I've been afraid of this.

The wife was a voice on an answering machine. The manager could not talk to that.

LYNETTE PLANS A SALE

When I decide to go it'll be ethnic, said Janice. Wine with meals, and the food should be better.

Imagine, just because you're old, not having wine with meals, said Lynette. What kind of ethnic do you have in mind?

Italian, I think. Though Greek could be okay. Lots of vegetables. Very healthy, said Janice. In her teens she'd turned herself into Jan, liking the laconic monosyllable, but in her fifties she decided she preferred the prettier Janice after all. It had been years, and people were still not used to it.

Not that we're going to need it for a while, of course.

Oh no. But you have to plan, so you don't get carted off to some substandard hole. By the way, have you talked to Jilly Parker? She's telling everyone about this marvellous Chinese medicine person she's found, cured her menopause with herbs.

Cured her menopause! That's something. They both laughed.

It's enough to make you laugh like a drain, said Lynette.

She must be pushing seventy, said Janice. Claiming to be menopausal is big-noting herself.

When they calmed down, Lynette said, We should start our own. No, seriously. Get a bunch of like-minded friends together and set up our own place.

Angus was keen on that, said Janice. He wanted to buy an old warehouse in Newcastle and convert it into luxury flats, with lifts and terraces, and a caretaker's quarters, to look after us. Could rent them out, be an investment, till we got old enough to need it. Too late, now. All the warehouses are snapped up. Already converted and costing millions. And now poor Angus has got too young to be thinking of retirement plans. He'll be working till he's a hundred to pay the school fees.

Angus had run off with one of the young interns in his practice. He had a new baby now. Janice liked to make bitter jokes about this but she didn't care much any more. She enjoyed her freedom from Angus's demands, and there was the shop, and a pleasant chap, a widower, younger than Janice though you'd never guess, well enough off, and he liked to travel. He'd have liked to live with her, too, but Janice said she wasn't having that, she'd been there done that, BTDT as her children had once said, but wouldn't now; an attentive companion and lover who didn't live in, that was perfect.

The business was a kitchenware shop, the scene of this conversation. It was Wednesday evening and the shop was closed, they were working on the sale starting Friday.

I think the melon ballers should go in, said Janice. Nobody ever buys them.

No, it's odd. I remember when I bought mine, how thrilled I was, such a good thing to have.

Do you ever use it now?

Can't say I do.

So, you see. I think melon balls are in pretty much the same league as radish roses. Far too artificial.

These wine sealers—down to half? Nobody likes them, it's obvious at a glance that the vacuum sets are better.

We need some loss leaders too. We can't just mark down the junk that nobody wants.

Even if it's the only reason for having a sale in the first place? Okay, what?

I wondered about some of the linen tea towels. People tend to resist them. Think they're lovely, but too dear.

Will that be a loss leader?

Not knives, said Janice. Never knives. What about some of the Moroccan tagines, down to cost?

Oh, they're so gorgeous . . .

I reckon the main point of this exercise is what we've bought that doesn't sell. And not do it again. Be ruthless on both counts.

Only up to a point. I think a good kitchen shop has to have a good range. Even if things hardly ever sell, we should stock them.

This was a conversation they had every time they had a sale. They always enjoyed it. Lynette thought they never came to any useful conclusions, but Janice said they did. And the fact was that the shop, called Batterie de Cuisine, was a good business, it did its job well and made a lot of money. Lynette was pleased that she had turned her old job of cooking and her fondness for buying curious objects overseas into a commercial success, especially since at the beginning their husbands, who were colleagues, had been hugely sceptical of the whole business and made endless jokes about it.

The graveyard of good money, they called it. The sink. Lynette's husband called it the Junket Shop. Angus said it would be a failure even as a tax dodge. Aren't you lucky we give you a chance to sharpen your wits, said Lynette. They need it, said Janice, being so very very dull.

Janice and Lynette were equal partners but Janice did not ever feel so equal as Lynette. Janice had wanted some sort of business; Lynette had wanted this one. The shop's name was her idea; Batterie still gave Janice the notion of fighting going on, cannon shots and shouting, the racket of instruments of war. And it was Lynette who loved the things they sold, all the intricate, erudite, abstruse objects, for which there was such an enthusiastic market. Janice never ceased to be amazed by the people—it wasn't just women—who coveted these things. Lynette walked through the shop touching them for the sheer pleasure of it. The nutmeg graters, in the form of lids to small satiny steel boxes in which the nutmegs could be kept. The new range of baking pans that looked like rubber and were as flexible, so you could cook little cakes or tarts or whatever and with a bend of the pan out they would pop. In gorgeous colours, especially a dark crimson. Supposed to come out of space technology somehow. Dozens of whisks; just to look at them made your wrists want to start beating something. A big copper jam pan, with two black iron handles. If somebody didn't buy that soon Lynette would. Janice teased her: how could she make any money if she kept buying the stock? Iron omelette pans; Lynette already had several, but not in every size. Quasi-professional espresso coffee machines; her family already had one of those, too, she'd given it as a house present last Christmas. Wooden spoons: never can you have too many wooden spoons. The naming and ordering and pricing of these things, laid on industrial metal shelving or in big willow baskets, gladdened Lynette's heart.

There was something spiritual in this accumulation of objects. They were material things, but somehow the number and diversity and usefulness ancient or modern of them transcended the mundane, gave them power.

It's a cult, kitchenware, said Janice.

Down the back were the foodstuffs, the jams and preserves, the olive oils, the vinegars, the array of marvellously named pastas, the black cooking chocolate, the tiny tins of truffles, the foie gras, the goose fat.

Beautifully packaged heart attacks, said Janice.

Not the way the French eat them. In moderation, with a little red wine.

Sometimes Lynette's daughter Erin came into the shop after school and they went home together. Lynette didn't often stay until the end of the day, she came in the morning and liked to get home to make dinner. Janice didn't care for mornings and didn't do much dinner-making. They had people who worked for them, but they liked to have one or other of the owners there. Sometimes they had lunch together in one of the local cafes; they teased one another and laughed a lot. Lynette enjoyed Janice's insouciance. No husband, children nicely settled, she didn't care for any of the old rules she'd once lived by.

You're not really thinking of a retirement home yet, are you? said Lynette.

Not of doing it any moment soon, but you've got to think ahead. Especially if we create our own. I like that idea. Who'll we have? We should make a list.

We're organising a sale, remember? After that's done.

I'll send Angus an email and ask him does he want to be in it, said Janice.

Oh, are we asking ex-spouses?

Could be fun.

Malice often is.

Malice? Generosity, I'd have thought, said Janice. But her smile was malicious.

Janice became aware of dark figures at the doorway of the shop, peering as though they wanted to come in. She shook her head and waved her arms to indicate it was closed. The figures didn't go away. She noticed that the cumquats on either side of the door hadn't been brought in. It was dark outside. The figures loomed. The light inside shone on the glass, making them dim shapes in the darkness. Now one was knocking on the glass.

Lynette stopped sticking on cut-price labels to look. They don't believe no, she said.

The door rattled with the knocking, making it very loud. I'll tell them to go away, said Janice.

When she got near the door she saw that the figures were police. A lean young woman and a stocky man. The woman asked for Lynette by name. Would you like to sit down, she said. Perhaps your friend would like to make a cup of tea? I am afraid . . .

Lynette said, Erin? in a voice that rasped in her throat, and the woman said no, that it was her husband, and explained about the swimming pool and William being found dead.

There were no chairs in the shop so Lynette slumped against the counter. No, she said, not William. Not William. Saying his name as though it had a particular music she'd spoken before. And a magic that would not let harm come to him. The policewoman said, Tea? And Janice got the step stool for Lynette to sit on and made a mug of peppermint tea and brought it to her, thinking it is always the same: bad news, disbelief, tea. She put her hand on Lynette's back and rubbed it gently; Lynette's head sagged against Janice's hip bone.

She didn't cry, she just repeated small phrases in a faint, disbelieving voice. Not William . . . so much . . . so much . . . he can't . . . dead? . . .

Janice kept rubbing. Drink the tea while it's hot, she said. I know you don't like sugar, but I put a bit in, it's good, you know, when there's shock . . . The policewoman nodded.

Desolation. And always now the sweet minty sharpness of this tea will be the taste of desolation. Lynette sitting on the step stool in her shop tastes the absence of William. Words come into her head. *He is drowned. Oh he is drowned.* Where do they come from? Drowned, drowned. William will know. And with a flush of peppermint nausea to her throat she sees: no William, ever again.

To know, to tell, to smile, to offer words like jewels heaped rich and gleaming in her open hands. He's taken the marvellous words and left her with desolation. Loss. Grief. But first of all, drama. The production of death and funeral. The command performance. For whatever else you thought you were going to do, like having a sale in your shop, is suddenly not any kind of consideration. The burial must take place. William is dead, the peppermint tea is harsh in her throat, she must bear it. All the curious and erudite objects on their shelves, in their baskets, mute as always, but no help any more. Smug, impervious, quotidian, and grief does not compute. William is dead, who kept the words, and they have gone with him.

Is there someone you could stay with tonight? asked the policewoman. You shouldn't be on your own.

Come home with me, said Janice. I'll look after you.

Erin. Lynette jumped up, pushed the mug into the nearest hands. Erin. I have to go home and tell Erin.

She stopped and sat down again. Erin would be at home, doing her homework, watching the television, talking on the phone. Safe in the fixtures of her world. No need to hurry to tell her that one of its pillars is gone, that it is all tumbling down.

I have to try to hold it up, said Lynette. But it's going to be lopsided. She swayed. She felt dizzy. Can't even hold herself up and she the only prop in this edifice of family, friends, work. Former wives. Other children. Breathe deep, strong reviving oxygen. Be strong, to tell Erin that her beloved father is dead. And then, all the others.

What's Erin's favourite takeaway? asked Janice. You go, I'll finish here and come round with some food. It's late, you need food. Turkish? Okay. These people will drive you home.

Mostly Lynette walked down to the shop. Her house was just about as close as parking.

The phone rang. Janice picked it up. Your ma's on her way, she said. Food's coming. And to Lynette: Off you go. I can manage here.

Death. Hospitals. War. They are the same. A mixture of boredom and fear. Terrified boredom. Bored terror. And it is not you dealing with it, it is another person that you have become, that has taken you over, whom you watch with your chest caving in and wonder, what is happening? What is she doing? The real you is happy, her loved ones are safe in her care, this other person is demented and bereft. Poor thing.

Erin cried. She sat at the kitchen table and sobbed. Not my daddy, she howled. My dad. He wouldn't do that. She hiccupped. Not my daddy, she said, over and over. Lynette put her arms around her and the girl buried her head. So many tears. They were both soaked.

You did say Thai, didn't you? said Janice, carrying in a plastic bag packed with boxes of food and another clanking with bottles of wine. Lynette picked up morsels with a fork but her mouth didn't seem to want to take them in. Though it readily swallowed the wine.

Don't let me get drunk, she said to Janice.

Best thing for you.

No. Then I'd have a hangover tomorrow. No.

Enough, then. Not too much.

Erin pushed her bowl away. How can anyone eat at a time like this, she said.

You need to keep your strength up, said Janice. And Thai food, your favourite.

Erin looked surprised. She said, The food's delicious. It's me. I'm not hungry.

I should telephone, said Lynette. She sat at the kitchen table and pictured herself doing that. Crossing the room to the telephone. Picking it up. Pressing the buttons for the numbers.

Shall I get the phone? said Janice.

The picture: dialling the numbers. It froze there.

I don't know the numbers, she said. Ex-wives. Who knows the numbers of her husband's ex-wives?

I'll look in the study, said Janice. But when she saw the impossibly tidy room she wasn't hopeful. It was a nominal study, a space furnished by a wife for her husband because that's the appropriate thing, but not looking as though it was ever used. A cedar desk, on it some beautifully bound notebooks with marbled covers. All empty. A stand with pens and an antique inkwell. A small colour-coordinated notebook computer. *New Yorker*s in a pile. Bookshelves. The armchair in the corner beside them looked as though it might have been sat in, sometimes. She looked in the desk drawers: sticky tape, a stapler, paper clips, a tray of perfect sharp pencils. No addresses.

Lynette pictured William leaving the house in the morning. Picking up his wallet, keys, phone from the *vide-poche* on the dressing table. He laughed at that, saying, How very posh. I can't help it if there isn't an English word, she said. A pocket emptier, he said. It was of course a present from her. A present for the man who has everything. Very useful it had turned out to be. It was a ceramic bowl, made by Vic Greenaway. If you put things into it too roughly you might break it. So, William picking up his bits from the dressing table. His satchel from the chair in the hall, which would have his Filofax in it. The satchel. Where was that? In his car. Where was his car? At the pool.

Tomorrow, she said to Janice. I'll have to get his car. And I have to go and identify . . .

All those grim movie moments. The trolley wheeled in. The drawer rolled out. The sheet pulled back. The stricken face which perhaps a second before had been hopeful: of course it was all a mistake.

Janice made Sleepytime tea. Fifteen somniferous herbs. Have you got sleeping pills? she asked.

Lynette shook her head. I'm asleep on my feet. I won't need pills. She gave Janice a nightgown and a new toothbrush. Use any of the gunk you feel like, she said, waving at the shelf of bottles in the bathroom. There was a big fluffy towel on the heated rail. Excellent *House and Garden* orderliness. Janice wished her own apartment was quite so just-so. The sheets smelt of lavender. The books by the bed looked interesting.

Lynette lay for a long time in a scented creamy bath, her

head on a pillow, inert while the water cooled and had to be topped up with more hot, picturing William. Pushing back the chair in his office, standing, tidying papers, putting things in his satchel. Turning off the lights. Walking down the corridor. Past the reception and waiting room. Calling the lift. No, walking down the stairs. He liked to exercise when he could. Down to the parking lot. Pressing the button on the remote to unlock his car. Plucking the knees of his fine wool suit to keep the creases sharp. Wearing his cashmere overcoat? The weather was cold. Driving to the hotel. Picking up the bag with his swimmers, the shampoo for washing his hair after. The pool . . . No. Stop there. With all those small daily acts, and not ever thinking they would be the last time ever.

She shivered, and got out of the bath. She was too tired to dry her body. She wrapped herself in a big bathrobe and sat on the edge of the bed. Janice had turned the doona back. Not quite chocolate on the pillow. She gazed at the tall cedar chest of drawers. One of the knobs had a little V-shaped nick in it. At what stage of its life, spanning two centuries now, had that happened? In anger, somebody throwing a heavy object? Or accidentally, on one of its moves in or out of the many houses it would have lived in? So many things you couldn't know, and each one of them part of a narrative that had been important to someone.

She pulled her nightgown out from under her pillow and let the bathrobe fall off her shoulders. She was so tired, if she didn't lie down soon her flesh would slide off her bones and slump to the floor in a glistening mass of folds and coils, leaving her skeleton sitting there trying to work out how to put it on again, one foot into the leg, the other; pulling up the shapeless weight of her hips, fitting it to her buttocks; shrugging her arms in; then smoothing her face on to her skull, shaking her hair into place. Arranging her breasts. Making sure her heart was in the right place. Her lungs, her stomach. What a frightful effort all that would be. She'd never manage it.

The bed, her bed, didn't have William in it. Never would again. But if she began to think this, William not here, or there, never ever again William anywhere, each absence would be like a footstep in quicksand, sliding away and swallowing her up. She tipped herself over so her head was on the pillow, dragged her legs up on to the bed, pulled the doona over. Asleep before your head hits the pillow, her mother used to say, though she had never been so easy a sleeper as that.

Wynken, Blynken and Nod one night
Set sail in a wooden shoe—
Sailed on a river of silvery light,
Into a sea of dew.

Her mother had said that, too, in a voice soft and low, making a soothing music to send her to sleep. But they weren't asleep, Lynette said, they were sailing away and having adventures. And so can you, my precious, sail away into sleep and have lovely dreams. Dreams are adventures, you know. And you can tell me all about them in the morning.

Sometimes it worked, sometimes she sailed off into sleep. Tonight she waited for tides of unconsciousness to carry her into oblivion. She heard the gruntling roar of a motorbike speeding past. The man up the road. The midlife-crisis Harley, William called it. And suddenly she was bolted awake, her bones skittering, her skin itching. Full of anger.

William! her mind shouted. What have you done? He should be lying in bed beside her, curled up warm and comfortable, not making love with their bodies—William's health, she worried about that—but close, so close, with the loving threads of their voices weaving the tough gorgeous fabric of their marriage. And now William had destroyed it. William, how could you!

Linnet. He always called her Linnet. His sweet little singing bird. The first time they met he said she looked like a portrait of Iris Murdoch painted by Gauguin. She didn't take a lot of notice at that moment because she was flat out doing lunch, but when she thought about it she was suspicious. Iris Murdoch she'd heard of but not read, Gauguin she knew painted idol-like naked brown boxy women. Later she asked him, and he said, It was the planes of your face. Carved, and dreaming.

He'd stayed behind, after the others had left, and complimented her on her food. It's a miracle, he said, after the stuff we've had. I was convinced that boardroom lunches were the nightmare of modern times. The desiccated and diabolical open sandwich.

Lynette knew about bad boardroom lunches, which was why her business was successful, offering fresh vegetables, salads, fish dishes. Busy executives didn't need stodge, or wodges of heavy protein. She smiled at William, and he made the Iris Murdoch/ Gauguin comment about her face. Her hair was dark, then, and cut in a shapely twenties bob, whereas Murdoch's—she thought when she saw pictures of her—looked as though it was cut with a knife and fork.

After that he often stayed behind and talked to her while she finished up. One day he kissed her. Then they found themselves making love on the floor between the island bench and the sink. Anyone could come in, she said. I know, he said. Isn't it wonderful?

Danger, and passion. It was hard to tell them apart.

Found themselves. It's a good way to put it. Sounds as if they had no choice. So lovers like to think.

Danger. Passion. Damage. In the end. Other people suffered. They couldn't help that. Couldn't help themselves. They needed to be together. William's wife; the man Lynette was living with: couldn't they understand that? It was too strong, they couldn't resist, love couldn't be denied.

Ah, William. Lost lover, lost husband, lost father.

Ah, Linnet. Her little-bird round smallness, her neatness, her smooth brownness. All lost now, too. Nobody to see that, now. Nobody to call her sweet singing bird Linnet.

William found it amusing that someone as little as Lynette was so good at her job, cooking for large numbers of people. Lugging heavy pots. Great bowls. Iron griddles. Trays of food, utensils, plates. I am strong, she said. Fit. A tough little urchin. Lucky. The shop wasn't any easier. Still lugging heavy pots. Boxes, now, of utensils, food, plates. Janice was rather vaporous when it came to this kind of work; she faded away. She was the money, the figures. She balanced the books, a weighty job in its way. Lynette always imagined two tall piles of books on the brass pans of a pair of scales, teetering, tottering, one side overbalancing, falling down, smashing things as it went. Dangerous things, unbalanced books. Never the case with Janice. Her books always balanced, impeccably. Always healthily in the black. The shop made money. Lynette would lose her way of life by the death of William, but not her livelihood.

She didn't cry. Her bones skittered in her body, her flesh twitched, her head was swollen up, fragile and aching, her eyes, shut or open, itchy and awake. As though they were filled with sand. And not the soothing sleep-giving sand of the Sandman— once she'd asked her mother, Why does sand put you to sleep? Sand in your eyes hurts. Her mother replied, It's magic sand, it melts and brings you beautiful dreams. It's not the kind that hurts so much when it is blown into your face by the sea wind. Tears could flush out that stinging sand, but she didn't have any.

William was ten years older than Lynette; it wasn't unlikely that he'd die before her. But not yet. Not at sixty-four. Why not seventy-four, eighty-four, ninety-four? His heart was okay; he had angina pains sometimes but they needn't be a problem the doctor said, diet and exercise were the answer there and William paid attention to both. Lynette cooked vegetables and fish, made salads, used olive oil, avoided butter. William was trim and fit. He worked long hours, often didn't finish until eight or so, but that was good for him, he'd claimed, it wasn't stressful dangerous work.

Ah, William. The life we were going to lead. The travel. The six months in the French countryside. The Greek islands. The boat around the coast of Turkey. Over dinner together they had talked of the voyages they would embark on, next year, why not.

Ah, William. You have left me. You have abandoned me. I am bereft. I am betrayed. Her anger mounted in her chest, tasted like metal in her mouth.

People say that a death like this, a quick death, sudden, no warning or portent, really no pain to herald it, such a death is a good death, lucky. There is even sometimes a suggestion that it is a reward, for a life well lived, for goodness, and noble behaviour. She'd said it herself in the past. And yet, to have your death, that is, you might say, what life has been lived for, the culmination and the end of it, this death that everybody knows and nobody under-stands, the experience that everybody ever born must have, has had or will have, to have this happen so that its protagonist hardly notices, since by the time it has begun to happen it is already over, is a kind of waste. Shouldn't death be prepared for? Not in linger-ing pain, not that, nor in terror, but with enough awareness to allow the dying person to put his mind in order. Last rites, not to stop you going to hell, but to show you that you are prepared for this next step in life's way. The great adventure, Peter Pan called it, to die will be a great adventure, and people remember that, even though if you look at it in context you can see that Peter was not keen.

That's for the person dying. And for the people left? The quick death, the sudden death, is the worst kind for them. Their life is changed utterly, in a moment; everything has to go on as it was before, work, eating, keeping house, bringing up children, yet nothing can be the same. If you have nursed a beloved person you can say, perhaps devoutly and with gratitude, It is finished. You have a chance to put your joined existences in order, to remember with care the past, to recall joys. The beloved says, I will never see Paris again, but you can remind him how many times he has already, and with what pleasure, visiting it again in this new conversation. The past can live in your recollecting of it, become more vivid than the present that is about to stop existing. He can say, You are the love of my life, and it is true, at this moment.

Lynette was suddenly angry at this suddenness. No goodbye. No farewells. Just this terrible guillotine-quick not-being whose events kept crashing on to her like huge waves that dumped her, knocking her off her feet, rolling her over in scouring sand, slapping the breath out of her, and when she fought her way to her feet again and tried to catch her breath, another wave crashing down on her and the same thing happening over. Maybe in a while she wouldn't make it to her feet again. Maybe she'd drown.

Like dying of a broken heart, she knew it wouldn't happen.

And so much to do. The identifying. The car. The address book. The telephoning. The lists multiplied in her head like bacteria. They'd make her sick.

She turned over. The doona was too hot, the sheet was rucked. The pillow seemed to have bricks in it. She began thinking of the calls she'd have to make. She hadn't ever thought much about William's wife, the one he'd been married to when they kept having to make urgent love on the kitchen floor, with its black rubbery covering printed in a pattern of raised coin-sized dots. You've got spots on your bottom, the man she was living with remarked. What? she shrieked, imagining red pustules, but when she peered over her shoulder in the mirror she realised it was the indentations from the kitchen floor. Where's that bottom been? the man had laughed. Sitting on something dotty, I suppose, she said. Dotty, that'd be right, he laughed again. She was pleased and hardly at all guilty that he didn't suspect. Later she sometimes thought of him, with pain for her bad behaviour. Passion, and damage. But William's wife, well, she was William's wife. People said a woman couldn't come between a happily married couple. For Linnet and William there was the overwhelming need, irresistible, ungainsayable (the William word), they had to do this, this fucking on the kitchen floor, they had to do it now and keep on doing it, all their lives they would need this. There was this beautiful necessity to it. Love asks all, and demands that all be forgiven. She didn't think about the wife, she only thought of herself, and William. Though she knew the wife had been devastated. How had she known? Lynette had side-long glanced at a tall still figure, composed, heartbroken, like a ghost seen only from the corner of the eye. Or like a statue, a still pale figure, carved as a monument to grief, in the graveyard of another life, left further and further behind and disregarded, as the helpless ardent lovers galloped harder and more headlong on the joy and gaiety of their own passion.

And now she would have to look at her, turn and discern where she stood. The passion had stopped galloping some time ago. Now Lynette had lost William too, and the other wife—she did not ever say her name to herself, though she knew William kept in touch, and there was the boy, whom she loved more than a stepmother might, for his own sake and his father's—that other wife would now have to be told that William was lost again, but maybe she would be glad in a vindictive fashion, thinking that now Lynette would not have him either, though she told herself she had no reason to believe that the woman was mean-spirited. But she would have to ring her and tell her, the woman she saw in her mind as a slender statuesque figure, its stone pitted from years of standing in a seaside graveyard, and blotched a little with intricate small growths of yellow lichen. And the stone hands would grind together in the wringing motion of sorrow, and the carved tears would slide down the worn cheeks.

She hadn't thought to pull the curtains. The sky began to lighten. The birds began their chortling, soon to sound like a distant schoolyard of children playing. She drifted into a fitful sleep. She was still in the seaside graveyard; the statue stood with its back to her, but she could see that it was beginning to turn with a stone slowness. She walked away down to the shore, on to a jetty, out to the end and stepped off. Her sleeping self stepped too, and woke up with a violent start, her whole body recoiling as it saved itself from the fall. The light was bright now, it was the next day and so much to do. She was still exhausted but that couldn't matter.

She went into Erin's room. The girl was asleep, the salt of tears like snail trails on her cheeks. The child was half an orphan, and Lynette was a single parent. The man she'd been living with when she fell in love with William wanted them to have a baby but he wasn't keen to get married and she thought he wasn't committed; to a child maybe but not to her. When it was she who went away and broke his heart, he said, and she knew he believed it to be true. Whyever would anyone think marriage would save you from single parenthood? And Erin in the early days of her teens, the traditional difficult time. She'd been funny about food lately. Not hungry. Lynette knew she had to pay attention. Not that she was thinking of anorexia or anything like that.

Janice was in the kitchen making coffee. It didn't occur to Lynette how uncharacteristically early it was for her to be up.

Look at you, Janice said. Did you sleep a wink all night?

Not many, said Lynette.

We'll get you some Normies. You need to sleep.

Sleep that knits up the ravelled sleeve of care, said Lynette. Astounded. Her mouth gaped. She didn't know she even knew such a quotation. It was William who came in with the neat classy words from his vast lexicon of useful quotes for all occasions. Was this him, still here, speaking through her? Maybe she was channelling him. Perhaps he was still nearby. People said the souls of the dead didn't depart instantly, they hung around their old haunts for a while.

Ravelled, said Janice. I thought it was unravelled.

Maybe Lynette is unravelling. There was a thread got loose, and someone is pulling it. And all the stitches, so firm when the thread is fastened, so tightly locked, just slip apart, faster and faster, whole rows and chunks coming undone. Until in the end there is a tangled mess of threads and no sign that once they had been knitted up into a person.

I'm pretty sure it's ravelled, she said. Though I don't know . . .

Erin came stumbling out, her eyes half closed. Janice poured juice and made her some toast, buttering it and spreading it with Vegemite. She cut it into thin strips. Soldiers, she said. Erin picked one up and sat with it between her fingers.

Erin, said Lynette. The girl turned her head and lifted her face, but her eyes didn't meet her mother's, they looked emptily to one side, as though Lynette was not to be seen. The mother saw a little thin snake of hunger peering from her daughter's eye, playful and deadly, ready to feed on her from within, eating her insides out into a cave of rib bones, held together by cracked and desiccating skin, her rosy flesh consumed, her head a skull. Erin, she said, almost shouting. Your father would want you to eat. Be strong for him.

Erin's eyes focused, the skinny snake blinked away. She said, My father wanted me to be happy. But she put the Vegemite soldier into her mouth and took a small bite.

They made lists. Things to do. People to ring. Lynette remembered days when she'd happily made lists and added things she'd already done, so straightaway she could tick them off, as if a list was not a reminder of things to be done but a pattern to be completed.

By evening she'd rewritten it several times, ticking things off, crossing them out, but always adding more. The pattern was far from complete. It never would be. However much was crossed off there would always be more to add. She could get one of those rolls of paper from the till and still the things to do would spool out, never ending.

When she got into bed she decided to imagine that William lay there beside her, asleep as he sometimes was by the time she came. But she could not see his face. She had forgotten him. Barely a day dead, and she had forgotten him. Even though she had looked at him just that morning, said, Yes, that's my husband, because it was certainly him, though he was cold now and waxy. A friend who'd lived among Buddhists said that they kept a body in the house for three days and no corruption happened, and then after the three days the spirit left, and the body was taken away. Less than one day, and William wasn't there any more. When she finally got to sleep, the endless spool of lists wound through her dreams, and though she woke up often it didn't ever go away, it turned and rolled out in its endless spiral, trapping her in its stiff papery folds. It wasn't lists at all, it was William's spirit, twisting away, away.

Janice had gone into the shop and discovered that she'd forgotten to take in the tubs of cumquat trees on either side of the door. They stood on wheeled metal stands so they could be pushed inside the door at night, for fear of vandals. Or strong robbers. Yesterday they'd been covered with shining globes of fruit. In the night all the fruit had been ripped off and squashed under

30

feet wearing shoes with treads like a truck's tyres. A crushed mess of muddied orange skin and pulp carpeted the pavement. Janice felt sad, that what was beautiful had been destroyed, that people could look at something beautiful and see only something that could be destroyed, turned into an ugly mess.

Lynette had often wondered if it would be safe to leave the cumquats outside. Several years ago, she said, she'd stayed in a flat in London, just off Jermyn Street, and walking around at night she'd noticed that all the shops had wonderful flowers outside, iron stands with terracotta pots of cyclamen, tubs of polyanthus, of azaleas, all sorts of elegant flowers, just sitting there, not fastened down or anything, and nobody touched them.

Jermyn Street's very posh, said Janice.

Yes, but that's the point. It's pretty quiet at night, not a lot of people about, certainly no guards or anything. You'd think it would be a good place for disaffected people to come and destroy things. Or steal them. I couldn't see what was stopping them. But night after night, the same marvellous displays of flowers, unharmed.

Well, here was Lynette's answer. Manuka was quite posh, even if it wasn't Jermyn Street. And it wasn't safe. One night, and the pretty cumquat trees had been violated.

Janice got a bucket of water and a broom and washed the smashed fruit into the gutter. She trimmed the broken and bent branches of the little trees, sprayed their glossy green leaves with water. They were still quite handsome, if you didn't know how they'd looked, yesterday.

JACK GOES FISHING

When they drove down to the house at Eden on a Friday afternoon they took sandwiches and a thermos of tea. Rosamund always carried the milk and sugar separately, in little jars she kept for that purpose. This meant that the tea tasted fresher, not stored and stale.

Later Jack dropped the jar for the milk, it broke and he was bereft. You should not be bereft by the loss of a small useful but otherwise valueless article, but he was.

They left Cooma on Friday during the afternoon and always stopped just past Bombala, where the high country starts to shift down to the coast, leaving behind the yellow grasslands rubbed and dusty like the skin of a mangy old lion in the zoo. Leaving behind that hard clear light, without softness or distraction or movement, the light that burns in summer and freezes in winter. Entering the forest, almost rainforest, turning off on a dirt road threading its way through the tall slender-trunked trees, where the light falls in shafts and shadows, and trembles and shivers as the leaves move. In the distance there are smooth layers of mountains blue in the oiled air. It is not the coast, which has different light and trees, glittering with prickly sunlight in the morning, shrouded in luminous watery mist in the afternoon. Nor is it the high country. It's the space between and they always stop there, eat their sandwiches and drink their tea, and go on refreshed.

Bill and Jack were brothers, Jack the older by several years. They had idyllic childhoods in those days when parents didn't work such long hours and rarely bought objects and loved their children with a certain amount of benign neglect. Those days before the phrase 'stranger danger' was invented, when children were almost never driven anywhere, even if their fathers owned cars, being expected to make their own ways, on buses or bicycles or their own two feet, and telling your mother you were bored during the school holidays wouldn't have crossed anyone's mind. So they played on abandoned railway lines and crawled through culverts spiky with lantana and the thrilling odours of dead things decaying. Once a goat, which was a bit too thrilling. They climbed crumbling sand-stone cliffs in bare feet. They made cubbies in deserted huts, and in the intervals of swimming in the sea collected a certain kind of small pointed shell that a friend of someone's mother could sell to a chinaman for a lot of money.

They fell down ditches and off bikes, their legs were always scratched and scabbed, their clothes which were once-good garments wearing out and growing too small were dusty and their skin grubby, they had that hot dry feral smell of physically exerted boys which made lady teachers wrinkle their noses when they got too close.

Strangers might still have been dangerous: Jack playing hide and seek had once been accosted by a man who pushed him against the concrete pylon of a bridge and pulled out his willy which was big and purple and waved around in the watery light. He never found out what the man intended to do with it. Jack's mates caught up with him and the man ran off. You never told your mother things like that. They didn't worry you but they'd worry her. In fact you had to protect her from the knowledge of a lot of things that happened. Mothers were innocent, it was wise to keep them that way.

Jack is the dreamy one, grown-ups said. Jack is always dreaming. He stared at things in a kind of trance, the sea, a gravel path, the bark on a tree, looking at its blueness, or redness, the peeling roughness, but not making anything of this, simply gazing. Sometimes adults gazed at him too, because he was a beautiful child and an even more beautiful young man, as though one of those Greek marble statues had had life breathed into it and turned rosy and golden instead of stony white. But nobody talked about this because it wasn't the sort of thing to discuss, really.

It was a kind of paradise, our childhood, said Jack to Bill when they were both middle-aged, and Bill who was William now said, Do you think so? I suppose it was.

Jack was still much better looking than Bill, than William, but it hadn't done much for him. When he was young Jack didn't know he was not ambitious. It didn't occur to him to think about it. He gazed at life and when things offered he took them, if they seemed like a good idea. It wasn't until Bill began to make something of himself, their father's phrase, that Jack saw he wasn't doing that and didn't know how to. By that time he was working in the county offices in Cooma, married to Rosamund. A good job, honest and worthwhile, finished with when he left the office and walked home to a good meal. Sometimes he went away for a weekend with a colleague; they walked high into the mountains and caught trout. They tied their own flies, painstaking in the long winter evenings; they camped by the rocky fast-flowing streams and went their own way, up and down the river banks with their tall rods, casting the flies dancing across the water. They constructed a device for smoking the fish, so they could preserve some of their catch. Do you ever think of moving on, Jack asked his companion, I mean, going somewhere else, getting a better job? Because everyone knew that the hierarchies in the council were set, there was unlikely to be any movement for years. And the colleague, whose name was Clarrie, replied, No. Why?

Though he clearly continued to consider the question, because several times over the weekend he referred to it. Where would you go you could catch fish like this? At the time, they were frying two beauties in butter in the old iron frying pan. Cooma's a bonza town, said Clarrie as they hiked out, laden with sleeping bags and fish and the smoke box. Joyce likes it here, her family's all about. And the kids. Jack felt comforted by that. Less guilty with his own contentment.

Rosamund understood Jack's absence of ambition. The way she saw it he was making a kind of pact with life: he would be modest and life would be good to him. By not asking a lot he would be entirely in control of what he did have. She doubted that life worked like that, she knew that chaos could waylay the most methodical and careful and undemanding of people, but she hoped that Jack would not ever find this out. She thought the pact was something not conscious. She loved him, she would keep him safe. She understood how precious their kind of happiness was. She said to herself, absence of ambition goes with presence of contentment.

Rosamund worked in the council too. She was a tall girl with long brown hair, and the first time he saw her he was struck by her graceful good looks. As she was struck by him, but neither let on for a while, or they thought they didn't. They exchanged words about work and sometimes had a conversation over morning coffee, and then it seemed to be they were often walking home at the same time. He asked her to go to the pictures, and then they were courting and within a year getting married. What a handsome couple they make, said their friends, and so they did, in every way, they loved and looked after one another. They never had a cross word. Jack was always finding little ways to make Rosamund happy, to show he cared about her, and she did the same for him. They were known in the office as the lovebirds.

They bought a house, a solid old house with high ceilings and good verandas. It wasn't very expensive because it was pretty much on the flood plain, but it didn't seem to flood these days and the soil was rich, the garden already flourishing. Rosamund fell in love with the fretwork round the veranda, its wooden lace patterned in scrolls and loops. A bit was missing and Jack made a new piece to fit, cutting out the wood in the same scrolls and painting it white so you couldn't tell new from old. In the good soil Jack grew vegetables, and Rosamund's flowers were a marvel. Jack painted and mended and maintained the fabric of the house, Rosamund made curtains and cushion covers. The lovebirds in their cosy nest. They planned to have a number of children.

It took them a long time to get pregnant. They'd reached an age when everybody assumed they never would, since in those days almost nobody had babies in their thirties. It wasn't for lack of trying; Jack even wondered if frequency reduced potency, and plucked up the courage to ask the doctor who was a golfing friend if this could be the case, but the doctor pooh-poohed the idea. Just keep going, he said, it'll happen if it's going to. And eventually it did. Rosamund blossomed. She bloomed with health, was even more beautiful pregnant than before. The baby grew strong and lusty. Jack put his hand on the enormous taut egg of her belly and felt the child's violent kicks. Egg, the embryo was called. Sometimes Jack bent his head and laid his ear to his wife's belly and listened to Egg at play. They didn't know if it was a boy or a girl. If she was a girl she'd be Louise, but they hadn't decided on a boy's name.

Rosamund carried the baby to term. Her waters broke early in the morning and she went into labour. Everything was normal, until suddenly it wasn't. Everything went wrong. The baby could not be born. The doctors broke the bones of Rosamund's pelvis but they could not get the baby out alive. A perfect little girl. They called her Louise; Jack had a faint pang that now this name would only belong to a dead child. They had a funeral service; Rosamund had to go in a wheelchair. It was a long time before she could walk again. He said, We have to get pregnant again, as soon as you are well, and he nursed and cosseted and cherished her. As soon as you are well, he said, we'll get pregnant again. But they didn't.

Sometimes he wondered, if they'd been in a bigger city, with a fancier hospital, whether the baby might have been saved. He did not think he could ask the doctor that question, who had worked so hard and been distraught that he could not save the child. He once said something to a nurse but she shook her head. No, she said, everything was done, you couldn't have had better care.

Rosamund didn't go back to the council. She got a job in the chemist, three mornings a week. That left her time to look after the house, and Jack, to bake and cook good dinners, and busy herself over the knitting and sewing that she liked to do. She was a thrifty woman, and her housekeeping was impeccable. Meantime Bill was forging his career as a lawyer and making money. He was on to his third wife. What sort of a life is that? said Jack. Three wives, and who knows if he's got it right yet. Some people, he said, putting his arms around Rosamund, some people can get it right the first time.

There was an occasion when Bill and Jack stood together at a family party in a backyard in Sydney, one of those scruffy seaside backyards with buffalo grass and a frangipani tree. Each had a glass of beer in his hand and Bill was holding on to one of the metal bars of the Hills Hoist as though he was strap-hanging in a bus, as though life might suddenly lurch and he fall over, staring rather morosely at a derelict swing. It was the funeral of one of their uncles, not someone they knew well at all, they were there out of family piety, because he was their mother's brother, and his death wasn't the cause of Bill's moroseness. He was newly divorced from his first wife. Do you ever regret . . . said Bill. Do you ever have regrets, I suppose I mean.

No, I don't regret, said Jack, I don't think things are for regretting. How can that help? You do what you think is the right thing at the time and you have to stick with that.

You're a lucky man, you know, said Bill. He was hanging on to the Hoist with his arm raised and his body slumped as though he would fall to the ground if it wasn't holding him up. You don't know that, of course.

Jack said, I think I do. This conversation was a good while ago, before the baby died. But his answer would probably have been the same, then.

Driving back to Cooma in the car, he said to Rosamund, I suppose Bill does regret things.

He does seem to be a discontented person, said Rosamund.

Do you think that's his nature? asked Jack.

Nature, habit, I don't know, said Rosamund.

I think it's greed, said Jack. Greed, ambition; are they the same thing?

It was certainly sad that they didn't have any children, and Rosamund would have been such a good mother, but Jack was sanguine. Who knows, we might not be so perfectly happy if we had children, he said to himself. They'd be a lot of work, and we might have to worry about money, and the right way to bring them up, and what if they went off the rails? Because children did seem to do that, these days, not like when he was young, when kids could be a bit rough but settled down okay in the end, quite quickly really, and turned into decent citizens.

Jack was still in much the same job. More money, more responsibility, but basically the same job. Clarrie did move away, after all, he got a position in Canberra, in Treasury, with a much higher salary, and Joyce was thrilled; she boasted to all her friends and family about the new house she was going to have. There didn't seem to be anybody else to go fishing with, and it was a fair hike in to the river anyway, not something to do on your own. He didn't even think of suggesting that his wife take Clarrie's place. When they were first married they used to go skiing, but they gave it up when Rosamund got pregnant, and never took it up again. They bought the cottage in Eden intending to retire there one day, in the more kindly climate of the coast; Jack fancied ending his days as he had begun, by the sea. Of course retirement was a while off, but they could go for weekends and holidays.

The house in Eden was a little old wooden cottage, in a street off the main road, the hub of town, quite a lively little town, with everything you could want, baker, butcher, post office, dress shops, hairdresser, hardware, several pubs. A decent hospital in Bega. The street ran along a ridge and was quite high, so the house had a view two ways: it looked out over Aslings Beach and Calle Calle Bay to the ocean and also through trees to Twofold Bay. Not big: two rooms at the front, a parlour and a bedroom, under the high-pitched roof of the old cottage, and a large lean-to at the back, quite solid, which was kitchen and dining room. There was a bathroom off this and some good sheds. They did not need a lot of space; there were no children or grandchildren to visit, Bill was unlikely to come down, and though they were friends with half of Cooma they were not really on terms where you would say, Come and stay.

It was a small house but a big block. Vegetables for him. Flowers for her. Books. Fishing. The quiet life they both liked. When he had an image of this in his mind it was like looking at a children's picture book, with beautiful illustrations making glamorous and mysterious the fairytale domestic story. The little wooden house, painted cream with a green trim. The fat cabbages and the scarlet runner beans. The meadow garden. The dog, the cat, the fire. The little old woman and the little old man, rosy-cheeked and robust. The blue blue water of the bay with its frilled edges, the wooden rowing boat. The fishing fleet painted in primary colours. The rocky breakwaters, the smudged indigo of the enclosing mountains. Turn the pages slowly so you can enjoy the intricate detail of the drawings, the tall foxgloves, the tiny violets nestling round them, the brass knocker in the shape of a lady's hand. The sleeping cat on the round rag rug. The round little old woman with her apple cheeks, throwing grain to her chickens.

If he had ever put these pictures into words somebody might have said, But you and Rosamund aren't nuggety and apple-cheeked. You're tall and willowy and more pale biscuit than red apple. And of course the fat cabbages and the scarlet runner beans would have to wait until they were living there permanently, though the meadow garden was showing some signs of life. But the pictures never got into words, not even in Jack's head.

And so they drove from Cooma to Eden most weekends and always stopped just past Bombala, where the high country has begun its descent to the sea, where the light is filtered through the slender lacy-leafed trees, and the tea tastes fresh and the sandwiches are juicy. Some people don't like juicy sandwiches, but Jack and Rosamund did. She always put in some tomato, or soft-boiled egg, or pickles with the meat. Maybe some home-cooked beetroot with cheese. And when they got to Eden, Rosamund cleaned and aired while Jack maintained the fabric of this house and went fishing; they usually had a good feed of fish at Eden. And the fish and chip shop was good if the fish in the bay weren't biting. They went for walks and had a drink at the pub and swam when the weather was warm enough.

They liked the walk down the hill to Aslings Beach, through the cemetery, a pretty little white-fenced marine cemetery with a lot of flowers, brightly coloured plastic mainly but quite new. There were nearly always several people looking after it, gardening and tidying, and the old graves of the seamen and whalers and timber getters were gradually being restored. They'd often stop and have a conversation with one or other of these people, and Rosamund liked to read the inscriptions on the graves. She wept when they were tiny, for babies. Their inscriptions said things like, Too good for this earth, God wanted our treasure for His own, or

A little angel loaned us for so short a time and now gone home. Parents often had a lot to say on infant tombs.

The people working in the cemetery were mostly volunteers, and Jack thought when he retired he'd become a volunteer too. Pottering about in the bracing wind from the sea. A good cemetery is a sign of a flourishing town, said Rosamund; if they neglect the cemetery it is because they are too depressed to care. There were still some plots left to buy. One day Rosamund said, Maybe we should buy one of them and be buried here. And we could bring Louise down too. The thing that worried her about moving to Eden was leaving Louise behind in the Cooma churchyard.

Yes, said Jack, let's do that.

They did everything together, of course they would be buried together. Everything except fishing. The old days, with the trout, Jack had gone with Clarrie, and when he married Rosamund he wouldn't have dreamt of expecting her to walk that rough track deep into the Snowies. Now, when it would have been easier in the boat, she still didn't go. She thought it was a good idea for him to do something on his own, and she liked a kind of busyness, knitting or sewing or even reading, that you didn't get with fishing.

Jack had bought an old launch, a sturdy wooden clinker-built boat, called the *Campaspe*, probably after that river in Victoria. He took it out, just in the bay; he didn't venture through the heads, that was for the rough and tumble sport of the big-game fisher-men, not his gentle pastime. He sat in the boat and didn't think; it was a way of simply being. If he had thought about it he might have called it a meditation, and there could have been something for a Buddhist to envy in the success with which his mind stayed emptied of cerebral activity. He sat with his line out, felt the sun warming him, the damp cold of the winter sea mist, without ever even needing to name them to himself. Occasionally he had words in his head. Not much good, this bait. Getting late. The water is roughing up. See there's a new roof on the old house. Often just Rosamund. Her name in his mind like her presence in his life, always there, warm, luminous, enormous, leaving no room for empty spaces.

Fishing was a pastime, and there was skill. It was also killing. Only what you need for food, like a hunter. But the killing was important.

The years passed, and Jack retired. They sold the house on the flood plain in Cooma, and moved permanently to the coast. They had quite a bit of money and could have bought a fancier boat or a bigger house. But the house they had was in such a good spot, and did them. They could have extended it, but what would have been the point? Occasionally one of Bill's children came to visit them, so they invested in a sofa bed to put in the parlour, which was quite suitable for infrequent guests. The vegetables were planted in their regular seasons, the meadow garden blossomed. Rosamund grew climbing roses over the verandas. Jack did his volunteer work in the cemetery, and gradually learned the names of the families buried there. The pages were turning on the picture-book life of the children's story.

Jack, whose favourite reading was thrillers, ought to have known that even a story for children needs a narrative, and narratives need worry, threat, disaster, despair, or at least some shadow, some menacing promise of everything going wrong. Until the last pages, when the sun comes out, the bay is blue again, the roses nod on the trellis, and the old man has his arm round the old woman's waist and everyone is safe, and we can shut them up happily in their world of the book and put it on the shelf. Taking it down whenever you like and reading about vicissitudes because you know they will all be overcome by The End.

Well. The story went well on the first pages of the book. But then Jack shut it up and put it on the shelf and never wanted to look at it again. The vegetables fattened, the meadow garden sowed itself, the bay was blue and the fish biting, there was Jack robust and sun-browned. But there was no Rosamund.

Her skin, which had so delighted him by its pale gold silky smoothness, remained unblemished even into her sixties. But a melanoma suddenly grew on her arm and though it was removed and the doctor was fairly certain he'd got all of it, he hadn't, and the cancer shifted to her spine and her lungs and in no time it was clear it was going to kill her. The small pebble of gladness in this was the time it took. Time to learn her thoroughly all over again, her face, her voice, the movement of her hands, the special sweetness of her smile, time to make sure his memory had hold of her. Time to talk about the past, to retell the story of their life together, to store up its details. Rosamund said, You know, never having a baby: I was sorry. And yet it has meant us being together; with a child we might not have had that. Yes, said Jack. She said, Mind you, if there was a child, there would be somebody for you, now. He put his arms around her and hugged her, delicately, for she was frail, and her body hurt. Words he was never good at. Pictures he had in his mind. He imagined her going out and being bowled over and never coming home again, that was the worst thing. She was ill, and in some pain, though she had morphine she took in pill form, and a bottle to sip when she needed it, but she was here, and imprinting herself deeper in his mind, his heart. The year he nursed her was his most precious possession.

He didn't know that Rosamund had always hoped that he would die first because she couldn't bear to think of how he would manage on his own. He didn't think he could, either, he didn't think he could bear it, but he did. He went on being methodical and orderly and doing things properly and keeping them in their places, and since he had to clean the house as well and do the cooking he was kept busy, too busy, he decided, to keep up his volunteer work at the cemetery. Though he always tended the grave where Rosamund and Louise were buried, with space for him beside them.

You say *I cannot bear it*, but you do.

Maybe it was the fishing that saved him from despair. Fishing was what he did and he was good at it. That afternoon he took *Campaspe* out, with several short boat rods and a supply of bait. He mostly caught more than he needed, especially as now there was only him to eat it; there was a limit to how much fish one person could eat and give away to his friends, who were not usually short themselves. He used barbless hooks so he could release them without too much harm. It was a winter's afternoon, still and grey, it could have been twilight already though it was not yet three o'clock. The dusk was his favourite time for fishing. The sea mist veiled the hills and headlands so they lost all their lineaments. In the morning the sun lit them up cleanly and all their contours and the patterns of trees stood out sharply, but in the afternoon they retired into mystery.

He took his car to Quarantine Bay where he kept the boat. Most of the other craft were gleaming and shapely: svelte yachts, sailing boats with tall masts, ravenous-looking big-game cruisers with their wireless aerials and global positioning systems, hungry as sharks but less handsome. There was only one other boat as old as *Campaspe*, but it was a good deal bigger. He fetched his coracle from the shore by the beach shacks and rowed slowly across the water to his mooring buoy. The water looked very smooth, but there was quite a lot of movement in it; the pontoon was riding up and down and creaking at its hawsers. Anybody watching him could see that he was a slow man. Now more than ever he enjoyed the not-thinking, carefully stowing the oars of the coracle, loading the boat rods, the small chilly bin of bait, his tea things, starting the motor of the old launch and putt-putting out through the misty silence, out into Nullica Bay, more or less opposite where the Nullica River came out. He had brought live squid for bait; with a bit of luck there would be mulloway in this spot. Mulloway, that used to be jewfish when he was a kid; his father had considered it an excellent fish.

He could see across to the long pale stretch of the beach at Boydtown, and dimly through the pines and palm trees the restored and expanded towers of the Seahorse Inn. He knew that it had been built in the 1840s by Ben Boyd as part of the empire that was to begin with whaling at Twofold Bay and take in pastoral leases and banks, an empire which collapsed and was abandoned, though the Seahorse Inn survived, and was now supposed to be emerging as a luxurious resort for rich people. So grandiose at birth and now again in this latest incarnation. The locals were sceptical about its likely success. He knew these things but did not particularly think of them as his eyes gazed at the mist-shrouded edifice.

The boat rod dipped. He reeled in the line: a mulloway, but too small. The minimum length was forty-five centimetres, and he could see that this one was considerably shorter than that. He didn't pull it out of the water but left it just below the surface, in order to shock it as little as possible. Fish have delicate skins; nets and hard surfaces quickly damage them. And of course the unbreathable air. No point in putting them back if you traumatise them. He tried to grasp the body of the fish and pull out the hook but the fish struggled and he could not get a purchase. Even with his needle-nose pliers he could not get near or steady enough to extract it. Instead he cut the line with scissors, and the fish, released, gave a quick flick and was gone. Sometimes if the fish was very fatigued it was necessary to hold it and push it through the water so that it got oxygen through its gills, until it was strong enough to swim away on its own. The hook should easily dissolve in the stomach acids. So the old fishermen said.

Several more times he caught too-small mulloway and then a trevally. He let that go, even though there was no legal limit;

he wasn't particularly interested in trevally. He poured himself a cup of tea from the thermos, added milk from the jar that had replaced the one he broke. He'd tried various different jars and none of them poured as well as the old one. He ate a Turkish pastry from the deli, oozing honey and knobbly with walnuts. Then another mulloway took the live squid bait. A good big one, at least fifty centimetres. He reeled it in gently. The barbless hooks required a certain skill. When he got it into the boat he clocked it on the head with a small billet of wood. It was a trick an old Frenchman had shown him for killing trout quickly and painlessly, so they didn't bang about and bruise themselves and drown in air. The old man didn't do it because it was humane but because he believed the fish tasted sweeter if they hadn't suffered.

When that was done he realised that the sounds about him were changing. The soft quietness of the mist with only the mild lapping of the water against the wooden timbers of the boat was being invaded by a faint distant groan, and the air felt altogether different, disturbed. And it was no longer the sunless mistiness of a winter's afternoon but the real twilight of the end of the day. Soon it would be dark. The invisible sun would have set by now. He could feel the weather changing, the storm promised for tomorrow coming early, the wind rising and the formerly tranquil water heaving and slapping; soon it would be choppy and then rough. Twofold Bay was remarkably sheltered, but Nullica Bay was opposite the open sea, the enfolding headlands couldn't protect it. It would take a while for the storm's force to hit, he'd have plenty of time to get back to Quarantine Bay. And he had his fish.

He stowed his gear in the careful way that gave him pleasure. He took the hatch off the engine and pulled the cord to start it. It never fired on the first two pulls, but reliably always on the third or fourth it broke into its slow comfortable putt-putt. He pulled up the anchor, turned the boat around and headed for home. The waves were beginning to slap quite hard against the timbers and soon the boat's forward movement was slowed by her wallowing from side to side. It wouldn't be a quick trip back.

And then the engine stopped. It had never done that before. Jack took the hatch off. It was almost completely dark now. There was a torch but when he shone it into the compartment he couldn't see what might be wrong. He pulled the cord again, a number of times, but it didn't even turn over. Old it was, the engine, probably as old as the boat. But as reliable, he'd thought. He had it serviced, it always worked. Engines weren't Jack's thing. Carpentry, painting, any kind of work with wood, but not mechanical.

He knew how dangerous his position was. In a small boat, in a gathering storm. He wasn't sure what the tides would do; pull him out into the open sea, probably. At least here was no bar, as there was in the ports farther up the coast, Merimbula, Narooma; even in good weather a boat could easily be wrecked on a bar. There was a technique for crossing these sand barriers, pausing for the right moment then moving quickly. And of course the tide had to be high. But no bar was very little comfort in bad weather, rough seas, in a small boat which could make no way, could only toss at the mercy of the waters. He put on his life jacket.

He did have a sea anchor. He'd never used it before but he knew where it was, properly stowed in its locker. That should keep him nose to the waves. He fastened it to an iron ring in the bow of the boat which was probably for that purpose, and it was successful. *Campaspe* rode nose to the waves, and though the motion was violent he stayed afloat. He used the dipper to bail out the water that drove over the bow. The little craft was seaworthy but not proof against water splashing in. It had a little half-cabin that formed a kind of shelter, but not against the wild seas and the rain that had begun to fall in sheets. The sea water splashed into his face, he could feel his skin becoming crusted with salt and when he licked his lips he got the thirsty gritty taste of it. He tipped his face up to the rain but it did not seem to wash away the saltiness.

He was perfectly safe. He could ride the storm and sooner or later somebody should come, even if he had to wait for daylight, which would be a long night. Some vessel might pass in the meantime. He huddled down into his life jacket. Already quite a lot of time had passed. There was a creaking and scraping noise that worried him and when he shone the torch in its direction he realised that the hook that held the sea anchor was working loose from the old soft wood of the boat's prow. He made a lunge for it but a fraction too late. The loop flew out and the sea anchor was lost.

He could try to hold *Campaspe* head on to the waves using the rudder but he knew that would be almost impossible. The boat would keep turning side on to the waves and he could easily be swamped. Nevertheless he had to keep trying.

It was exhausting work. His body was fit and did not often remind him that he wasn't a young man. But tonight it felt very old. He also felt calm. His child had died, his wife. They had slipped without complaint into whatever death was. It was the least he could do, to follow with the same dignity, if that was what was required. Perhaps it was the desirable thing. There need be no more striving. The thought of peace seemed beautiful.

Just the same he readied a flare. He carried two, had never used one before. When would be the moment? There was no sign of any other boat. He hadn't reported his trip to anyone. He never did, since he never went out into the open sea. Would somebody on shore see a flare? He had only two chances. Fate would decide.

He thought he heard the sound of a motor; it was hard to tell through the groaning of the elements. He let off the flare; when would he know if anyone had seen? It lit up his boat, the churning water, his engine but not its secrets, hung for a little while, then went out.

Time passed. He could no longer work out where the Seahorse Inn was. It didn't seem to have any lights. There didn't seem to be any lights anywhere. Was it the weather, or had he been washed away from any habitation? The shores were quite empty for much of Twofold Bay, what houses there were hidden among trees. He wondered if death meant he would see Rosamund again. He had never thought he knew anything about death, whether there would be life again, and people you loved. Louise might be waiting too. A baby. Or a little girl. Or just a soul. Rosamund was still always there in his mind, still luminous but not so enormous as she used to be, there were hollows and empty spaces that she could no longer fill. Rosamund. He wanted that she be there, waiting for him.

He saw points of light away across the water, and heard the faint roar of a powerful engine. He let off another flare. He heard the boat slow, and then it was circling, and a searchlight shone down on him. It was one of the game-fishing boats, plunging up and down in the waves, no longer cleaving through them with the speed of its passage.

Hello there, an American voice called. Trouble?

Engine failure, shouted Jack.

Hold on. Here come the marines.

Another voice said, There's gotta be a rope here somewhere. Try that box.

The game cruiser towed him into Cattle Bay. That was its destination. That okay, buddy? the first voice asked, and of course it was, any shore would do. His rescuers moored his powerless boat to their buoy with plenty of slack and he put out his anchor to stop it bumping against the big boat in the storm. Unlikely: the bay was tucked into Snug Cove and sheltered. The Americans offered him a lift in the four-wheel drive they had parked there but he refused. He lived just up the hill, he said. It was true, more or less. He was cold, and his legs trembled as he set off. A walk would steady him. And he didn't want to talk to cheerful Americans full of the sport of the fish they had nearly caught. He had his fish in his bag, though it was far too late to clean and fillet and cook it tonight. He was for a tin of soup, some toast, bed. He'd have to get down to the cove early, he'd left his tackle in the boat, which normally he'd never do, and he had to get the engine fixed so he could sail around to Quarantine Bay and get his car. He should have accepted the lift, he hadn't realised how tired he was.

You know why it's called Quarantine Bay? said a voice, a quavering rusty voice that sounded as if it hadn't been used for forming words in a long time, then after a while they came out in something of a rush, as though the first ones had primed the machinery.

Quarantine Bay, muttered Jack. He didn't care why. He was tired and worn out and all his limbs trembled, but even rested and well he wouldn't be especially interested. Things had names, you used them but didn't concern yourself with them.

The smallpox, said the voice, coming creaking out of the deep-set hood of a duffel coat, while a light and bony hand had fixed itself on Jack's arm and a pair of round-toed boots kept slow pace with him on the path up the hill.

The smallpox, the voice repeated. A boat came in to the bay and her passengers were infected with smallpox so they made her anchor there, instead of round in the cove. A lot of them died. She picked up the smallpox in India, see, along with her cargo of silk. They buried the silk along with the dead bodies just up the beach there. He pointed.

The man's hand was bone-white on his arm, not heavy, but when Jack tried to pull away he couldn't. Weak as a kitten, he was.

The man said in his disused voice, If you'll allow me. My sight's not good . . .

Jack just wanted to get up the hill, which felt even steeper than usual. And though there was no weight in the man's hand he seemed a burden that Jack had to drag up as well as himself.

'Course, straightaway folks dug it up, the silk, and sold it up and down the coast. All the grand ladies in mortal silk dresses. Mortal silk. The man's chuckle was even rustier than his voice.

Jack said nothing, needing his energy for the climb. But the man kept on talking. I'm an Eden man myself, he said, an Eden man, man and boy, and beyond. Spent m'days as a whaler, on the boats.

What he meant was, he went to sea to catch whales, rather than wait for them to come into the bay and harpoon them there and haul them ashore, which had been big business in Eden. Jack knew there'd been no whaling in Eden since the thirties of last century. I thought you could only watch whales, these days, he said.

We watched 'em, sure enough. The man chuckled again. I'll tell you a story. It's a strange story, and a true one, though maybe I wouldn't believe it if it hadn't happened to me. It was back when I was on *Star of the East*. Way out at sea we was.

Jack wondered if maybe the man had been a whaling pirate. In the pay of one of those countries people suspected were breaking the whaling ban. *Star of the East*: the name could have sinister implications.

She was chased by a huge sperm whale. Three of us whaleboats put out after him and got a harpoon into the mighty creature, what dived eight hundred feet before the line slackened. It's all quiet when that happens, and you sit there in a funk, I can tell you. You know he's lurking, and you know he'll break again. Where will he come up next? They're angry, these whales, they're mean beasts, they fight. Well, erupt he did, under my very boat, tossing it into the air and smashing it into matchsticks with one blow of his tail. The other boats picked up the survivors, but two men were missing.

That tail, said the man. You know what they call it? The hand of God. The hand of God, down it comes, whack, and you're destroyed.

Well, by sunset the harpoon had done its job and the whale was dying. They winched it to the side of the vessel to start work on it. They flensed the blubber from the carcass, and then they hoisted its huge liver and stomach on board. The paunch was breathing. In and out. In and out. Well . . . how could that be? The whale's carcass was cut up for blubber. Its organs weren't even in it any more. How could they be breathing?

The men sliced the paunch open. Out came a man's foot, boot on, and a trousered leg. Here the man stamped his round-toed boot on the ground. That was me. I weren't conscious. I been inside that stomach for fifteen hours. Think of it. Fifteen hours inside of a whale. M'flesh was white as death, bleached by the creature's digestive juices. The skin of my eyes were damaged, so I can't see too well. I were delirious for a month. But I lived to tell the tale. What it felt like, the monster's huge teeth grating across my legs as I slid down the tube of his throat. Jonah, they call me.

Tell us the story of the whale swallowing you, Jonah, they say, and they buy me a drink. Used to.

They were at the top of the hill now and walking along the street that would lead to Jack's house. Well, he said, sorry about that. The pub's shut and I've got no drink. He heard himself sounding ungracious. I can give you a mug of soup, he said, much to his surprise. The last thing he wanted was this stranger in the sanctuary of his house. The rain was sluicing down and his meant-to-be-waterproof jacket no more use than an old shirt. He had to blink hard to shake the water out of his eyelashes.

I thank you, said the man, but I'll not trouble you. He paused, not far from a street light that was tossing wildly in the wind, and raised his head a little, so the light briefly illuminated his ghastly white face and the opaque glitter of his eyes, then retreated again into the depths of his hood. He tapped Jack twice on the arm with his bone-white hand, a tap Jack saw rather than felt, then slid his hands into the sleeves of his coat, nodded, and ambled back the way they had come. When Jack looked again he was not even a shadow in the dark and rainswept night.

He heated soup and buttered some toast and ate them in a deep hot bath. The warmth calmed the shivering of his body but didn't overcome the trembling of his limbs. Though that didn't keep him awake when he went to bed. He fell asleep and stayed there long past the time he had meant to get up. And was only woken by the ringing of the telephone.

*

It was Lynette, his sister-in-law, number three. To tell him that Bill—William—had died. Last night. Drowned in a pool at a hotel gym. Jack heard himself say, in a kind of wonderment, What time? I nearly drowned last night . . . too.

Lynette said, It was a heart attack that did it. She was thinking, trust Jack to put himself in the picture. Slow Jack. Maddening Jack. William's energy and spirit snuffed out and Jack who was older as well still maundering along. So far she was more angry with William for dying than she was grieving.

Jack was saying something about his little brother and how hard it was to grasp the idea of losing him, he'd never even thought of such a thing. She interrupted. I'm sorry, Jack, I've got to go. I'll let you know about the funeral.

By the time he'd arranged for the mechanic to look at the boat and got a mate to drive him to Quarantine Bay—remembering the story of the silk and the victims of smallpox being buried there and how there was no sign at all of such events—and brought his car back and filleted the fish and put it on a plate in the refrigerator, the early evening was closing in. The house, which he had been finally managing to find cosy again, after Rosamund's death had made it bleak and empty, seemed forlorn once more. Even though he didn't see much of Bill he was his brother, he did not need to keep visiting him to feel him part of his life, and every winter he wrote him a long letter which Bill eventually always answered so they knew what they were up to. And now that comfortable warm presence whom distance couldn't diminish had been turned by death to an ache and an absence. He felt hollowed out, and it was as though all his bones and muscles still so sore from yesterday's fight with the elements were strung together in a flimsy skeleton housing nothing. Oh Rosamund, he said, why did you leave me? He needed her now to console him for the death of Bill. Nothing could hurt him while Rosamund was there to look after him. Now it seemed that everything knocked him about. He could turn into a complete wreck.

Just feeling sorry for myself, love, he said, and went up to the pub. It was warm in the pub, and a couple of stouts would take the cold out of his inside, and there'd be some blokes he knew. George was there, and Leon. George had been on the trawlers. He enjoyed Jack's story about the engine breaking down and the loss of the sea anchor and being rescued by the game cruiser. You were lucky, mate. Lucky them fuckwits knew one end of the rope from the other. Jack wanted to tell them about his brother dying, but Leon got started on some yarn about how his truck drove up the mountain to Canberra faster when there was a tailwind, and used less fuel too. Should be even better coming back, said George, it's all downhill. The word downhill made them laugh.

There was another round of beer, and Jack said, Speaking of downhill. Or should I say up. He told them about the bloke who'd materialised at Cattle Bay. The Americans went off in their four-wheel drive, he said, and suddenly there was this bloke. Just appeared. He told them how he'd sort of had to walk up the hill with this bloke, and related the long story he'd told, of the whale swallowing him, and being got out after fifteen hours. He didn't mention the skinny bone-white hand that had rested so lightly and yet so relentlessly on his arm, or the strange glitter of the man's eyes when the light of the street lamp fell glancing upon them.

George gave him a curious look. How old was this cove?

Dunno. That white skin. Kind of half-digested somehow. Hard to say how old he was.

That story—the bloke being swallowed by the whale, and people calling him Jonah. That's up on the wall in the museum.

Jack had always meant to go and look at the museum, every time he went past the pretty blue and white building on the hill, but somehow he'd never got round to it. Plenty of time, he told himself.

He reckoned he was a whaler? George said. You don't get whalers no more.

Not legal ones, said Jack.

He said he was in the paunch, and it looked like it was breathing, and they cut it open, and out came this foot with a boot on it.

Yes, said Jack.

It's all writ up on a board in the museum. Doreen! George called to a woman at the next table. What year was it that bloke got swallowed by the whale? In the museum.

Doreen turned around. Eighteen ninety-one, she said.

Knows that museum off by heart, Doreen does, said George. Eighteen ninety-one. I reckon he'd be pretty old by now. George and Leon broke into wheezy laughter.

Maybe he was his own ghost, said Leon.

George shook his head. I reckon you was conned. Bloke spun you a fancy one. And you fell for it.

The two men looked into their empty glasses.

Looks like I'd better buy the next round, said Jack. Gullible and all as I am.

Why would he of done it, though, George? asked Leon. What was in it for him?

Conning, said George. Your good con man, he cons for the fun of it.

But Jack, walking home through the cold night and looking up at the sky washed clean by last night's storm, wasn't so sure. The stars sparkled, a long way away, explained by science but not really understood. Not by people like him, who were happy to look up and let gazing at the sight be enough for them. The blackness so smooth, and the points of light so prickly and brilliant; he slowed his pace and bent his head back to let his eyes rest on them. On the day that his brother had died Jack had perhaps nearly died too. That was something to think about, but what might you make of it? And the hooded bleached-white stranger . . . perhaps he had really survived swallowing by a whale and lived to be called Jonah and bought drinks on the strength of it. He hadn't got a drink out of Jack. Had refused a mug of soup. Perhaps he was even now sitting in a warm room somewhere laughing at the way a stranger toiling up a hill had swallowed his yarn. Though Jack had been so exhausted he didn't think anyone could tell what he made of it. Except he had listened. He'd heard every word. He hadn't wanted to, but somehow he couldn't help himself. He'd heard every word, and remembered it to tell the blokes in the pub.

And Quarantine Bay, with its buried bodies and poisoned silk sold up and down the coast? Was that a story on the wall of the museum, too?

FERDIE AND BERENICE GO ON A PICNIC

Now he was a student living in London, Ferdie was in the habit of saying to women he fell in love with: Sometimes I'm afraid I'm just another Casaubon.

He was waiting for one to say, No, of course you're not, anything but, no way—any sort of ardent denial—but they never did. They never had. They said, Casaubon . . . ? Sometimes they just said, Cas . . . ?, looking at him with big liquid eyes waiting to be filled with the knowledge.

So then he would say, *Middlemarch*? George Eliot? Adding more and more details as they looked more and more solemn. The story of Dorothea? A novel? Published in 1872?

Probably the best novel written in the nineteenth century, he would say. Dorothea is a rich and beautiful and good woman who wants to do something important with her money and intelligence. She marries Casaubon, a biblical scholar, who is working on a great book, a key to all mythologies. She thinks she can love him, cheer and help and support him, be a handmaiden to the great work. And her money will be used to noble purpose.

Do you mean you're looking for a handmaiden? a girl might mutter.

It's a mistake more terrible than you could believe, Ferdie would go on. He's supposed to be a man of God but he's so cold he's wicked. He denies her love. He won't even have sex with her, so we understand; it is a Victorian novel, but that's clear. He steals her money—legally, of course, but still wickedly. When he dies, which he does after a while, you think thank God, but then his will stipulates that she can only inherit her own money, her fortune which she brought to the marriage, if she does not marry a certain person. The person, it turns out, that she falls in love with. On top of it all, Casaubon is a bad scholar. The vaunted work of many decades simply doesn't exist. He can't do it, he hasn't been doing it, it's all pretence; it has to be above criticism so he's too frightened to even try, and maybe there you should feel sorry for him. It's ego that drives him, not scholarship.

The stolen money and sex denied often interest women and they will sometimes question him about what else happens in the story and he can explain how it is about wrong choices made from the best of intentions, and how the plot coils inexorably and squeezes lives. In fact, he says, it's about two very bad marriages. There's a character called Lydgate who's a brilliant medico; he falls in love with Rosamond who is very pretty (if you like that blonde pink and white stuff) and frivolous and extravagant, and to keep her he has to become a fashionable doctor instead of doing research. He and Dorothea would have been a great couple, intellectually and idealistically, and she could have seen her money doing the good she wanted.

Well, said one girl, people never do fall in love with the right people.

Another said, Seems a bit cold-blooded. People being good people to marry, better people to marry.

He'd never met one who knew straight off who Casaubon is.

He wondered if he knew the reason for this. He always fell for girls who were pretty. He liked women who looked as though they lived in Pre-Raphaelite paintings, with masses of springy red hair—though blonde or chestnut was okay, provided it did the right springy thing—and milk-white faces with round chins and a sense of rich and flowery garments. Not one of these girls had ever heard of *Middlemarch*, so he was beginning to wonder if he would ever find Pre-Raphaelite beauty and his kind of cleverness going together. He considered this as a possibly sexist thought, but told himself it would be sexist to assume a pretty woman couldn't be clever, or a clever woman pretty. He was sensitive to perceptions of sexism, his mother had brought him up to be so, occasionally offering his father as a model to be avoided, in a moderately scientific manner, not particularly emotional—as in *that mad old sexist, your father*, said in a calm voice—and he was glad of this education, it came in handy in his present circumstances. He decided that the solution was to persevere: sooner or later there would be a woman beautiful and bright. Well, he knew they were bright; he wanted one who knew the things that interested him.

He wished he was a man like George Henry Lewes, who could fall besotted with the truly astonishing mental beauty of a George Eliot, and ignore or maybe not even see her equally astounding ugliness, at least if photos are to be believed. Dorothea Brooke, beautiful and rich and good and quite clever, makes a disastrous choice. Mary Ann, or Marian she decided was less vulgar, before opting for the oomph of the masculine George Eliot, Marian Evans, plain and poor and gifted, has her disasters but finds a man who not only loves her for herself but lives in sin with her for years. Ferdie admired George Henry Lewes, and hoped that one day he might be like him. He examined the women he saw in the corridors of the university, looking for someone plain and clever and adorable, but so far had failed to find one.

Berenice worked at a place that dealt in computers, providing technical support, she had a good brain, she'd just never heard of George Eliot. He offered to lend her *Middlemarch*, but she said she wasn't a great reader. But she did say, Was Dorothea in love with Casaubon?

A good question, said Ferdie. She thought it was a good thing to do, that she would come to love him.

Berenice shook her head. It's wrong not to marry for love, she said. Coming to love, what a joke. Didn't George Eliot know that?

She was a Victorian novelist.

Didn't they know about love?

Oh yes, they did, but they didn't always trust it.

George Eliot. George Sand. George seems a good name for a woman to take on when she wants to assume a masculine persona. There's George in *The Famous Five*, too. You read Enid Blyton, said the girl before Berenice, my god. Why not? he asked. It was on the shelves at home, would have been his mother's when she was a girl. There was a time when he read everything on the shelves at home. Including *Middlemarch*.

Berenice had red-gold hair and big grey eyes. She was slender, waif-like even, with a touch of nineteenth-century tuberculosis chic, but of course she was healthy. He wondered if her pubic hair was the same precious metal colour but when he got to look he saw that she was completely shaved, like a bluish marble statue. Her cleft as bare and linear as a child's. You should try it, she said. All that hair, yuck. It's so free and clean and lovely without.

He did not say, I don't feel dirty and imprisoned in my pubic hair. He liked the way it curled, softly stiff and brown, around his penis.

I'll do it for you, if you like, said Berenice, but he said, Not now, thank you.

He knew he wasn't a Casaubon. He was younger, for a start, and much handsomer, much livelier. He liked sex and expected to manage love one day. He had no intention of marrying to get a secretary. He would not punish a woman who loved him for having flaws. Would he? He thought that being aware of the situation would make him able to avoid it. And no way would he do her out of her money, should she happen to have any. But he also knew that it wasn't any of these things that made him truly fearful. It was that matter of his ambition being greater than his intelligence, which had turned everything to salt and ashes and dung in Casaubon's mouth and might do so in his. The whole lifetime spent in not doing what he claimed to be doing because he had understood that he could not do it.

Ferdie's PhD money would run out after three years; there'd be a bit more time after that but not much. He thought he could do it; so presumably did Casaubon, at the beginning. And he wasn't exactly working on the key to all mythologies, though the topic seemed equally large. He'd got the idea when he read some words in an essay: *The gods never die. None of the gods that ever lived has ever died.* 'The gods are dead: long live the gods' was the title he had chosen. A working title, he called it. There was a lengthy subtitle which changed from time to time.

At one time, dipping into *The Golden Bough*, he wondered if Eliot had modelled Casaubon's enterprise on James Frazer's, but the chronology wasn't right, *Middlemarch* being 1872 and *The Golden Bough*'s twelve volumes taking from 1890 to 1915. Perhaps the idea had been in the wind for some time. He knew that some scholars didn't think a lot of Frazer, being critical of him because he got all his material from secondary sources, but Casaubon who had never intended to do anything else couldn't manage even that. *Even that* . . . There was a phrase. Ferdie was doing his work on literature, not anthropology, so by definition he was looking at people's writing on his subject.

One person who would have known what he was doing in invoking Casaubon he didn't tell his fears to. That was his great-aunt Pepita, on his father's side, who had given him her car. She was ninety-four and thought it was time she stopped driving. It was a 1930s Sunbeam Talbot roadster with a canvas hood and a dickey-seat. It was called Pegasus.

Has it got wings? he asked.

It is a trusty steed, she said, with many powers. It may be given to you to see them.

He was pleased to have a car at all, since he didn't have the money to buy one himself. Even better, for you, she said with her still-wicked smile, is its having had only one careful little old lady driver.

You weren't very old when you got it, he said.

True.

She didn't seem very old now, either. She had been a teacher of elocution, still had a few special clients, and would produce scrapbooks of correspondence from grateful and often surprising ex-students. Good grief, said Ferdie, what a catalogue of the great and the good. Ever thought of blackmail?

Pepita's face said she did not consider this worthy of an answer.

The letters were not just one-off notes of thanks. Her former students seemed moved to send her postcards from time to time, just to keep in touch. I expect it will all end up in the tip when I go, she said.

She knelt on the floor to get out the Rockingham cups from the bottom of the china cabinet. Not these, of course, she said. She stood up in a quick graceful movement. The cups didn't even clatter. She boiled water in a spirit kettle to make tea in a pot round and ribbed like a pumpkin, and poured it into the shallow precious cups. There was thin bread and butter and dark fruit cake.

You will have to leave me soon, she said. I have to prepare for my date tonight.

A beau? he asked.

She smiled mysteriously. Oh, she said in a pensive voice, a dear boy. I taught him in, let me see, the late fifties. He was quite a lad then. These days . . . he has a fondness for grand restaurants. A taste acquired when he was at the embassy in Paris. I think I shall wear my black lace fascinator with a diamante clip, nearly hidden. It's always seductive.

Pepita held her fine wrinkled cheek to be kissed. It was soft and scented and faintly rosy in the rich dim light of her house. This aunt, the tea party, her blue eyes shining on him; he suddenly felt immensely lucky.

Come and see me, my dear, from time to time, and bring Pegasus to visit. I shall pine for news of the dear old boy.

Pepita had never married, but it wasn't for lack of the flirtatious arts. Ferdie could remember odd remarks from his father about his aunt's adventures. She was supposed to have claimed she didn't ever feel like marriage at the time. I like my own company, she said, and there is no shortage of men should one feel in need of a little masculine diversion. Ferdie wondered if he could understand the pleasures of a lifetime's coquetry. What do I know? he said to himself. Maybe she slept with all her clients. She certainly dined with them. Bet you could tell us a thing or two, eh Pegasus, dear old boy. He eased his foot on the clutch as she had warned him, but still the car leapt forward.

Berenice thought Pegasus was wonderful when she first saw him but after driving for a bit she wasn't so sure. When it rained and she got soaked before Ferdie got the hood up, she hated it.

Next time he visited Pepita he talked to her about *Middle-march*. Ah, poor dear Dorothea. Silly girl, how could she be so taken in by that frightful old bore? And if she had to get married, why not Lydgate? Of course that's what we all think, but there'd be no story if she'd done that. I often wonder if that is why people marry. There'd be no story if they didn't. I'm lucky, she said, with a wicked little smug air. I've had plenty of stories and no need of wedlock.

She said 'wedlock' with such a snap of finality that he laughed.

I'm still planning to live happily ever after, she said. And what about your generation? They're doing quite well without.

Oh, we mostly get caught eventually.

In the trap, she said.

She was wearing a jumper in a pale cream colour, so fine it had to be cashmere, with a cream silk shirt and a soft tweed skirt. She had gossamer stockings on her slender legs and polished brown shoes with a small heel. Once again she had to go and get dressed for dinner, another old pupil, on a flying visit from New York; she was planning to wear her ashes of roses cocktail gown which had quite a daring neckline; it seemed the occasion for it. And her new pashmina, in a slightly deeper rose colour. She'd already had her nails painted to match. Ferdie wished he had enough money to take her out to a grand dinner, one that would warrant the ashes of roses cocktail dress. Whatever that was. With the daring neckline. He wondered, were these proper thoughts to have about a great-aunt?

He got into the habit of calling to see her most weeks. She lived in a village but it wasn't far to drive and though Pegasus

71

drank petrol like water he decided to forget that. He liked to talk to her because she knew what he was talking about.

The sin of Casaubon, she said one day, and it gave him a start, he thought she might have guessed how that failed scholar troubled him, the sin of Casaubon was envy. I know despair is supposed to be the most terrible sin of all, and it is bad, but it doesn't hurt others, except as they love you. Which is an occupational hazard of living. But envy, resentment of the happiness or good of others, so that you desire to do things to harm them, that is very bad. Other sins—lust, sloth, gluttony, even covetousness—are benign in comparison.

That's only six.

I can only ever remember six. A different six each time, usually.

Ferdie counted on his fingers and thought. Wrath, he said.

Ah yes, wrath. There you are, a good honest sin. And often, I should think, appropriate, even necessary. I have been wrathful and most righteously so on occasions. But envy, no. A mean and withering and poisonous sin. Self-poisoning.

To be feared, worst of all, then.

Yes. And avoided. You must train yourself out of it, if you notice any tendencies. As I am sure you do not.

He felt comforted. Maybe he was a Casaubon in his talent falling short of his ambition, but he had not caught himself in envy.

How had Pepita known his fear of being Casaubon?

You are something of a sport, she said. Aren't you. You know all the old cultural references.

So do you.

I'm seventy years older than you. It was the thing, even for teachers of elocution. But not any more, not for anyone much, these days. *You are a sport.* I said something like that to one of my really young pupils and he said, Oh no, I am not at all good at games.

Yes, I know I'm a sport, said Ferdie, and believe me it doesn't please me. There's nobody left to talk to.

We're living in a world that is narrowing, and darkening, said Pepita. Its mental furnishings are reducing to a minimalism that is becoming painful. It's a kind of sensory deprivation—a form of torture, if you're used to something grander, richer, more full of light.

Old people are always supposed to be saying that kind of thing, she sighed. But sometimes it's going to be true.

Berenice didn't much like economical outings but she was quite keen on the idea of a picnic on a warm day. He took boiled eggs and ham with some very good bread and butter and peaches, with cider to drink. Berenice had brought a bottle of champagne. Daddy keeps me in champagne, she said. He thinks it's the only suitable drink for a young woman.

Your father must be rather rich.

He doesn't think a young woman should drink a lot of champagne, said Berenice.

It was a lovely summery day with zephyrous breezes and the leaves massed dark green on the trees, very still except when they twirled in little eddies of wind. Everything calm, and then suddenly a little cluster of leaves twirling in an invisible wind. The trees were oaks, with trunks larger than a person could hug, and branches beginning above head height and spreading in a horizontal fashion, like arms stretching out. Ferdie thought of the word benign when looking at them. Their sheltering arms. And also the words that had become associated, like hearts of oak. Solid, trustworthy, keeping you safe like the sturdy ships that were built from them. And winning battles and gaining empires.

He was being fanciful. It was necessary to pay attention to Berenice. Would she want to know about the sixteen-hundred-year-old oak in Yorkshire that could hold seventy people in its hollow trunk, or the one in Sherwood Forest called Robin Hood's Larder, that was a thousand years old when it was blown down in 1966?

Fancy being in a forest so close to London, she said.

It's not very big, said Ferdie. But big enough for our picnic.

He'd brought a rug and a faded Indian cotton tablecloth, the only one he had and which he never used at home. He had glasses with long stems and blue and white china plates.

This is all very proper, said Berenice.

Of course. No point in doing it if we don't do it proper. What did you expect, takeaway chicken in a box?

For a while he'd been in love with a girl called Alison who'd wondered if his desire to do things properly came out of his study of English literature. Its provenance is so essentially domestic, she said. He thought of Spenser and Pope and Shakespeare and Congreve and Tennyson. Domestic, he said. Don't you mean—life? Okay, said Alison, domestic life, if you like. The thing is, you pursue it in rooms, you sit in a room and read, in a comfortable house—or an Oxbridge college—you read and you look about you and you want what you see to look good. To reassure you that you can keep on reading. That you don't have to get up and change things.

He was a little bemused that what he had imagined was going to be a penetrating comment on his life's work turned out to be really only about interior decoration. That did not stop him considering her remark as if it did have cultural and philosophical significance. He did like orderliness and elegance—no wonder he'd fallen in love with Great-Aunt Pepita—but did that come about because he was a student of literature, or more fashionably these days of cultural studies (he had the terminology if not the intention), or was he such a student because it was in his nature to appreciate the ordered and elegant?

His father had been enraged when Ferdie told him, somewhat after the event, feeling the need of accomplished fact to deal with the anger he expected. Medicine was what he was intended for, in his father's eyes. Failing that, the law. Architecture, at a pinch; it was a bit arty but still potentially a prestige- and money-generating profession. Ferdie knew that had his father looked closely at his results he would have seen that they were gradually excluding the medicine option, if not law entirely, but he was happy when Ferdie reported high distinctions, and did not enquire with any rigour as to what subjects they may have been in, his own money-generating profession not leaving much time for paying attention to children. When he registered them it was too late; Ferdie was set in his course.

His father looked at him with hostile eyes. You realise, I hope, that you are condemning yourself to life as a second-rater?

I'd never have got into medicine, so there I'd have been a failure. I might have made it into law, but that's where I'd've been truly second rate. I'm good at this, top rate. Studying top-rate stuff.

Only because nobody with any ability wants to do it. Where will it get you? A schoolteacher. A dominie. A poverty-stricken usher.

Ferdie admired his father's vocabulary and took it for the beginning of an acceptance of defeat. Well, he said, after a while I'm expecting to be a poverty-stricken PhD student, and then, who knows. I'll be doing what matters to me. I know you probably think I'm an idiot idealist, but doing what I love is more important than making money.

It's easy to say that now. Wait till you're as old as me.

Of course Ferdie wasn't going to say, I hope I'm nothing like you when I'm your age. He didn't know his father well enough to be so rude. He did mutter, Isn't it supposed to be you telling me that money can't buy happiness? Now, reclining on a rug while a woman as beautiful as Berenice poured champagne into a glass that in her hand became a goblet, he didn't feel poverty-stricken.

She was wearing a sundress in a fine cotton Liberty print of silvery green willow fronds that owed a lot to William Morris, with a hooped skirt and thin straps over her white shoulders—she'd carefully chosen a shady spot to keep them from getting sunburned—and carried a small white curly-fur jacket. With her springing red-gold hair and silvery-grey eyes she looked enchanting.

Berenice was a quiet sort of girl, given to occasional brief and sharpish remarks. If Ferdie had thought about it he would have noticed that she didn't have a lot to say, but he didn't think about it at all. Not then. He had plenty to say; she gazed at him with her large grey eyes and he was entranced by her beauty and his words. He was telling her about Pan. Pan was where he was up to in his work.

He's a terribly important god, he said. He was the god of woods and fields—which is a fair bit of the ancient world—and shepherds and flocks, but more than that, the name Pan means 'all', so that he comes to be seen as a symbol of the whole universe, as a personification of nature.

Wasn't he half goat? Horrible hairy haunches, and cloven feet?

Handsome hairy haunches, he said. Yes, exactly, so he unites the animal with the human. The ancient world valued that, animals were significant, and they liked to be inclusive, not chop things out and get rid of them. And he played a pipe, a syrinx, which he invented—that's another story—played it brilliantly, though maybe not quite so well as Apollo. He was lustful, of course, but that's also important, it means fecundity. You have to admit, that's an issue these days. Ferdie was thinking of his half-sister Aurora, who at thirty-six was very miserable failing to get pregnant.

Here in the woods, said Ferdie, this is the haunt of Pan.

So far north? said Berenice. I thought he was Mediterranean.

In ancient times. But the Romans came to Britain. They brought their gods with them.

The Romans were driven out.

That's not to say the gods went too. Anyway, there's this marvellous story. At the moment when the angels told the shepherds—watching their flocks by night and all that—about the birth of Christ, at that very moment there was a deep groan, heard through all the isles of Greece, crying *Great Pan is dead!* All the gods of Olympus were dethroned and all the oracles ceased at that very moment.

Berenice looked at Ferdie.

Milton wrote a poem about the nativity and it has this really sad bit, of weeping and lamenting, mourning for the old gods. Elizabeth Barrett Browning, on the other hand, positively gloats.

Is she the one who spent her life on a sofa until Robert Browning came and married her?

You know? said Ferdie.

Obviously all she needed was sex.

Possibly. They eloped.

The idea of sex.

He could have seen this as a suggestion, but he was too keen to talk about his gods. Anyway, he went on, Elizabeth wrote a long poem rejoicing in the death of Pan, how we don't need him any more, we've got Christianity and Truth, with a capital T, and all that. Ferdie shook his head. It's sad really. Sad and simple-minded.

I don't know. I'm with Elizabeth. Entirely a good thing. Much better stick with Christianity. Much safer.

Suddenly she raised her white arms, slender and sculpted as a statue, tipped her head back and cried in a loud voice, Great Pan is dead!

She ran her fingers through her hair so it sprang even more wildly and looked at him out of the corners of her eyes. She leaned forward and picked up his glass, pouring more champagne.

Ferdie looked at her in amazement.

Who needs oracles. Animal insides and all that. Great Pan is dead. And a good thing too.

Are you a Christian?

I live in a Christian society. I'm not a pagan.

Yes, but a real believing Christian?

Aren't you?

No, said Ferdie. I like all the stories, the myths, the music, the art. But there's too much wickedness in the religion.

Wickedness? She gave a dramatic shiver.

Someone walking over your grave, said Ferdie.

The sun going behind a cloud, said Berenice. She pointed upwards. But it wasn't just a summer cloud flitting over the sun. The sky was no longer blue, it was the colour of lead, and seemed heavy, like lead. Oh poo, said Berenice, I hate these summer storms.

The air was still, not the summery murmurous stillness of earlier but an anxious and waiting pause, almost a paralysis, as if time were holding its breath. The light became more lurid, a strange light that changed the colours of things, made objects unlike themselves, as if night were about to fall, though it was far too early for twilight even to begin.

Do you know, said Ferdie in a distracted voice, in English we talk about the fall of night, and the French call it the fall of day? Different sorts of logic.

There's going to be the godfather of a storm, said Berenice. Quick! She started throwing food and plates into the basket. Ferdie drained his glass, thinking it was criminal to glug down good champagne like that. Berenice tipped hers on the ground. He caught up the rug and cloth, grabbed the basket and ran with them to the car. Berenice was trying to get her arms into her little fur jacket and hurry to the car at the same time. She got it twisted and was writhing around in a panic trying to pull it on and trapping her arms so she couldn't escape. Ferdie pulled it off and was straightening it to help her put it on properly but she was jumping in the car. Hurry, she said, hurry. I hate storms.

Ferdie hurrying did not go through the usual solemn rituals of getting Pegasus's engine going, and the car wouldn't start. Berenice hitched her jacket round her neck, buried her face and moaned.

There were pebbles, not falling, flung from the sky. Hailstones. Occasional and, of course, random, except that it seemed somebody was taking aim and deliberately slowly pelting them. Ferdie got Pegasus's engine to turn over but still it wouldn't start.

I'll put the hood up, he said. He was wrestling with it when Berenice was struck on the head by a hailstone as big as a walnut.

She howled, and covered her head with her hands. Blood ran down her forehead, she brushed it off with her fingers and licked them, then gagged.

He'd put the hood up only once before. Pepita had shown him; his fragile old great-aunt had nimbly unstrapped and unclipped and folded out the stiff ribbed canvas without a scratch to her long rosy nails. He found himself fighting with it. It caught his hand as it snapped shut like a trap and he had to dance around with his fingers in his mouth yelling to make the pain go away. It was too late to realise he should have practised this at home first.

Sorry, he said to Berenice. She wasn't there, in the car. She was running crazily, awkwardly, very fast, through the grand spreading oaks of the wood. He called, but she didn't stop. He started after her. She was very swift. She had lost her shoes, her feet were bare. The wood had seemed quite small when they entered it with their picnic but now it seemed to go for sinister miles.

He caught her when she fell down the bank of a small stream and lay wailing in the water.

You are in a state, he said. He pulled her out and held her in his arms, speaking soothing words to her until she stopped shivering and stuttering and trying to twitch away from him and resume her flight. There was a strange deep groaning sound that filled the sky. The branches moved with a restless creaking noise. It began to rain hard. He cajoled her back to the car. Her sobs dwindled to hiccups. The little white fur was snagged on a bush and he picked it off. He wrapped her in the picnic blanket. *Nice and cosy*, he said. Slowly and carefully he manoeuvred the hood into position.

There, that's better. He imagined himself one day with a small child, consoling her with these meaningless comforting words. *All fixed now.* Slowly he worked on the hood and this time he got it up. *There*, he said, *not wet now*.

He knew he'd flooded the engine trying to start it too hastily. He went slowly, remembering Pepita's instructions, her thin little old hands, the fingers coaxing. When it started he slowly eased in the choke, giving it time to warm up. Then he let in the clutch and Pegasus began his slow progress along the winding track through the woods.

My shoes! said Berenice.

He remembered the little glittery mules with curly heels she'd been wearing. Funny footwear for a picnic, he'd thought, but since they'd only strolled a short distance across spongy mossy grass that was all right, and he had admired the slip-sloppy way they made her walk, and how her bottom rolled as she stepped gingerly in them.

They were Jimmy Choos, she said. If you knew what they cost.

He braked. I'll go back and find them.

No! No. Let's just go.

The rain drummed on the roof. She combed her hair with her fingers. She didn't look bedraggled, her hair sprang as energetically as ever, but she did look woebegone and fierce at the same time, her eyes trembling and even more silvery under a film of tears, her eyelashes clotted with them. I don't know what possessed me. A picnic! I'm an urban girl. I hate nature.

He couldn't remember the track winding so far into the woods. They were very dark green in the rain, sombre and tossing like horses' manes in a slow gallop. Of course the trees themselves weren't moving, they were fixed and immemorial. But didn't his sideways glance seem to catch a sly sidestepping? He was sure this was not the sunny path that had led them to the grove for their picnic. They were in an impenetrable net of trees. A cage. A trap.

He stopped the car and jumped out. He spread his arms wide and tipped his head back. Great Pan lives, he shouted. He turned around. Great Pan lives!

What are you doing? said Berenice.

Leaving no stone unturned.

The leaves stirred. Ahead was a gap in the canopy. The leaden cloud cover began to shred, a scrap of blue sky showed. Soon the track brought them to a country road, and the light had become summery again.

Ferdie supposed that Pepita invited her friends to tea and was taken out to dinner. He liked to drink tea with her, he liked the blue spirit flame under the kettle, the teapot shaped like a silver pumpkin, the arc of golden liquid pouring into the Rockingham cups. In these constant rituals was a whole history of tea-drinking, in fiction and in fact, in pleasant rooms where polite conversation gave no indication of the anguish or bliss, the sorrow or simple calm contentment, of the couples, the families, the visitors gratefully sipping. You could not lay waste to a tea table, no matter how angry or grief-stricken or hurt you were, it stood inviolable and as a measure of your own disorder. Pepita pouring tea: if it had been a painting it would have been an emblem of a way of life, that understood a need for order on the surface but by no means mistook that for what was really going on. He sipped at the hot tea, milkless, with lemon, pale, astringent, refreshing; one more sip, it seemed, and he would understand, but then there was the gilt and roses of the emptied cup and he doubted he was any wiser. He sat in one of the upright armchairs and Pepita sparkled at him, her dark blue eyes teasing sideways, her small mouth pouting into laughter. He thought, this is conversation, and it is an art that Berenice does not have. But perhaps, when she is ninety . . .

It's a dead art, said Pepita, with her uncanny gift for reading his thoughts. Tea-drinking.

I thought it was quite popular . . .

As a beverage, perhaps. As a ceremony, quite dead. Maybe little pockets still practising, but they are doomed. There'll be none of us left soon.

Maybe people will put it into theme parks.

Indeed. And that's a sign of death. Interesting: it's progress, which is almost never civilisation.

He told her about the picnic in the woods, the sudden leaden sky, the groaning, and Berenice's terror. Told it as a story, polished and offered as a gift in return for tea out of Rockingham cups.

So, she said, you went on a picnic and a storm came up. This is England, after all.

Yes, he said. I know.

Ah, but you don't. None of us do. And perhaps it was dangerous of Berenice to deny the great god Pan. To insist on his mortality.

Then, you think it was a good idea for me to . . .?

I think a great many things, all at once. The older I get the more strange things I can hold in my head simultaneously. I take great pleasure in it.

He was thinking about how to answer this when she went on, And it is your thesis, is it not, that the gods still live?

I hope so . . .

I have known many theses, and there was always a great deal of hope involved.

Successfully?

Generally. Though it was usually difficult to have faith, at the time.

It got dark, so suddenly—but then it usually does in summer storms, doesn't it? Maybe we should have made a libation.

Didn't you?

Berenice emptied her glass, at the end.

Emptying your glass isn't the same as a libation. No ritual. And it should be the first thing.

I suppose so.

Do you think the oracles really did stop with the birth of Christ? she asked.

Do you know? Did they?

That's what the death of Pan is supposed to mean. Not that oracles ever were a lot of help. Entirely dangerous advice, since it could mean one thing or its opposite: what you wanted to happen, or most feared.

The ambiguity always strikes me as very clever.

Oh yes. But who wants clever? When I was young I imagined growing into a sibylline old woman one day. It hasn't happened yet, but it might. She giggled. I think perhaps I am too frivolous.

You seem wise to me.

Oh Ferdie. You are falling into two fallacies. One is that the old are wise. They are not. They are often not even old. I am mostly not much more than twenty-three. On a quiet day I might be twenty-seven. I know I look older, but it's the feeling that counts. And one cannot see one's own wrinkles.

Ferdie could see her wrinkles, but he believed her when she said twenty-three. She seemed younger than Berenice, most of the time.

Two fallacies, I said. Ah yes. That the oracles were wise. They were not. They were cryptic, to disguise the fact they hadn't a clue, which made them cruel. The king asks, Shall I win the battle? and the oracle replies, The king shall win the battle, and so he does, but it is his enemy the king of the other side who wins, he the consulter of the oracle is defeated. The oracle doesn't care.

As I said, clever.

But not wise. Or good.

Wisdom would be in ignoring the oracle, said Ferdie.

You couldn't, said Pepita. When people tried, the oracle turned round and trapped them. Not always straightaway. Look at Oedipus. Took several decades, but the prophecy that he would murder his father and marry his mother did come true.

I suppose so. Trying to subvert them only made them worse.

And yet one should not submit to a callous fate, said Pepita.

Maybe, since you reckon you're frivolous, don't you think, maybe that makes you truly wise.

Her face became unusually sombre. I may feel twenty-three, but I know I'm not. I know too well what the future will bring. Death. When you're as old as me everyone has died. Every one of your fellows. I'm lucky, I've got young pupils, otherwise I'd be as solitary as a pillar in the desert.

What about family?

She held her hand out to him and he found himself taking it and kissing it. One of her rings was a half-circle of large diamonds held in strong gold claws. That was my grandmother's, said Pepita. Perhaps I should give it to you, for your Pre-Raphaelite girl. Nicely of the period.

He laughed, in shock. It had not occurred to him to give Berenice a ring.

Pepita tipped up the kettle and poured more water into the teapot; he passed her his cup. Steam rose.

The fumes of Yunnan tea, said Pepita.

Maybe I shall become possessed, and start to prophesy. The oracles at Delphi came from fumes out of the rock.

The navel of the world, said Pepita. I suppose you also know, the most ancient oracle in Greece was the sound of oak leaves rustling? The oracle of Zeus at Dodona. Did your oak trees tell you anything about the future?

Probably that there isn't likely to be any with Berenice. I'll be lucky if she ever talks to me again. I doubt she'll ever forgive me the Jimmy Choos.

Jimmy Choo shoes. That could be a very good test.

*

In fact Berenice didn't seem to have given him up. He'd dropped her at her flat for a hot bath and cocoa and bed, all of which she'd refused his help with, and supposed that she would never ever want to see him again. But when he rang her she was quite civil, and when he offered to take her out to dinner (thinking he would give up going to the pub and live on boiled potatoes for a while to finance it) she said she'd like that, to call her in a few days and make a time.

Berenice. He wondered what it would be like to say that name, think that name, every day for the rest of your life, your tongue forming its syllables and knowing its meaning for you that very few other words could ever have. When he said it now, wondering, doubting, it seemed to mesmerise him. It was like a spell. It robbed him of power. Maybe this was how you knew you were in love. Applying logic was no help at all.

He was making a list of all the gods that, according to Milton's ode, died 'On the Morning of Christ's Nativity'. Apollo leaves Delphos with a 'hollow shreik', there is weeping and loud lament from the 'Nimphs', the Lars and Lemures moan, Peor and Baalim forsake their temples. And so the list goes on, not just the classical gods, but also Ashtaroth, Hammon, Thamuz, Moloch, Isis and Orus, the Dog Anubis, Osiris, Typhon: they are all cancelled out by 'the dredded Infant's hand'. The poem before the Ode in his book of Milton was a vacation exercise, and he couldn't help suspecting something of that kind of necessity behind this one.

When Milton described it, in his last stanza, as 'our tedious Song', Ferdie wasn't inclined to disagree too violently.

He knew he wasn't really concentrating on this. The word Berenice kept sounding in his head. And with what ambiguity. Berenice: love, or dread? He looked up her name in Brewer: she was the wife of one of the Ptolemys, she vowed to sacrifice her hair to the gods if her husband came back home the conqueror of Asia. Presumably he did, for she hung the hair in the temple, but it was stolen; the king was told that the winds had wafted it to heaven. And there it is, it still can be seen, near the tail of Leo, forming the cluster of stars known as the Coma Berenices.

He thought of Berenice's frizz of red-gold hair shining as stars in the heavens. A good sacrifice, and worth stealing. He could write a poem about it. He saw again her sculpted white arms raised, heard her voice shouting the death of Pan. She'd surprised him, and he liked that. A sonnet perhaps. Or a villanelle. Maybe a stanza for every star. His father didn't know about the poetry. William liked poems but they weren't something he valued as an activity in the present. Ferdie pushed aside the Milton list. A fuzz of red-gold stars to dim the night. Dim? Star the night. No, that was a repetition. Light? A tittupping rhyme. His father would be certain that no good could come of such a wastrel occupation. At least a schoolmaster had a salary, which was more than could be said for a poet. A party; somebody says, And what do you do in life? Me? Oh, I'm a wastrel. Would anybody know what it meant? Fuzz, or frizz? Frizz, perhaps. His mind's eye saw her lying on the olive-green satin of her bed, naked, luminous, her bare childish cleft (taking him back twenty years to kindergarten and the girl next door, stepping out of her knickers and lifting her dress in the cubby house at the bottom of her garden, letting him look but not touch), her narrow hips barely curving into her waist, her tiny round breasts and then the high colour of her lips and hair, her mouth slyly smiling, her teeth pinching her lip. Such nakedness seeming a gift, but also a tease; not really a gift, not even an offer, more a glimpse of what might be, if . . . what? He passed a test? Made the right bargain? Negotiated a suitable price? The gods were happy with a swatch of hair; what would Berenice want?

He suddenly thought of Ruskin, how different his life would have been if his bride Effie had done as Berenice and shaved herself. Poor Ruskin, scared off consummating his marriage, any consummation with a woman then or later, because of the shock of Effie's pubic hair. What a different person he might have become. He imagined writing a neat little metafiction, with Effie shaven and Ruskin happy.

A poem, anyway. A naked woman, childish in body and mind, a swatch of hair turning into the cluster of stars near the tail of Leo, the lion, the fifth sign of the Zodiac. A good poem, tight, mysterious, a bit old-fashioned. He wished he lived in a time when the old ideas which so excited him had been everyday currency. He worked on it for an hour and then rewarded himself with a call to Berenice in the flesh, though only at the end of a telephone line, Berenice certainly not naked, being clever about computers in the campus shop. Yes, she said, they could meet but not this week; give her a ring later, this week there was too much on. Pepita's diamond ring: tell me when you need it, she had said. He went back to Milton and the ode 'On the Morning of Christ's Nativity'. Not a cheerful poem, not joyful, not a carol or a celebration, being about the way Christ 'Forsook the Courts of Everlasting Day, and chose with us a darksom House of mortal Clay'. Very heavy and sticky it sounds. And all the good that will come of this will have to wait till after 'the bitter cross', and even when the terrible pain of that has been borne, humanity has to go on waiting for 'the wakefull trump of doom' to 'thunder through the deep'. Moreover, loss comes at the very moment of birth: 'the Oracles are dumm', Apollo flees from Delphos, the nymphs mourn. And Berenice lies on her bed like a constellation in the night sky, for gazing, not touching. So he fears. Coma Berenices: Berenice's hair.

And he remembers that she chose this Christianity, repudiated Pan and his pagan works. Even Milton doesn't sound too happy with the choice.

In the dead of night when he is fast asleep the phone rings. He wakes in fear, his heart like a large slimy trout jumping into his throat and stopping him breathing; the phone in the night is always bad news. Unless it is your mother in Australia getting the time wrong again. Ma-ma, he starts to protest, but this time she is not apologising. Ferdinand, she says, which in itself is grim enough, Ferdinand . . . your father . . . and the trout jumps in his throat again.

Your father . . . he's dead.

All these years of 'your father', never his name. And now this final notice, and still no name.

Dead? he asks, as though he doubts; he doesn't, but the brain needs schooling in such a difficult idea. How?

Lynette rang. His mother pauses so he can take this in. The second wife and the third never talk, normally. She wasn't making much sense, his mother says. He seems to have drowned and had a heart attack.

Ferdie says, You mean, had a heart attack, and drowned?

Perhaps that's what she meant. I don't think it's what she said.

Ferdie listens, to hear if there is any sorrow in her words. All those many thousands of kilometres they've travelled, and yet the person speaking them could be in the next room. But that doesn't make detecting the emotion in them easier. He knows his mother has never forgiven his father for leaving them when Ferdie was small, and for an older woman; it was the huge fact of their lives. Ferdie keeps a commonplace book in which he writes thoughts and ideas, quotations and shaped sentences of observation. *My mother lives in a cocoon*, he wrote once, *a tight little cocoon of bitterness; she collects scraps of grievance with which to make it cosy. It fits snugly and protects her, she will never fight her way out of it and grow into something else—something beautiful and free.* It was a good image, he thought, but he also doubted you could capture your mother like that and get her down in metaphors. She was a teacher at a smart girls school, she liked the job and did it well, but at home, in private, she worked on the cocoon. When he was small he was afraid she'd marry again, give him another unsatisfactory father, then as he grew older he realised with sadness and dismay that she never would. He told her often enough that she ought to, but she shook her head and smiled sadly like a saint. Except the time, when he was about sixteen, he announced that she should get a boyfriend. A crimson bruising blush of anger suffused her face. Ferdie! What a shocking thing to say. Never—never!—say that again. I am married to your father.

She had her own language for telling him the story of herself and his father; it was the high old language of romance, with noble terms for sad human weaknesses and failures. She was the heroine of the narrative, steadfast and true; the subject matter was her betrayal. His father was the brave knight who had failed to be faithful to his vows. She had offered a great love, rare and incorruptible; it had been misprized.

The facts were: his father had married a woman called Nerys and they'd had a daughter called Aurora. At some point Nerys had left and gone to be an Orange person. In his mother's story this marriage was a false start on her lover's part. Nerys was never going to be suitable and the most sensible thing she could have done was take herself off. And lucky too, for her own happiness. Then he'd met Helen, that was Ferdie's mother, and they had fallen fathomlessly in love and lived in bliss until William had fallen into the clutches of Lynette, an evil and predatory creature who enticed him away from his true love. A kind of witch, in fact. When he was small Ferdie had understood that it would not be long before William saw the error of this course and broke the spell; he saw the movie of *The Wizard of Oz* and knew that the bad witches were always defeated but it was a long time now since he had realised this would not happen. The true lovers would never be reunited.

Lynette had provided another narrative, a precise grid to lay over his mother's plaintive tale. Lynette was making a family tree so her daughter Erin would know her ancestors. Its straight neat verticals and horizontals allowed a quite different scope for the imagination. His father's marriage to Nerys, for instance, had taken place in 1968. Aurora had been born in March 1968, which meant they'd only just made it before the baby was born. Ferdie felt a faint prickle of shame run through his blood, not because of the out-of-wedlock conception—his best friend's parents were living in sin, as their son Daniel described it— but that the need for a hasty marriage was a fact on an official document for everyone to see and know. Nerys was born in September 1949, which meant that she was eighteen when she married, seventeen when she got pregnant, seriously young, nine years younger than William.

It didn't say when she left to become an Orange person. Helen used to say she still was and had made a go of it. Rather a hippie upbringing for a child, said Helen, communes and such, but Aurora had left all that behind, for a degree in economics and a career in investment banking—she was often on the television when the dollar moved—and was now also in an IVF programme trying to get pregnant.

There was Helen's data: born 1956, married 1977, Ferdie born 1978. And then Lynette, born 1950, married 1988, Erin born 1991. The symmetry of the three children, born every decade or so, and the last two conceived in wedlock; pregnancy wasn't why William left Helen for Lynette. Lynette born 1950: that was what enraged Helen, that her beloved husband should have left her for an older woman.

A cool catalogue of births, deaths and marriages, and enough anguish for half a dozen nineteenth-century novels.

On the telephone Helen says, I suppose you'll want to come for the funeral.

He feels the trout jump in his chest again. What is the fear now? Time? Money? The kind stepmother? The now forever lost father?

Of course you will, says his mother. I'll send you the money.

He is about to say, No, don't do that, I don't need to come, a funeral is no help with grief, though as the words shape themselves he wonders what is a help with grief and furthermore what is the grief he feels? For the father dying now? Or the father whom he had loved and who had loved him, they both knew that, but not in any way that was a comfort or a balm or a delight but rather was an awareness, a desolation even, of what might have been, ought to have been, that people more clever, more diligent than they might have created. When he tried to think of his father he recalled Lynette being cheerful and affectionate and making holidays good fun, demanding to know what his favourite meal was, what could she cook that he liked best, he must have some special thing, surely, and William coming late for dinner or not at all, giving him ten-dollar notes to go and enjoy himself, asking him freighted questions about his school-work. He feels the tears prickling in his throat for a loss that isn't much to do with death.

His mother is saying, I'll like having you to go with me. And there he is again, being his mother's little man. His mother's big man. I think you should call me Helen in public, she said when he was thirteen. Mama is all very nice in private, but a proper name is more grown up, don't you think? The name was heavy in his mouth, and clumsy; he forced himself to use it, thinking it must get easier with time, but it never did. When they went out she linked her arm in his, he had to hold it bent like a solid bar for her to hang on to, and sometimes she brushed his shoulder with her cheek and gave a pretty little laugh. He had a creepy thought that if he had been a girl she might have looked for a new man to fall in love with. He said to himself it was a miracle that he had escaped to the other side of the world. No, not escaped, it was too cruel to say escaped. It's only for a few years, she'd said, with visible bravery. And I can come and visit.

He hears himself letting her pay for him to come home. You should be able to get quite a cheap fare from your end, she said. And stay for a while. Make it a holiday. I'm sure you need one. Oh, and Ferdinand, can you tell your aunt Pepita? Lynette thought that would be best. She's a bit old to hear it long distance on the phone.

Whenever Ferdie sat in an aeroplane trundling down a runway trying to build up enough speed to achieve lift, he thought of the words *flying in the face of nature*. It was a phrase his mother used, borrowed from the old lady next door; the old lady said it in all seriousness and his mother as a joke but they both meant it. His mother was just pretending that she didn't. He was doing exactly the same thing. The various layers of the phrase pleased him. Flying in the face of nature. Not because he didn't know the physics of planes becoming airborne; he didn't, but believed other people did. He heard Berenice say, I am an urban girl, I do not know what possessed me.

He sat upright in his seat, trying to arrange his legs. His eyes were closed. He had a number of books with him, but he never read when the plane was going up or coming down. He thought instead. When he'd told Pepita his father was dead she stood still and gazed at him. She said, Drowned . . . oh he is drowned . . . her voice plangent and tearful. Oh my dear, she said, holding his shoulders, the words quivering between them, then she put her arms around him and held him. He rested his cheek on her head. He could smell her perfume, something delicious out of a bottle but also herself, odour of Pepita. Now in the plane he could smell it again, its gentle memory in his nostrils; it had become the smell of comfort. Maybe that was how you knew you wanted to marry someone: you smelt her, and you thought, this is the person I want to spend the rest of my life with. Like a secular odour of sanctity. Except of course that was dying and this was an odour of life. Pepita was sad for his father's youth. It is not proper that one generation should bury a younger, she said. It is not part of the fitness of things.

Did you know my father well?

He came to see me when he was in England. A most charming man. He seemed fond of marrying. And no, not well.

Neither did I. Periods of living with him, and then it was Lynette, really. She was nice. He always seemed to be at work.

Work, said Pepita. Her tone was musing.

Don't you think it was work?

Oh yes, it would have been work, and work it may have been that killed him. But work . . . it's a word of such power, we all have to bow and worship, it's so grand and noble and necessary, but does anyone peep through a finger and say, But—it's got no clothes on!

Ferdie laughed. Not bad coming from a woman of ninety-four who hasn't retired yet, he said.

Pepita said, Don't get me wrong. I like work. I just don't believe it's the emperor of all.

She fell silent. There were a lot of silences in the conversation that afternoon, as though they could laugh and talk and tease as usual, but every now and then had to stop and think about mortality. Pepita sat with her hands in her lap, turning the half-hoop of diamonds. If it had been her grandmother's it must have been his great-great-grandmother's. It was loose on Pepita's little spotted hand. He wondered if it had belonged to the grandmother as a young woman, had been slid on to a firm and fine-skinned finger with promises of love and a life together. Whatever had happened, whether or not the promises had been kept, here was the ring still, its unchanging self, while its first owner, and her children and all of their children except this one rather supernaturally old woman, were dust and ashes. Why don't you give it to Berenice? she said. It's the right period. He imagined Berenice's granddaughter saying the same words to her great-nephew. A ring would be marriage and he wasn't thinking of that; what he needed to know was if he was in love with her. Berenice. He couldn't smell her any more, though he knew her perfume was an American one called White Linen which seemed curiously wholesome. If he went to a duty-free shop on the Singapore stopover and smelt it, would she be there? He was not even sure he could picture her; what he saw in his mind's eye was that earlier recollection of her, her narrow white body on satin sheets the colour of extra virgin olive oil. Fluid and fruity. A memory of a memory, already distracted by irrelevant images of olive oil, how it would stain the satin sheets. He'd telephoned to say he had to fly back to Australia. Forever? she'd said, a note of fright in her voice. Oh no. Just for the funeral. I'm sorry, she said, so sorry, her voice sounding tearful. Come with me, he nearly said, come and meet my mother, but something that wasn't just common sense stopped him.

My little man. My big man. His mother wouldn't say that any more. But she wouldn't be happy to give up her son's arm, bent like a solid bar to hold her firm, to another woman. Ferdie knew he would have to get it right before he did that to her. It. What was it?

Suddenly he imagined Berenice as the protagonist of a novel by George Eliot. Beautiful, clever, with a useful job. What conversations would she have with destiny? What expectation, what hopes, what desires? What trouble, what mistakes? Would Ferdie be a monster in her life, ruining it? Or would he be the right thing to do, and thus destroy the story before it could get really under way?

His mother, like Dorothea, had married the wrong man. He could see that, though she wouldn't; she believed she'd married the right man who had behaved wrongly. And that stymied the story, nothing more could happen, there was forever that pointless stalemate. The man betrayed her, and she suffered, frozen forever at that quivering moment. Whereas William; William had gone on, his narrative had continued to unfold.

The plane had levelled out. His seat was at the beginning of some invisible queue, and there was a flight attendant offering champagne. Australian bubbly.

BARBARA WAITS

The mistress is waiting for her lover.

She was stretched out on a pale sofa with matching ottoman, in a tall bright room in what would otherwise have been a poky flat. She was dressed in a white satin nightgown with wide shoulder straps and a sash tied under her breasts. A nightgown Rita Hayworth might have worn. Perhaps even had worn; Barbara had bought it from St Vincent de Paul downstairs, it was of the right vintage, quite fragile now. She imagined it making a complicated journey from Hollywood to Canberra: why not?

The mistress is waiting for her lover.

An archaic sentence. An old-fashioned sentence. Women when they are their own person aren't supposed to be mistresses. Mistress claims mastery but implies its opposite: submission, being owned. But Barbara was choosing this; he had offered, she had accepted the term. She wanted things to be turned around, upset. To subvert where she could. She thought it was accurate enough, in its antique ramifications. Except she wasn't kept by her lover. And only occasionally was she a mistress—which is traditional. She had another life. Well, a job. Cecil liked to murmur variations of the term. You are an odalisque, he said. A houri. You are *une grande horizontale*.

A grand horizontal? she asked.

He laughed. Grand? Great. Like a great singer. A great dancer. A performer of genius.

Certainly with him she performs. As she had never thought or known to do with Greg.

Cecil does not pay her, but he always brings her a present. Sometimes a bottle of wine, for the cellar; the wine they drink she provides, though now and then a case is delivered from a distinguished merchant. Sometimes flowers, loose bunches of gorgeous blooms, a cyclamen in a pot, an orchid with great flowering spikes. Perfume. For her bath he brings unguents made for half a millennium by nuns in Tuscany. Imagine: Catherine de Medici could have used this bath oil. Though it hadn't, by all accounts, made her beautiful.

One day she had cause to think: his presents were always ephemeral.

The mistress is waiting for her lover. Not: I am waiting for my love. She did love Cecil, in a way, a mild affectionate way, but he was not her love. Waiting was what she was doing. He was rarely very punctual, but tonight he seemed quite late. In a moment she would open the wine and pour herself a glass, though normally she waited for him. She lay back on the sofa, drowsy from her bath in Tuscan oils, warm in the well-heated flat whose double-storey north-facing windows had caught the winter sun all day.

It looked spacious because it had very little in it, and everything was pale, white stone floor, milky marble coffee table, the sofa and an armchair, the only colour a small yellow cedar table with two straight chairs. The bedroom was a mezzanine over the kitchen and spare room. Barbara had given up possessions. She didn't want to own things. Even the satin nightdress would go back to St Vinnie's when it had served its purpose.

She was sinking lower on the sofa. She'd had the nightgown dry-cleaned at a place in Kingston that took expensive care of delicate clothes. She did not want to crush it while she waited, she wanted it to fall in all the fluid viscid drapery of its rich fabric. When he came and stood and looked at her. Friday nights are play nights. On another evening he may call, perhaps for tea, always by arrangement, she bathes and looks pretty, is charming and interesting. Fridays are a game, a ritual, a celebration. She dresses up. She is always herself, but one of many selves, none of which may possess her for too long. She likes to see his eyes gleam as he takes in the person she is tonight. He stays till nine o'clock, when the shops shut, he hates shops, and then takes his wife out to dinner.

After he goes she stays in bed. Finishes the wine. Maybe opens another bottle. Eats fruit. A piece of cheese. Watches a DVD. Old Fred Astaire movies are good. More dress-ups and games. The life in them is a dance less complicated than the routines that take up most of the film's time. Ginger Rogers in gorgeous frocks. Once she'd said to Cecil, because she'd read it somewhere, Ginger did everything that Fred did, plus backwards in high heels. Ah, but she needed him to lead her, he said.

Or Hitchcock movies. Black and white and infinite nuances of grey. She likes noir films, partly because although they are so dark they are also particularly luminous, you can see what you need to, as in Welles' *The Third Man*. Sometimes the women in these films are mistresses. More often they are virgins, ready to become brides. Perhaps the charm of these is that they have no idea what will become of them, and everybody likes to go back to a time before the desperate outcomes of their narratives would be revealed. Cut, the end, and there you are, forever united with the lover.

Ah, Barbara, says Cecil, Barbara, this spiky name she's never cared for, and in his mouth it is given the full lilting music of all its syllables. It fills his mouth as she does. Barbara, he says, like a spell, and she always falls under it. But only while he is there; after he has gone she thinks, well, that was fun.

She got off the sofa, feeling the smooth slide of the satin against her naked skin, remembering that Rita Hayworth did not have a happy life, that men adored her but were not in the end good to her. She wondered if creating a world on the screen where you achieved a marvellous happy life or at least managed to suffer grandly and tragically would compensate for a life of the usual stuff-ups. She opened a bottle of New Zealand sauvignon blanc and poured herself a glass; even only a third full it held quite a lot of wine. She walked across the warm stone floor, holding the glass by its long frail stem. The street outside was full of Friday after-work drinkers, happy hour going on being happy for a long time. Soon the restaurants would be full. The buzz came muted through the double-glazed windows.

When she and Greg split up the main lucky thing was the discovery that they'd bought their house cleverly. The old spacious, shabby, high-ceilinged, inner suburban, large-gardened renovator's delight that they had renovated, if not always with delight at least lovingly, had improved in value quite enormously, obscenely even, so when they divided the money, even after paying the mortgage, she had enough to buy this apartment, right in the shops and a bike ride from work, teaching geography at a school ten minutes away along a path that followed what used to be a creek but now was a concrete drain.

She made Greg take the car. He said she was perverse. How could she live without a car? She'd need it. Since the split wasn't very kind or amicable she suspected he wanted her to have the car so he could buy something more exciting. Midlife-crisis convertible. A snappy hatchback with go-faster stripes.

No, she said. I'm going to become a proper city dweller. No car.

You're mad, he said.

Quite possibly, she replied. She meant it, she thought she might be mad, in her anger, her violent rejection of things that had mattered to her. Left to Greg they'd still be married. It was she who said no, it was over. She'd be even madder if they'd stayed together. Not having a car she was certainly more fit. And she liked not having to worry about it, parking it, maintaining it. When the bike didn't work, if it was too far, or too dark, or very wet, she took buses, and sometimes taxis. That was useful: if she went out to dinner she could drink as much wine as she felt like. Not always a lot, but it didn't matter.

Her mother couldn't believe that she and Greg could stop being married at such a time. But Greg is such a nice man, she said. He's kind. He's suffering.

Barbara agreed. Yes, she said, he's suffering. But he's not nice, or kind.

Loss brings clarity, and truth. Things always known but never considered can now be said. After loss there is nothing to lose.

It's so easy to say someone is nice, Barbara said. And they almost never are. They're selfish and self-regarding. But we go along with the fictions. He's nice. You're nice. I'm nice.

Her mother said, I try to be a nice person.

Yes, said Barbara. I've given it up.

Where was Cecil? She'd been standing at the window staring out at the neon signs above the restaurant opposite. She'd had canvas blinds made to cover the windows in case she wanted to shut the outside out. But often she liked the scruffy high-coloured view of shops and commercial buildings, ugly and thoughtless or over-elaborate, as in the ersatz art deco of the bistro. They were like a framed picture on the wall, to be looked at but not needing any other attention, offering a contrast to the pale bare order inside the apartment. She poured some more wine into her glass and walked up and down, swishing her body so the cool satin caressed her limbs. Cecil was seriously late. He wasn't nice, or kind, particularly; he was tough and ruthless. He was nice and kind to her but that was because they had made this small fragment of life together that gave them both pleasure, and they were mutually grateful. As well as punctiliously courteous about arrangements.

She'd gone to see him on the recommendation of a colleague to talk about suing. Cecil's the man you want, said the colleague, and it was some time before she realised that was his surname. She kept on calling him that, as though it were his Christian name; it pleased her. Do you want money? Cecil had asked. She considered: I think . . . revenge. Ah, he said, what you need is Bacon.

She was puzzled by this; she thought, maybe I am crazy, or he is. She thought of breakfast, and then of Francis Bacon's meaty carcass paintings. Cecil was standing up and going to the bookshelves that filled the walls of his office. Here, he said, do you know it? Bacon's essay: *Revenge is a kind of wild justice* . . . Very succinct and beautiful. She thought, a wild justice; yes, that is what I want.

She never did know any of his references. He was full of other people's words. These became part of their elegant erotic games. I am no longer much interested in sexual gymnastics, he said. He'd be delighted with the Rita Hayworth nightdress, when he arrived.

Of course the idea of being a mistress is part of the play. She'd not have thought of it herself. She'd have thought, an affair, perhaps, that they were lovers, though even that was rather a grand term for her. The first evening, when he'd come for a drink, that's all it was, he'd looked at her over his glass and said, *Time turns the old days to derision, Our loves into corpses or wives*, and she thought this was maybe how lawyers spoke, this was what law training did for you, made you hold forth like a character in an old play. Swinburne, he said, isn't it fine? It was fashionable to sneer at Swinburne when

I was at university. How stupid was that? He repeated the lines again, and added two more: *And marriage and death and division Make barren our lives*. Barbara had a good memory, the words he quoted stayed in her mind. *Our loves into corpses or wives*, she said to herself, and shivered at the truth of it. Wives being husbands too, the poem meant both spouses. *Marriage and death and division*. The bleakness of the poem, and its clarity, chimed with her own feelings, and made her look at Cecil as someone who could help her. Even if only in providing words to recite, words to parcel up her feelings and remove them to their own small distance.

She imagined he might bring her a copy of Swinburne's poems, leather bound, with gilt, and a fond inscription, but he never did, never anything not ephemeral. There was never any paper with words on it, nothing ever written down. Just his voice, sonorous, persuasive, its cadences staying in her mind.

I am a melancholy person, he said. I think you are too. And she thought, yes, though it had not occurred to her before. Melancholy is making a form of pleasure out of pain, he went on; it is necessary if we are to bear it.

I don't think I have got that far yet, she said.

No. But you are a quick learner.

She knew that was an important part of their relationship, his telling her things and her taking a grave interest in his words, listening with respect, giving them back to him sometimes, hearing them in new ways, asking questions so he could expand on them. She had been to university, she had an education, it was just that you did not come across a lot of poetry when you did geography.

O my America, my new-found-land, he said. There was always some poem. She had not imagined any man saying the things that were in that poem.

She was a quick learner when it came to the games too. Greg is a nice kind man, said her mother; he needs comfort, he needs to comfort you. But Barbara did not want that. Cecil had shown her she wanted this sensuous play, this elaborate erotic pleasure that coexisted with the melancholy that ravished the heart and together could sometimes offer hope for ecstasy. And yet could be put back in the cupboard of sweets and toys and taken out the next time. Not forgotten, but not pined for. Having their place.

Once when the kids at school had put on *Antigone* she had borrowed one of the costumes. The art class had dyed muslin in rich dark colours for the chorus—Antigone herself was pure white—and she'd borrowed a crimson one, pleated and falling like a classical column. She'd always had a statuesque figure (over-weight, Greg could say, you should lose a few kilos), and now with all the cycling, not to mention the absence of family meals, she had fined down; she still had breasts and hips and now a small waist as well. The dress skimmed her body and floated about her legs. Cecil was charmed by this, he held out his hand and said, *There are many wonderful things, and nothing is more wonderful than man.* She widened her eyes and pouted her mouth, and he added, Sophocles of course meant women by that, as well. We've lost a lot by insisting on the exclusively male gender of man.

Every time he came he told her something new. One time he asked, did she know about the cardinal's death?

Poison, I suppose.

No. It is dying in the act of making love, he said. A heart attack, a stroke, while fucking.

Like Billy Snedden?

So I believe. I've always thought, what a good way to go.

What about the woman?

Less good for her, certainly.

They laughed, thinking of the farce that could result, the covering up, the pretending, hiding.

People still don't know who the woman was with Snedden, do they?

Oh, I think they do. They just don't say.

I wouldn't be a party to farce, she said. I'd put on a gown and call the ambulance. You'd be dead and I wouldn't be ashamed.

Excellent, said Cecil. You should be proud.

Why cardinal's death? Were cardinals particularly prone to dying in the arms of their lovers?

That's really interesting, said Cecil. It's possibly a corruption of carnal, is one suggestion. Dying in the carnal act.

Oh, I like to think of cardinals. How wicked, dying in mortal sin.

Dying as they'd lived, most of them.

Rotting in hell, while the beautiful girls, or boys, repent and go to heaven.

Of course, he said, carnal is a received Australian pronunciation. As in Carnal Pell.

That evening she'd been wearing black silk pyjamas, which Greg had given her for their seventh wedding anniversary. Her idea. She'd not ever really worn them, before. Perhaps that was a sign. Greg hadn't ever remarked upon the fact; perhaps that was a sign too. Maybe she was waiting for him to suggest them. They were Cecil's favourite; sometimes he asked for them. He liked to unbutton the jacket and slide it aside just a little and contemplate the whiteness of her breasts inside the black silk. They both enjoyed the sensuousness of the fabric sliding over her body.

Sometimes Barbara wondered how long this could go on. This apartment cocooned by the hushed noise of the street, this sense of time suspended, her costumes, his conversation, the wine, the gifts. All of these things she thought of as belonging to this present moment, not to be depended on, likely not to exist as suddenly as they had begun. So she had told herself. But now she was feeling put out, disappointed, worried. She poured some more wine and ate two grapes from the bunch she had put on a white plate. *I have been faithful to thee, Cynara, in my fashion*, he often said, and she could see this meant not really at all, but she took it as a kind of promise. We will tell one another the truth, he said, we will not lie or cheat, there will be no deception, and she had believed him, though once she did think it would be perfectly possible for a liar and cheat to promise to tell the truth always.

The wine was becoming warm. She put the bottle in the fridge, thinking of the cardinal's death. Thinking that if he had to die that would be a good way because then he would belong to her. The little death, the big one. If he died in the act he would always be hers. But that wasn't supposed to be what she wanted, for him to belong to her. What if a woman conceived with the sperm that burst from the man in the moment that he died? A child born out of death. That was irrelevant too. She was not going to get pregnant.

The kitchen window looked over a car park. She saw a man walking across it hand in hand with a child. Greg. She'd know that big craggy head with its thick pelt of hair anywhere. But it couldn't be, he'd gone away. Though he could have come back. Greg was a teacher too. After it had happened he'd said, Let's go somewhere else. Travel. Move to the country. Orange maybe. We could buy a terrace house, you've always wanted a terrace house, they have really good ones in Orange. Barb? Let's do that, he said. You could have fun, furnishing it with local stuff.

Remarkably garrulous for Greg. No, she said, it's too late. Too late for talking to her, this man whose idea of foreplay was the old joke: You awake, love? That wasn't fair. There was no reason to be fair, nothing else was fair, no other thing, why should she worry about being fair? But in fact he had talked to her. Sometimes.

We love each other, he said. We can get through this.

But she knew that Greg couldn't console her. She said, Do we love each other? I don't think so. She turned away from his bewildered face.

But you said . . . you always said . . . right at the beginning.

When we got pregnant, and you said we should get married. Yes, I did say I loved you then. Maybe I did. But I think, mainly, I wanted to . . . it was the least thing, to start a marriage. I said it, and it worked . . .

It can work again.

No. I'm not that person any more. Everything's changed. We can't go back. Make it undone.

That was when she said she didn't want the car or any furniture from the house, or objects, or appliances.

You'll regret it, Greg said.

I plan never to regret anything again.

She'd kept only the cedar table, the small schoolroom table, that had belonged to her grandmother. Its honey colour was startling in the flat. That wasn't why she kept it, though it was a bonus. She'd thought she should keep just one thing from an earlier life, but not hers. Two generations back.

Poor Greg. She was thinking too much, drinking too much, wandering about the apartment filling in time she hadn't expected to have. She organised her life to allow no time for filling. It was tight and efficient like the apartment. She did no entertaining of the cooking kind, there were all the restaurants downstairs to eat in. She grilled vegetables when she got bored with the restaurants. The cupboards contained wine glasses, a few plates, vases. I want none of my old possessions, she'd said, and Greg had looked at her in a kind of terror, as though she'd turned into a monster. She was monstrously different from the person she'd been, in her house furnished with antique furniture she'd restored, its dressers stacked with plates and cups and bowls for every kind of dish, any mood, all the recipes she was always trying out for constant parties of friends. Even Greg had learned to follow her round antique shops, markets, bazaars, junk shops, looking for the odd things that Barbara was famous for unearthing, things that no one else would have noticed but that in her hands became wonderful, unusual, bizarre, useful. She wasn't that Barbara any more. Barb, he said, Barb? His voice trembling. His big craggy head, his heavy footballer's body, this head, this body that she'd loved once, hadn't she?—she'd said she did, believed she did, and now didn't even want to look at, as he gazed at her, in terror, in bewilderment, wanting her to comfort him, and she looked away and didn't care. Had it been him, hand in hand with a child, walking across the car park?

Walking across the car park, undoing the past, making it all right again. How often she wanted to think that. How often had she realised it could never happen. Waiting, looking, thinking, in the waning of the day. When the ghosts come out.

She put more wine in her glass and went into the spare room that was a kind of study. When she turned on the television there was a crime thriller with impenetrable Scottish accents. She wandered back to the sitting room. It was nearly nine o'clock. Cecil wouldn't come now. Another channel had a tall handsome Asian man cooking. She used to love cooking programmes, even if they were bad she liked to watch them, now she couldn't be bothered looking. Cecil had never let her down before. Friday night, and he was there, with glamorous presents and even more glamorous words, with not very many glasses of delicious wine and delicate erotic games. He was twice her age. He did not ask anything of her, in love or constancy, just these small portions of her time, the brief occasional visits during the week, the longer Friday night play. Our *cinq à sept*, he called the weekday visits, and she didn't understand what he meant, he had to explain even that it was French. It's a time, he said, five o'clock to seven o'clock, it's when you visit your mistress, it's when work is over but before it is the hour of dinner, and you immerse yourself in this small artificial perfect world, with no worries or cares or responsibilities. It is fucking, he said, if you want, but it is also conversation. Tea, perhaps, or an aperitif. It is whatever sort of civilised intercourse takes your fancy.

Is it just men, she'd asked, or can women do it too?

Oh yes, women can visit their lovers, *cinq à sept*. Of course it is a high bourgeois activity, it implies someone is at home bathing the children and cooking the dinner.

Barbara had thought she was safe in this affair, so neatly defined by its time, so practical, so formal; not love or passion but pleasure and affection, not with expectations of forever after but politeness and good manners and knowing where you were. And so there would be no betrayal. Perhaps one day he would say, It has been very nice, or she would murmur, I think it is time to stop, and they would drink the wine and kiss goodbye in a melancholy way and she would do something else on Friday night. Go to the gym. Join another book club. Take in a movie with a friend. Now Cecil had broken the rules. Now there was betrayal. Now she was alone and drinking too much, thinking too much.

The cedar table glowed in the pale room, yellow as amber, old and rich and polished. Only one thing from that old life, which once had seemed so nourishing. She ate several more grapes, green on a white plate. She squeezed herself into a corner of the sofa, crunching up as small as possible. It didn't matter about the Rita Hayworth nightdress any more.

Greg in the car park. She had not been kind to Greg. She had to stop thinking about Greg because in a minute she'd be thinking about Chloe and that mustn't happen. Her life was organised so she never had to think about Chloe. Fleeting moments, of course, you couldn't do anything to stop them, but if you were busy you could move on, shake them off. But she was crunched in a ball in a corner of a sofa, she was a woman bereft and thinking about Chloe.

Chloe would be eleven now, still a pretty and clever little girl, though reaching towards puberty. She must be still, mustn't she. Nothing could have happened to stop that. Chloe still alive, smiling, funny, happy. But she wasn't. A freak accident, that's what they said. Freak. She didn't know precisely how it had happened, hadn't wanted to know, hadn't wanted to picture it as vividly as if she had seen it. But still she did, she invented it, there it was happening. Playing in her mind and no off button to get rid of it. The ferry. The children stepping on to the gangplank, crossing from the jetty to the boat. Not Chloe. Chloe somehow slipping, a lurch, a trip, her little body sliding down into the water, caught between the boat and one of the piles of the jetty, crushed and drowned in the oily cold algae-infested water, too poisonous for swimming. How could it happen? Such care. Such responsibility. Chloe such a sensible child. The class of nine-year-olds, the school excursion to the museum, the ferry ride across the lake an extra treat.

The daughter she had loved. The daughter who had married her to Greg, had made the three of them into a family full of love. Living in a big old comfortable house full of objects, full of friends, full of life. She hadn't really minded when the doctor told her there would be no more children, her cervix was damaged, she could not carry another child. She had her family, and it was perfect.

Such a rich life they'd had, and orderly, a beautiful complicated order that nourished them. She had a habit of saying, we must not leave anything to chance. About picnics or holidays or simply the next day's plans. We cannot leave anything to chance. And so it was as though chance, so rigorously excluded, grabbed its own moment, one so unlikely that Barbara could never quite believe it. But then she thought, it wasn't chance. It was some ancient and godly malice. Or devilish. It wasn't chance: there was fault, and blame.

You can't say that, said Greg. It was simple accident, terrible, but accident.

Yes I can. It was malice. It was jealousy. It was fate, jealous of us. And it worked. We're destroyed.

Greg thought he could eventually comfort her. That she would accept and grieve for the child. That the terrible anger would calm. But when he put his arms around her she was like a post and he could not warm or soften her. Barbara knew what she had to do, empty herself, get rid of all possibility of future hurt. She was furious with Cecil for showing her she hadn't anywhere near achieved that.

She had to get out of the sofa. She uncurled, and dragged herself upright. She stumbled over the long folds of the nightgown and dropped the wine glass. Her feet were bare, she walked round it in a wide detour, the glass had exploded like a bomb on the white stone floor. She poured the rest of the wine into a tumbler and got into bed, lucky she already had her nightie on, took two temazapam from her emergency supply and still did not sleep very quickly or easily. She was thinking of Chloe's terror as she slipped off the gangplank into the water, the terror that her mother could never comfort now, and of how the child would not have known that this was the end for her, not at first. Would that knowledge have come to her before she died? Would she have understood that her life was over? Barbara could not escape the sickening wash of pain and fear, as if she herself were her child, this nightmare that she could never wake up from.

I want to sue, she said to Cecil, recommended by a colleague as a useful lawyer; she'd got his name back to front but stuck with it anyway, it was another game. Do you want money? he said. No, revenge. And he'd suggested she read Bacon. Had lent her the book. *A kind of wild justice.*

In the end she hadn't done it. You can't sue fate, he said.

Greg in the car park with a child. Greg in her dreams with a head like a bear. Who was the child? The child's hair had been cloudy with curls, but pale, not dark like Greg's.

Then Chloe was in her dream too. They were in the kitchen. She was making toast. The little girl stood up from the table and got a favourite plate off the dresser, patterned with a lady in a crinoline dress under a trellis of pink roses, and in the distance a pond and a summerhouse. Chloe liked to look at this plate and think of the story of the lady in her frilled dress. It was a small plate, meant for dainty tea sandwiches, and the large piece of sourdough bread overflowed it. Chloe spread butter carefully right to the edges and then Vegemite over that. Black toast, she said with satisfaction, and took a bite. In the dream Barbara suddenly knew it was a dream, which might have been the nightmare, the usual nightmare of drowning and terror and swamping dirty water. Instead she thought, perhaps I should have kept that plate; it had belonged to her mother and as a small child Barbara too had thought it was marvellously beautiful; of course she had got rid of all such things because of the memories in them. But she also as she realised this was a dream felt grateful. In life Chloe had never said *Black toast* in that gleeful voice, so it was as if new things were still happening, as if she was still growing and changing. Her hair was longer. It was very curly and usually cut short but in the dream it had grown into ringlets, and as she bent over the toast, concentrating on spreading the butter and Vegemite, they danced in a springy lively way. Chloe was always dancing, she was a slender sprite of a child who was never still, and even as she sat and concentrated on her task the curls of her hair danced. The hair was quite fair and when you looked at it was striped with a whole lot of different pale brown and yellow colours that caught the light and sparkled in the sunny kitchen.

In the morning Barbara woke up fusty and grubby and heavy with wine and drugged sleep, but remembering Chloe curly-haired and gleeful. She had a long shower and took vitamin pills, and then as she always did on Saturdays went to a cafe for coffee and the papers. In the *Canberra Times* she read how a well-known Canberra lawyer had died in the pool of the hotel where he swam regularly. William Cecil, aged sixty-four, had had a heart attack and drowned on Wednesday evening.

Barbara thought, so he did not betray me, after all. It was death, again. Not the cardinal's death; death by water. She stared out the window and was sad. And frightened, as well. If she had not seen that little notice in the paper she might not have found out the truth of things, might have gone on blaming him for deserting her. Might still have been the bereft and victimised woman. Of course she still was that, if you put in fate instead of Cecil, but somehow fate didn't fit well, or perhaps it was not she who was the object of its malice.

FERDIE ARRIVES

Ferdie came out of the doors of the customs hall, knowing his mother would be waiting for him. He couldn't see her. Maybe something had gone wrong, she'd slept in, her car had broken down; it would have to be something drastic. But she was there, he had seen her, just not registered her. He had forgotten, and he felt sad. So few years away, and he had forgotten his mother, and yet she had not changed. Tall, and slender still, like a maiden in a tower, he used to think. There were a great many Greek people ahead of him in the railed-off exit, being met by even more relations, who crowded in and made it difficult for the people behind to get through. His mother stood back, patiently waiting. A maiden in a tower? No, he thought; she is the tower, she is the imprisonment, invisible, impenetrable. You shut the princess in a tower for long enough and she becomes the tower. And there's only one key, which she gave to William. She could have taken it back, or called a locksmith and had another made. She chose not to do either of these things.

She wasn't looking at him though he knew she could see him, and when he reached her and spoke she was silent, she put her arms out and held him with such passion that he felt her crushing him. Then she moved back a little and scrutinised him, tenderly, frowning. Oh Ferdie, you're so thin! You're disappearing.

No I'm not. I'm exactly the same. And who are you to talk? He put his arm around her and felt long, frail bones under meagre flesh. I'm your son, remember? I don't think we run to fat.

She smiled, and squeezed him again. He could see her eyes quivering with tears. It is good to see you, she said.

She'd always worn the same style of clothes, dark slinky fabrics, fluid, loose, but moulding her willowy figure. It occurred to him that they were not just the same style, they were the same clothes. There was a flight of little moth holes in the front of her top that she had embroidered with silk thread in a lazy-daisy pattern. He remembered her doing it, years ago. She still had the same car, and it was a wreck. After the majesty of Pegasus. The house in Banksia Street hadn't changed, either. Helen liked old things, liked to keep them. He supposed it was his time of absence that made all this so noticeable.

The house was small, red brick, in a seaside suburb with cliffs and ridges that made the houses huddle. The blocks were small and there were only a few left of the old houses, which had fitted them well enough. The rest had been vastly extended, or pulled down and rebuilt, into McMansions crowding out one another's light. Or else there were blocks of apartments. All this had been happening for a long time, but it seemed to have got worse while he was away. The vegetation stuffed itself in where it could, its dark green strappy leaves greedily swallowing the sunshine. His mother's had a great fig tree in the garden, which

was otherwise morning glory holding up the fences, scabby gera-
niums and patches of thick cushiony buffalo grass, coarse padding
that scratched at bare feet. She'd inherited the place from her
parents. Ferdie remembered visiting them, the house in Banksia
Street, thinking Big Bad Banksia Men, those hairy-faced many-
eyed thugs in his Snugglepot and Cuddlepie books, and he'd been
frightened, but looking forward to them too, because life as it
is in books isn't always available, and they didn't ever win, in the
end. But there were no banksias, not flowers or men. Big railway-
sleepered beds of vegetables in the backyard, broad beans, silver-
beet, lettuces, strawberries, and in the front, flowers, stocks
scenting the night air, marigolds, shastas, gerberas, vivid daisy-
faced flowers that glowed in the bright air of the seaside. Only
straggling ghosts of them left, now. Helen would have been
surprised had anyone suggested that she might cultivate a garden
herself. She taught in a school, she read a lot of books, she ate
frugal meals in a regular fashion. She was cracked, and broken, she
had to step carefully or she would shatter into pieces.

His room was as he'd last slept in it. The narrow bed, the Wagga
quilt his great-grandmother had made, during the Depression,
out of patchwork fragments of men's suits. The posters from art
galleries, their edges torn and yellowing. He'd never spent a lot
of time in it. When his mother came to Sydney to live, his father
had been furious with her: interrupting the boy's schooling, the
most dangerous thing that could happen to a boy in his teenage
years. Taking him away from his father when he so badly needed
a male role model in his life. William had organised for him to

board at his school in Canberra. His mother had protested, but it had happened. She'd lived in a tiny flat, her mother died and she'd moved in with her father, then inherited the house. Ferdie had lived here sometimes as an undergraduate, mainly in the vacations. The room was certainly his, but not in any affectionate way.

What would you like? she asked. A cup of tea? I could cook you a breakfast. Or do you want to go straight to bed?

Oh no, I'm not going to bed. The only way to cope with jet lag is to go to bed at the normal time for the new country. Early normal, he said, but not silly.

Helen looked alarmed. Oh.

I've had breakfast. But a cup of tea would be nice.

He'd seen the alarm. He knew she was wondering what she was going to do with him all day. She so much wanted to see him, but then didn't know what to do with him. Except unwillingly to get cross. What he'd like was to go to a decent restaurant by the water and eat fish, with a bottle of decent white. But he knew this would be regarded as wickedly extravagant, so he didn't mention it. He didn't think his mother was poor, exactly, but he knew she wouldn't choose to spend money like that.

He hung up his clothes in the wardrobe while Helen made the tea. He looked out at the brilliant sunshine. He imagined a table and chairs under the fig tree, enjoying the winter sun. He knew that were he to suggest a table and chairs in the garden she would say, But I never go out there.

They sat in the kitchen and drank the tea. It was some strong cheap kind, not anything like Pepita's. He told his mother about

Pepita and her tea ceremonies but the topic didn't turn into a conversation. He ate an Iced VoVo, which would have been bought as a special treat, even though he was feeling overfed on plane food. It had a very pink taste.

He said suddenly, with a harshness he hoped would be helpful, Well, you're a widow now, you can grieve, and move on.

His mother balanced her Iced VoVo on the rim of her saucer. No I'm not. I'm not a widow. I'm a divorcee. William's death doesn't change that. Everything is the same.

Ferdie was silent. I should have known, he thought. Nothing's going to change. He said, I think, as far as the church is concerned for instance, death, well, it frees you in a way that divorce doesn't.

What's the church got to do with it? I don't believe.

I meant it as a way to look at things. Oh Ma, I want you to be happy. Let it go. Live your life.

These things are not for deciding. They are, or they are not. Do you think I can change that?

She stood up, her head bent. She was a pillar of darkness.

Yes, he wanted to say, in a loud vehement voice. He wanted to shake her clothes and let the light in. But he stayed silent, and still. He poured out more of the dull tea. He said, Do you know what I'd like us to do? I'd like to go and walk along the beach. Blow the cobwebs away.

As he said it he heard Lynette's voice. *Let's take our bikes and ride along the lake. Blow the cobwebs away.* Erin would come, at first in the child seat on the back of her mother's bike, later on her own. Sometimes she had a friend with her, there were often friends of

Erin's in the house. Rarely did William come. They'd pedal the lake path, sometimes doing the circuit from bridge to bridge. There were always mobs of people doing the same thing, it was a cheerful public outing.

Would you like to come?

Oh, I don't think so, said Helen. I've got things to do here. You go.

So he did. Though he knew she'd be thinking, thankless child, hardly home before he's off again. She loved him, and was jealous of him. She wanted him beside her but would not go with him, so she sent him away. He walked the short distance through jumbled suburban streets to the seafront. She had said, Oh, won't you be cold? He'd kissed her cheek: Not after London, Ma. There was a fine bracing wind off the water and the sun shone hot through it. The Norfolk Island pines looked very spiky, the fringed palm trees rattled. He walked from one end of the beach to the other and then around the cliff path to look at the cemetery on the headland. Stone angels turned their grieving backs to the sea, or faced it with their arms outflung. They held flowers, or leaned against urns, or pointed to heaven. He'd never explored it, though it was always something he was going to do. After lunch, maybe; a melancholy walk and thinking about the death of the father. Perhaps there would be ghosts. He should come in the twilight.

He walked enviously past the restaurant in the converted changing pavilion, the terrace already crowded with fisheaters chewing, talking, laughing, pouring yellow gleaming wine out of bottles misty with condensation. He couldn't really afford it and his mother wouldn't. If William had been there they'd have stepped in, boldly sure that a good table would be found for them.

At the back of the restaurant was a takeaway. And on the corner a pub with a bottle shop. He walked briskly back to the house in Banksia Street. Come on, he said, we're going to eat fish and chips on the beach.

His mother demurred, but not very actively. Ferdie thought there might not be much lunch in the house, since she'd expected him to go straight to bed. But she wouldn't walk. They had to take the car. There was nowhere to park. Ferdie dropped her at the restaurant. He had to drive nearly to Banksia Street to find a place. He'd put two glass tumblers and a corkscrew in a plastic bag and stopped at the bottle shop to buy wine. It had a screw top, that was a new thing since he'd been here last, he didn't need the corkscrew.

They sat at a picnic table in a gazebo overlooking the beach. A bunch of wetsuited surfers waited out beyond the breakers for a good wave. He unscrewed the bottle and poured wine. Surely this is illegal, she said.

All those people are doing it, he said, pointing to the restaurant terrace. But I'll leave it in the brown paper bag. No one will ever know.

He'd bought grilled snapper; it was good. The chips were thick but crisp. The wine was heavenly. He tipped his head back to the sun and closed his eyes. He felt very clever as he said to himself, I have circumvented both poverty and parsimony. I am eating fish and drinking wine by the sea. He wondered if he wished Berenice was here. She would have expected the terrace of the restaurant, one of the best tables, right by the grassy edge of the sand. In his head he wrote a postcard to her that suggested this was where the fish and chips were happening without actually lying.

When they got back to the house he mentioned coffee but there was only instant. I don't really drink coffee, said Helen. Tea?

She made a pot of the strong cheap tea but he said he would just have water, sitting at the kitchen table keeping her company. Helen washed her hands under the kitchen tap and took a little silver metal tube out of a drawer. It had a label with purple writing. She squeezed a little on to her palm, it smelt dry, pungent, a bit like eucalyptus but not exactly. She rubbed it between her palms then over the backs of her hands, smoothing it to her wrists, pushing it down her fingers as though she was pulling on gloves; she squeezed a bit more out of the tube and worked it around the edges of her fingernails, and then polished them against the palms of her hands. She realised she was frowning slightly, and massaged between her brows with three fingers, her face settling into a serene expression.

Ferdie picked up the tube. L'Occitane, it said. Hand cream. Lavender of Provence. He'd always thought of lavender and old ladies going together, it being a genteel perfume far away from any sexy overtones, but this was different; elemental, somehow. Maybe it was coming from Provence.

Are you going to have a nap? asked Helen.

No. It's important to stay awake till bedtime. When you come to London to visit me I will make sure you fit instantly into English hours.

She smiled the small smile of someone who is safe from what is being proposed. Yes, she said.

So, said Ferdie. What's news? He was pretty sure she wouldn't know any.

Aurora is trying to get pregnant, she said.

Aurora, he said, pleased to be able to talk about her. Still.

Aurora was his half-sister, daughter of Nerys who became an Orange person. He didn't know her very well but he held a small shining memory like a drop of water . . . there was the honey scent of blossom, a girl who was grown up and a child, who played with him. The scent of the blossom released that little drop of memory, full of light but opaque. He didn't know when it was, or where, no flowers to go with the smell, no pictures at all, the whole thing a mysterious sense, not graspable, not readable, just the musical name Aurora and a small time of bliss.

Of course, said his mother, she's left it too late, the way girls do these days.

Was her voice smug? He knew she'd been twenty-two when he was born.

Do you see her?

Not very often. Sometimes on the bus. She lives a bit further out. Sometimes I get on the bus and there she is, so I sit next to her and she tells me what she's up to. It doesn't happen often, mostly she drives, and so do I.

Is she married?

Oh no. She's got a partner. He's older than her. He's a perfusionist.

What's that?

It's a kind of doctor. He does the heart-lung machine for open-heart surgery. She tells me he's writing a book about the dreams people have when their hearts are outside their bodies. Very strange dreams, apparently. Well, why wouldn't they be? It isn't very natural, having your heart out of your body.

And she's trying to get pregnant.

Yes. IVF, the whole lot. So far it's not working.

Maybe I should ring her up.

If you want to. Please yourself.

What's she doing these days?

A merchant banker. Still. They know where the money is.

And Nerys? Is she still an Orange person? I thought they came to an end. He knew it was safe to talk about Nerys, who had realised William wasn't for her and had gone on to another life.

I don't think so. That dreadful holy man died, but there are still followers. Communities, or communes rather, up Byron Bay way.

Helen emptied the tea leaves out the back door and washed her mug. Well, she said, you mightn't want to, but I think I'll have a nap. She picked up a book. There were a lot of books in this house. He went into the lounge room and looked along the shelves. Helen read mainly novels. There were books of poetry, rows of classics, and Booker Prize winners, and a lot of the kind called commercial fiction. He picked up a Jodi Picoult; he'd seen her reviewed a lot and knew that she sold millions of copies, while critics had the habit of sneering. He sat on the sofa and began to read, but it soon became clear that this was a mistake, he'd send himself to sleep. He went into the bathroom and splashed cold water on his face. In the mirror it looked pinched and bluish. He turned on the light above it and suddenly his skin was rosy. There was a shelf with more bottles of L'Occitane creams, lotions, unguents. Olive oil night cream. Angelica shampoo, a potion of vine clippings that seemed to be for the feet, almond oil for bathing in, mud for a face mask. All the containers were part empty, Helen evidently used them all. He unscrewed lids and smelt them; they were herby, potent, evanescent. Serious, somehow. The promise of desire was in them. The labels talked about the plants and odours of Provence as though there were magic in the name of the place, as though the air of that fabled province would wreath out from the bottles and encloud you with beauty. None of them recalled the scent of his playtime with Aurora.

He decided to walk down to the pub and buy a bottle of red wine for dinner, blowing some more cobwebs away. Helen would doubtless say, What, wine for lunch and dinner? Are we turning into lushes? He'd buy two, always good to have a spare.

The shadows were long. It was getting cold. The angels in the cemetery stood serene against the wind. He passed the bottle shop and went into the bar. It was warm and beery and the sport zapped soundlessly from a huge television screen. He sat at a sticky formica table and saw himself staring into a glass of beer thinking about his father and death and what his life was doing. He felt sad but wasn't doing a good job of thinking about William. It was his mother who filled his mind. Living in London he thought at times about her, inhabiting the house of her parents, going every day to her teaching job, reading her books, eating frugal vegetable meals, but coming back to it suddenly was a shock, the dullness of it, the emptiness. He was to blame, he'd gone and left her. But guilt was a lame horse, he'd done what children do, moved out into his own life, and that long before he went to England.

He bought two bottles of red, inexpensive ones, and once again walked briskly back to Banksia Street. When he opened the door he smelt his mother's roast chicken. It was her dish that she made whenever a grand meal was called for, and very good it was, always a free-range chicken, golden-skinned and succulent, with a whole lot of root vegetables crisply roasted. She was welcoming him home in her best style. He was touched, but his heart did not lift as it ought to have done. Roast chicken dinners hadn't always brought happiness with them. Still he stepped blithely into the house, cried, Lovely roast chicken for dinner again, and found his mother in the kitchen, smiling and pink. He grabbed her round the waist and hugged her, feeling her soft warm cheek against his cold one, but did not miss her small pout of disgust when she smelt the beer on his breath. Ah, but Ma, he didn't say, without the beer I would not be so cheerful.

Shall I set the table? he said, but it was done. So he opened a bottle of wine instead. Such bad habits, said Helen, but she took her glass.

Wine's a good habit, he said.

You'll end up an alcoholic like your father. Dying young.

He knew William wasn't an alcoholic. So did Helen.

Don't you have a glass of wine with your dinner? he asked. It's so cheap in this country, and so good.

I don't think it looks well for a woman living on her own to be putting out empty bottles, she said.

Ma, said Ferdie, who cares? What do you care?

It's a matter of one's role, said Helen.

Browbeaten by anonymous neighbours, he said. Imaginary neighbours. It's mad.

He praised the chicken extravagantly, but no more than it deserved. He talked about his life in London. His mother didn't say much but she seemed to absorb what he said. After a while he tired of his prattling narratives. He poured out the last of the wine. Helen looked into her glass before she took a mouthful.

I'm glad I don't live closer to the cemetery, she said. You know what I think? I think those statues walk about at night. Walk the streets, and if they meet you, you have to join them. That's why there are so many, and getting more all the time. People don't put up marble statues any more, yet look, every time you turn around there are more of them.

There do seem to be a lot, he said, uneasy; he thought her words a bit mad.

They finished dinner and did the dishes, she washing, he drying, but he no longer remembered where anything went.

There's an Agatha Christie movie, she said. On the television. It should be good.

But when he sat down beside her on the sofa he realised how tired he was. He had a shower—it was over the bath, antique and given to squirting, but hot at least—got into the old narrow bed and went immediately to sleep. He came wide awake at two o'clock and tried reading some more Jodi Picoult but it didn't work. He lay with his brain buzzing until the dawn sky lightened, then fell heavily asleep again. When he woke up, his mother had gone to school.

The house on Banksia Street was a gloomy house, and cold. The sun shone brightly outside, but its small windows let in little light, and there was no heating. And no real coffee. He went down to the beach. The fish restaurant in the pavilion was closed, but there were cafes, their sunny pavements crowded with carefree people eating big breakfasts. He wondered what they did for a living. The coffee was good; he had two cups, and a croissant, which wasn't very. They still can't make croissants in this country, he said to himself, as though he had been away for so many years they should have developed the skill by now. He watched a young woman with streaky blonde hair who took off her sweater and sat in a black camisole top, sunning her golden skin, eating eggs benedict. Her boyfriend had the big breakfast: everything the English sent over with their colonists plus hash browns. They were laughing and kissing with their mouths full.

He did ring up Aurora. She said she was driving down to Canberra and why didn't they all go, in her car. Ferdie thought that not going in his mother's clapped-out old Volvo was a good idea. But Helen said she couldn't, she couldn't take the time off school, but Ferdie could. He felt guilty at leaving his mother, but she said it would suit her to take the bus, and Ferdie could save the money. So they went first thing the next morning, Aurora turning up in a sparkling new BMW, a big one with leather seats.

I got rid of the Mazda sports, she said. Hopeless for a family. No I'm not pregnant yet. I'm thinking positively.

The BMW was a sleek silver colour. The colour of money, Ferdie said. Aurora laughed, a deep hiccupy laugh that made you want to join her.

He hadn't imagined she'd be such a tiny woman. He was remembering when she'd been a big girl. But she was short, with small bones and little flesh. She seemed frail. She had a soft deep voice and when she talked it gusted through her. She talked a lot, and laughed, catching her breath in a husky way. She seemed to remember her old affection for him and to start off from that. She had to sit on a cushion to drive the car, and held the wheel with small worn hands like paws. Hastily you might have thought she was a child, but not when you looked into her face. It was pretty still, but her mouth clenched when she wasn't laughing or talking, lines fanned out from around her eyes, and the line of her jaw was sharp as a knife.

Desperation, Ferdie said to himself. No, I am being fanciful. But he looked again and he wasn't. Aurora drove with swift darting ease through the traffic, accelerating past slow cars, sharply braking when the traffic blocked. She talked all the time but left space for him too. He told her about his thesis, and Pepita and Pegasus, and even mentioned Berenice; she gave her breathy delighted laugh.

Is it good being a merchant banker? he asked when they'd left the suburbs behind and were speeding down the motorway.

It is if you're good at it. If you're good at money. I mean big money, the idea of money, the theory of it. It's like singing, excellent if you can do it. I can. I get it from my mum. Oh yes, I know, everyone thinks she's a mad hippie Orange person, and, well, she is, an Orange person, although they aren't really called that any more, but she's good at money. People are always putting people in boxes. You can't do that, unless you chop off everything but the central little solid nub of them, nobody fits in a box. You could put me in a box labelled merchant banker, but you'd have to take a chainsaw to me first.

Or me . . .

Or you, into a box marked PhD student in literature, but think of all the bits that would dangle over the edge.

He was going to say that perhaps all the dangly bits are me, PhD student of literature, too, but he didn't get a chance.

I'm getting us to Lynette's for lunch. Not madly early lunch, I had to go to the gym before we started, but it'll be cool. I've told her about my diet. No soft cheese, no big fish, no raw fish, no prawns or oysters, no salads I haven't washed myself. Of course I told Lynette I'd trust her salad washing.

Heavens, began Ferdie.

Pregnancy diet. I know I'm not, but you've got to be ready. And of course no alcohol. Foetal alcohol syndrome, that's the least of it. You can't imagine. And no junk food, stands to reason, and no tea or coffee.

How did people ever have healthy babies in the past? They didn't not do all those things.

The world was a much purer place, then. Much fewer additives, dangerous chemicals. Women were fertile, men were potent. Now—we could wipe ourselves out. Become totally infertile. The end of the human race. It's not unlikely.

Aurora was overtaking every semi-trailer on the road. They can only do a hundred, she said, so we're okay.

Even though the speedometer said 130, Ferdie noticed. Being good at money didn't seem to mean being good at numbers. The car was happy at this speed, it glided effortlessly along.

I'm not staying with Lynette, said Aurora. I'm staying with a friend of mine. She works in Treasury. Great job, considering it's the public service, but they pay peanuts. She's no monkey, though. I have to tell you this story. Two years ago. February. I'd been in Tokyo for work and when I came back I had to go to Canberra. I had a bit of time so I thought I'd drop in and see her. I had the Mazda then. I should say, she was pregnant, I knew the baby was due in March, so I thought I'd just pop in and see how she was doing, not ring or anything, not make a fuss. I didn't want to disturb her. So, I go to her house, Saturday morning it is, and Flavia's there, sitting in the family room, with the cutest little carved wood cradle beside her, that she's rocking with one foot, and it's piled high with blankets, layers of them, layers.

She's cold, says Flavia.

I sit down in a chair and look at the cradle. I put out my hand and pull the coverings away from her face. The baby's a little wizened-up creature. I touch her.

She . . . she doesn't seem to be breathing, I say to Flavia.

No, says Flavia.

And cold she is. Cold, like frozen wax. I tell you, it's giving me a fright. Flavia is so calm, I suppose she's frozen too, in her way. Anyway, turns out the baby came early and was stillborn. She brought her home and keeps her in the freezer, takes her out and gets to know her . . .

Gets to know her?

That's the thing. Everybody does it. I mean, when the baby is stillborn. Apparently. Keeps it in the fridge, and cuddles it. Makes it part of the family. Of course you have to let it go, in the end. The baby, she called it Lola, had a funeral eventually and got buried in the family plot. Flavia's all right now, I think, but she was a bit dodgy for a while. The baby got a bit, well . . .

Ferdie couldn't think of anything to say.

I don't know, went on Aurora. Do you believe in God? Or the gods? I don't. But sometimes, well, you might wonder if there are sacrifices. A certain number required. I suppose you could see a baby's death as a sort of appeasement. Of course I don't really believe that. But there's a kind of safety in it, the odds, that's rather appealing.

For other people, not Flavia, said Ferdie.

No, not Flavia. Other people. That's the point, said Aurora. Others might be safe. It used to work, so why shouldn't it again?

I don't know about working, said Ferdie. People believed in it.

And if I believed?

Yeah. If you believed.

Flavia hasn't got pregnant again. It was frightfully difficult the first time. I don't know how many turns at IVF.

Perhaps she doesn't want to.

People can't adopt these days. My mother was going to put me up for adoption, and then she decided to marry William. Of course it was pretty not on to be a single mum in those days. And men would marry you.

Lucky for you.

What? Oh yes, I suppose. Yes, well, Flavia. Maybe she's decided not to keep on. Should get out of Treasury. Go for a real job in the private sector. Mind, I've got one of those and I'm still planning to have a baby. And Cezary's planning to stop home with it and write his book. Did I tell you he's a perfusionist? Like a kind of plumber, only of people's bodies. The book's about dreams. You should hear the dreams people have when they're on the heart-lung machine. And when they come off it. He goes round afterwards and asks them about it.

Maybe they make them up.

Have you ever tried to make up a dream? No, they're too truly weird. Cezary will fly down for the funeral and then we'll drive back together. He's already got three children but he's really keen to have one with me. If we'd had time I was going to stop off at this fabulous baby shop in Moss Vale. All these designer clothes for babies, so cute. Maybe on the way back. You can drive back with us too, you know, if you want to.

Thank you, said Ferdie. That's very kind. I shall have to see what Helen's doing.

He was pleased with himself for saying 'Helen' so naturally.

Cezary, he said, that's an unusual name.

Polish. He's actually a count. There's a family castle somewhere near Cracow. Not theirs any more, of course. His other children are all girls, so if mine's a boy he'll be the count, too. Have to make sure we get married, of course. And I can be countess. What larks. Like a story.

You read Jane Austen? she went on. I've never read any of those old books. Tell you the truth, I don't read books at all really. Just the market, and all that. It's a full-time job. And magazines. Flavia's in a book group. Once a month. They meet at one another's houses and talk about the book and drink red wine. Flavia loves it. I asked her how she managed to read a book a month. She said it was fun.

But that's it, isn't it, Aurora said; other people's ideas of fun are hardly ever yours. Oh yes, Jane Austen: a friend of mine belongs to a book club that reads only Jane Austen. Think of that. She loves it.

Do they start again as soon as they've finished? It wouldn't take them long to get through the whole oeuvre, would it.

Wouldn't it?

Only six books.

Your mum likes to read too, doesn't she? said Aurora. You know who she makes me think of? That statue in the cemetery, not marble, the black one, what would it be, granite? Do they make statues of granite? She's tall and slender, like a pillar, and she has flowing draperies and a sad look. I don't know how our dad came to marry your mum. He usually likes small plump women. You should see my mother, she's a round little ball these days, all the Byron Bay good life. I mean, she exercises, but not more than she eats. And Lynette, she's small and plump too. Whereas Helen, she could be a fashion model.

They were passing the heavy vehicle weighing station at Marulan. Aurora heaved a sigh and stopped talking. She offered him some gum and they chewed in silence. The old familiar grey-green scenery flashed past. At Lake George, Aurora said, You know the story about the lake in China that's full when this one's empty, and vice versa?

I've heard . . .

It's not true, you know. She waved her hand across the lumpy grasslands of the lake, the fences, the occasional sheep grazing. The one in China would be awfully full right now. There's a lot of weird stories about that lake, none of them true. Except about the people getting drowned in it. It's truly dangerous. When there's water.

He knew the stories, designed to account for the fact that sometimes the lake was grazing paddocks, sometimes a treacherous stretch of water, and he also knew that it was just a phenomenon, a quite natural happening. That was the kind of thing William used to talk to him about, when Ferdie was a boy and they'd driven to Sydney in one of William's Citroëns. He'd liked best the one where you had to wait for it to rise up before you could drive it. It was very special. He thought it looked like a shark, a friendly shark, a pet. William quite often drove him to Sydney, to his mother's place. Ferdie realised later that it gave them a quiet spacious time on their own, when they could talk, or just be silent together. When they arrived, William would stop the car and help Ferdie with his bags; he'd knock on the front door and say, Hello, Helen, nice to see you. She would say hello and never invite him in. At first he mentioned it, and then she said no, she didn't think it was a good idea. Ferdie knew that William was disappointed by this, that he'd have liked to have a friendly relationship with Helen, but his mother would never allow it. It was betrayal she nursed.

The first time he drove past the lake it was quite full, and he imagined the lake in China being empty, a grassy plain, with people in pointed straw hats planting crops. He wondered where the passage began that let the water drain from one side to the other; did it run out like a plughole, gurgling out quite fast, or did it trickle slowly so that suddenly you saw that it had gone? There was something magical in the process, there had to be for the water to go in opposite directions. Maybe it filtered slowly through predestined paths. Or maybe there was a spirit lived in the lake, a genie or even a bunyip, that liked to spend some of its time in Australia, some in China. He'd mentioned this China business to his father, and William had explained that it was all fantasy, based on ignorance. He told him the scientific explanation. Are you disappointed? William asked. Ferdie considered; I thought I might be, he said, but it's more important to know what really happens, don't you think?

William smiled, and Ferdie knew this was a good answer. Later William gave him a card with a beautiful coloured painting of how the new capital Canberra might have looked if it had been built there, at Lake George, as certain people had planned. His father pointed out the strange mixture of buildings, the castles, the gothic towers, the Greek temples. And look at this, he said, when you go to Florence you will see buildings just like that. Imagine this, with its water steps and little boats, in one of the terrible freezing gales that sweep through here. The whole thing is a fairytale.

But were they serious?

Oh yes, they were serious. Foolish, but they really thought they could make such a dream of palaces in that bleak spot.

Have you got anywhere to stay in Canberra? asked Aurora. I'm staying with Flavia, I can't really . . . but you could stay with Lynette, I'm sure she'll have room and she'd love to have you, she'll want family around at this time.

Oh no, he said, I can stay at the youth hostel. I thought I might be able to use William's bike.

Oh no, said Aurora, much better to stay with Lynette . . . I'm sure that's what she'll want.

They'd come to the first houses of the suburbs, and now there was city traffic. Aurora said, If I thought there were gods to see us I would make sacrifices to them.

What about your name? You're a goddess. Rosy-fingered, dressed in saffron robes, wearing yellow shoes.

Yuck, said Aurora. I can't stand all that new age stuff. Chants and bad poems and thanks for morning erections.

It's not new age, said Ferdie. It's Homer. Dawn rising before the sun; first your white wings, then your yellow robes, then your rosy fingers. And your nature is to awaken desire.

O-oh. That's nice.

He was working out how to say, if you made sacrifices to them, perhaps there would be gods. But they were pulling up outside the house. His father's house.

Lynette looked distracted, tired, older, sad. But she hugged him as she always did, holding him in her arms for some moments, her head tipped sideways against his shoulder, reaching up and kissing his cheeks. Then she held him at arm's length. How like William you grow, she said.

Aurora had brought flowers, a massive exotic bunch of powerfully scented lilies. Lynette looked around helplessly. Every vase, every container, every possible receptacle was full of large bunches of flowers. She put them in the sink while she thought. Janice can bring something from the shop, she said. We are living in a bower of flowers, isn't it lovely.

They ate lunch in the kitchen. Lynette carved slices off a huge ham. There was a bowl of tomatoes with oil and vinegar to make your own dressing and a plate-sized brie, with a loaf of brown sourdough bread.

I'm afraid I don't eat pork, said Aurora. Pigs are far too intelligent to be eaten by us.

This is a free-range pig from the eco butcher, said Lynette. It lived a happy life. Probably even had a name.

Anyway, it's processed meat. It's okay. Tomatoes will be fine.

The food's gone basic, said Lynette. It's good, but it's basic. Oh . . . I forgot, brie. Soft cheeses. I think there's some cheddar in the fridge.

No probs, said Aurora. She ate bread, and spread the pale delicious butter thickly. Lynette ate very little but drank white wine. She poured copious amounts into glasses like tall transparent tulips. Oh, she said suddenly, and jumped up and got starched linen napkins out of a drawer. Things have gone downhill, she said, screwing up her face.

There was a ring at the doorbell. She hurried out to answer it. A man carried in a wooden box and put it on the bench. Wine, said Lynette, wine from beyond the grave. She giggled. I expect it's meant for cellaring, who knows, she said, squinting at the label, which to Ferdie had a grand look. Coats of arms and Latin mottoes. I suppose it will have to be paid attention to, Lynette said, sitting back down to her barely touched food. Ferdie was hungry, but tried to eat as though it were a rather difficult chore, though not to a rude degree.

Lynette jumped up to make coffee. Sit down, said Ferdie, I'll do it. I remember. Lynette had taught him to use her various machines. Today it was plunger, grinding the right amount of coffee, left so long before plunging, left again to rest. Your coffee, he said, it smells better than anyone's.

Aurora said there was no point in going to Flavia's till she got home from work, so what could they do to help in the meantime? Lynette pointed to the sheets of paper on the end of the table. I've always loved lists, she said, and crossing things off, but they've got out of hand, they're a reproach. And every time I try to do something the phone rings.

She looked at Ferdie. You'll stay here, of course. No, no buts. I need you. She hugged him. He felt her plump body tense in his arms, strung out like wires; if one broke they'd all spring apart with a terrible jangle.

Anyway, she said, have a look, and see if you can make any sense.

Ferdie and Lynette drank coffee, and he was eating nougat, which he loved, he thought it began with the edible rice paper which had so intrigued him as a child, and they looked through the lists. Most of the things Lynette had to do. There was a lot of telephoning. Aurora cleared the table, put the plates and glasses in the dishwasher, wrapped up the ham in its cloth bag. Lynette began ringing up. I spend my life on the phone, she sighed. Ferdie went and got firewood from the shed by the garage and stacked it beside the fireplace in the sitting room. He began to sweep the back terrace, but Lynette said, Never mind that, I've got the gardening man coming tomorrow. Aurora fossicked around and found in William's study a big engraved silver cup which some long-ago Cecil had won for singing and arranged her flowers in it, putting them in the middle of the kitchen table. Ferdie remembered William intoning, *Lilies that fester smell far worse than weeds*. Of course these weren't festering yet. It was getting dark. He brought in the washing and was folding it when the doorbell rang.

HELEN COMES HOME LATE

The winter night had come suddenly. Fallen, yes, that was the word. There'd been almost no twilight, it seemed, and now it was dark. Helen didn't care for being out in the dark. She always arranged it so she was home before the light went. Shopping at the organic vegetable shop had taken an inordinate amount of time. She was cross, with the night, with Ferdie, with herself. Why had he gone off with Aurora? Why had she let him? She could have said, Darling, do wait and come down with me, and he would have, he did like to please her, but always she did this, pushed him to go when she wanted him to stay, and got angry when she had made what she didn't want happen.

And now her street was full of parked cars. She could always get a spot outside her house; not tonight. Somebody must be having a party. On a Monday evening. She had to park several hundred metres away, and carry the food, and books, and marking, and walk. The footpath was old, cracked and bumpy; she made her way carefully, fearful of tripping. The street trees were strange bushy creatures, surviving in the sea winds, with many trunks and spiky leaves and half-dead branches.

There was somebody hiding in one. Crouched up against the prickly branches. Grey in the night dark, formally draped, one of the kneeling angels from the cemetery, head bent, grieving. Neither man nor woman, the angel sex. Helen was hurrying past, not looking, remembering what she'd said to Ferdie about them obliging people to join them—had she meant that?—when a clear voice said, I know I dropped a shilling here.

Not very encouraging, since you could think only ghosts would talk about shillings, but Helen stopped. The babble of the party came from a house over the road.

A shilling, the voice said. I don't suppose it's very much money for some people, but it's a shilling. The shape moved. Helen saw a pale old face in the gleam of light that is always there in cities. Pale and old but childlike too. The voice wasn't querulous, it was patient.

Shall I have a look? said Helen. She put her bags down and bent over; she wouldn't kneel. I don't know, she said, I think it's too dark. Maybe you should come back in daylight.

Do you think so? But what if somebody else finds it first?

I don't think that will happen. It's quite a secret place. Hidden from an idle passerby.

I suppose it is just a risk.

You could go home and come back early in the morning. Which house do you live in? Shall I walk with you?

Ooh, I don't know. I don't live here. Do I?

Helen didn't know. Years she had lived here but people kept to themselves. She supposed.

Can you stand up? she asked. Then you can tell me where you live.

It took a bit of doing. The old woman, that's what she was, seemed reluctant to move, but it was because she was stiff from crouching. She had to lean all her weight on Helen to get upright. She had a kind of blanket around her shoulders; Helen decided it was a throw, the kind of thing you see cast over sofas in *House and Garden* photographs, that was what had fallen into a drapery as she squatted in the bush.

Helen had trouble organising her vegetables and books and marking in one hand so she could free her other arm to support the old woman.

What's your name? she asked.

The woman thought. Ruth, she said.

Hello, Ruth. I'm Helen. Where are we going?

Ruth had tottered several steps. Now she stopped. Don't you know?

Helen said, Is it one of these houses? Do you live in a house in this street? Do you have a bag? A purse?

I had a shilling. I lost my shilling.

They were walking towards Helen's house, but at this pace it would be a while before they reached it. It was really dark now, but the street lights seemed to be working better. More people turned up for the party. Helen wondered how you found out the identity of an old lady alone in a dark suburb. A car came past, driving slowly; it stopped, backed, double-parked. A man and a woman got out and came hurrying up.

Nellie, Nellie. What are you doing? the man said, in a kind but exasperated voice, an aren't-you-a-naughty-child voice. Helen and Ruth looked at him.

She's dementing, he said.

She's Ruth. Maybe if you called her that.

She's called Nellie. Come on, Nellie. Time to go home.

The old woman clung to Helen's arm. Helen said, How do I know you're not trying to kidnap her?

As if, said the woman from the car.

We're from the Strawberry Springs Retirement Village. Nellie's always wandering off. Looks totally decrepit but you'd be surprised how far she can get.

Helen wondered if the old woman was Nellie, or if she was Ruth. Maybe Ruth was who she wanted to be.

Ruth, she said.

The old woman turned her head and looked at her.

Do you want to go with these people?

She's got to. She's already missed her tea. We can't stuff about all night. The woman from the car was chewing gum, she moved it noisily about her mouth. She said, Who'd want to kidnap an old girl who's more trouble than she's worth? Come on, Nellie, get a move on.

Cindy, easy does it. The man pulled back his parka and pointed to the name badge on his sweatshirt. It said 'Strawberry Springs Retirement Village', with Troy in big letters.

We do have to get her back, he said.

Ruth, are you going to go with Troy?

Oh, Troy. Hello. Nice to meet you.

We're going in the car. You like the car. He held out his arm.

Ruth looked from him to Helen, and back, then let go of Helen's arm and took his. Are we going on a trip? she said.

You wish, said Cindy, opening the back door. Ruth took a bit of getting in, but not because she was uncooperative.

There, said Troy, that's nice and comfy.

I didn't find my shilling, Ruth said.

Helen said, I'll look tomorrow, when it's daylight.

Helen went home to her dark cold house. Ruth, or maybe Nellie, was going back to warmth and lights and people, but Helen preferred her own darkness and cold. There was leftover chicken and she had bought some beans to cook. She put on a warm cardigan and turned on the television. She sat on the sofa and ate with her fingers. The beans were luxuriantly green and crisp. The television was dull, so she turned it off and got her book, along with a pot of tea, and wrapped herself in a rug. She thought of Ruth. I suppose it is the kindness of strangers, she said to herself. It is likely we will all come to it. And gratitude will not be a consideration. The phone rang.

Hello, Ma. Just thought I'd ring and let you know I'm here safely.

Oh Ferdie. How lovely to hear from you. Did you have a good trip?

Ferdie described it, and Helen knew there were other people in the room.

I'm staying at Lynette's, he said. She sends her love.

Oh.

They talked on for a bit. Helen knew she was cold in manner, though she tried to be warm. Ferdie said, Lynette says she's glad I'm here. There's a lot to do. Tomorrow we're planting olive trees.

Olive trees? At a time like this?

Well, they were arranged before. So we have to do something with them.

Life goes on.

I suppose so. Tell you what, I could bring one back for you. Plant it in your garden.

Whatever would I do with an olive tree?

Eat olives?

They take months of processing. Even I know that.

When she hung up, rage possessed her like a tremor, complete with tidal wave that gushed through her, annihilating all in its path, and then washed out again, leaving her trembling and weak. The tea was cold, so she boiled more water to heat it up, and sat on the couch, wrapped in the rug, drinking this hot sweet companion of so many solitary days. Lynette sends her love. Planting olive trees. Life goes on. She went to bed and slept and dreamt strange dreams, and woke and recalled the perfusionist recording the dreams that occur when the heart is taken out of the body, and thought, I know what I will do, and slept some more.

In the morning she rang up school and said she was ill and wouldn't be coming in. She never was ill, she had a lifetime of sick leave accrued. She knew how difficult it was to replace a teacher, that her colleagues would have to do extras, spend their free periods minding her classes. She'd done a great many extras in her time. She hunted through the recycled paper bin and found the flyer she was looking for. She had automatically thrown it out, but registered it nonetheless. She made tea and drank it with toast and Vegemite, all the while staring at the glossy page on the table in front of her.

She took down from the mantelpiece the tarnished cloisonné box that had always sat there. In it were pins, buttons, a newspaper announcement of a death, useless coins. As she had hoped, she found a shilling. She walked around to the Strawberry Springs Retirement Village. Cindy answered the door.

When Helen asked for Ruth she said, What? Oh, you mean Nellie. She took her to a big room with four beds. The old woman sat in an armchair, a blanket over her knees, her hands folded. Cindy shouted, Nellie! A visitor for ya.

Nellie, if she was, gazed at the two women in wonderment. In the daylight you could see her hair, thick and white and twisted in a long schoolgirl plait over one shoulder. Her cheeks were pink and softly crumpled, her eyes grey, wide open and looking at the world. Helen said, I've brought your shilling.

Oh, you can't use those any more, she said. Then added, as if remembering her manners, Thank you, it's very kind.

Helen asked, Shall I call you Nellie?

The woman gazed. Helen said, Would you prefer I called you Ruth?

Ruth. Yes. Ruth died. Her eyes looked sideways for a moment. She smiled.

So Helen still did not know what to say. Cindy had gone off. To Cindy she was Nellie. And to Troy. Helen would have liked to call her by the name that made her happy.

Who was Ruth? she asked.

I'm Ruth. Isn't it a pretty name?

Yes, Ruth, it's a lovely name.

There was a silence. Helen said, And how are you this morning? You didn't take cold from your adventure, I hope?

Oh no, I never take cold. It's warm here. Very cosy. Central heating, you know.

She unfolded her hands and began to turn her gold wedding ring round her finger. Her hands were age-spotted and elegant, the fingernails manicured and painted pale pink.

Helen couldn't think of any more conversation to make. She thought, at least it is companionship, my sitting here.

Shall I come and visit you again?

Oh yes, dear, that would be lovely.

Helen felt baffled in her good intentions. She did not know how to talk to Nellie-Ruth, nor what to understand from her. Last night, in the dark, the cold, huddled by the bushes, the lost shilling, the difficulty of standing up, the tottering steps: it had all been simple compared with the near-empty dormitory and this pretty, limpid-eyed, mysterious woman.

Helen put the shilling on the table beside the bed. On the way out she met Cindy, and tried to talk to her. She's dementing, Cindy said. Nothing to be done.

Does anyone come to visit? Any family?

There's a daughter. Once a year if you're lucky. But then, why bother? It's not as if she knows anyone. Could be Britney Spears for all she'd know.

Helen walked along the street and round several corners to the cemetery. It was a high blue day, the sun warm, the world still. The coarse bright green seaside grass was thick and cushiony, soft to walk on. The graves sloped to the sea cliffs, since that was the lie of the land, but the headstones, the obelisks, the angels, the draperied urns, mostly turned their backs to the ocean. The marble of the angels was white and smooth, unaged, except for occasional drastic accidents, an arm broken off, a wing snapped and lying on the ground. She didn't pay attention to names, to the deaths of babies, to the intricate family connections to be read on the headstones, or the puzzling gaps in the narrative: why is that adoring wife, that dear son, not buried here? Where are the other three children? What happened to the loving daughter? There was space to walk between the graves across the slope, but up or down you had to look for paths, for the graves pressed against one another like terrace houses in a street. Helen walked along these streets and looked at the intense blueness of the sea, the different intense blueness of the sky. Just that azure was the colour of the glossy brochure she had rescued from the recycling bin, the colour of promise, the colour of hope. The angels patiently gesturing on their plinths would not have looked out of place on that shining paper. The angels, ghostly and not placid, who slipped out into those other streets, of the suburb, in the dark, and drew you to them, called you and carried you back, made you one of them;

155

she had thought that might be a pleasant thing. If you were so lucky. It was so still in the graveyard; you knew the teeming city was all around out there but you did not need to hear it or see it. A stout woman in a thick black coat knelt on a grave, pulling out weeds. She had brought a pickle jar of flowers, straggling winter blooms and evergreen leaves. There was nobody else in sight. The cushioning grass, the soundless sea, the marble and limestone and concrete, the one black obsidian figure she knew was there though it was out of sight, all hung poised in the blue silence of winter midday.

Helen walked to the bus stop and sat on the seat. She would not see Aurora on the bus today. It was not the right time. Of course, she was in Canberra. Helen thought this with a detachment that suddenly seemed angelic. What did it matter? She got off at Market Street and walked up to David Jones. She was thinking about how much money she had. Her salary was good, she had no mortgage, her meals were frugal, her clothes old, her car ancient; she hardly ever spent any money. It was time that she did.

BARBARA PAYS A VISIT

Barbara decided not to take her bike. After school she caught the bus to Manuka and then walked the route she'd planned from a map. The house was behind tall iron gates, which stood open; a paved drive forked and went around either side of the spreading brick building. Which way? She went to the right. Steps led up to a narrow terrace and French windows, but that didn't seem to be the entrance, there was a sofa halfway across the door. She kept on. More steps, lined with tubs of white camellias in bloom, and this did seem to be the front door.

She rang the bell. A young man answered, tall, with dark soft hair falling half across his face.

I'm looking for Mrs Cecil, she said.

Oh yes, he said. Won't you come in?

She wondered about his accent. Very posh, it was, upper class. He stood back, and pointed to the seat against the side wall of the hall. It was like three rush-bottomed chairs put together, with carved cockle shells on its wooden back and cushions in Provençal Indian prints. I'll tell Lynette, he said.

Lynette was on the phone. Bring her in here, she muttered with one hand over the receiver. Ferdie supposed she knew who the visitor was. Lynette flapped her hand and grimaced; the person on the other end was doing all the talking.

Ferdie said, Shall I make some coffee? Barbara said thank you, and Lynette nodded. She had her eyes fixed on the great silver singing cup of flowers. Barbara looked at the flowers too. They were different sorts of lilies, with a powerful smell. Then she looked about the kitchen. It reminded her of her old house in Ainslie. The same sort of space, full of things, plates on dressers, jugs, copper bowls, saucepans hanging, a kitchen for serious cooking and eating. Plus odd curious things that were antique objects, useful once, decorations now. Thank god I have left all that behind, she said to herself, remembering with a pang the pale emptiness of her flat. She sat very straight on her chair and looked out of the corners of her eyes at Lynette, the searching gaze of the mistress at the wife, as though there are questions whose answers will be found in her mien. Small and plump, short dark curls, an urchin face under its overlay of tiredness and sorrow.

She'd practised her opening lines on the bus. Hello, Mrs Cecil—may I call you Lynette? (Nobody, nobody, said Mrs any more; the plumber, the bank person, should you find one, the flight attendant, all said Hello Barbara, yes Barbara, no cheques please Barbara, have a nice day Barbara.) I know about you, but I expect, it's quite likely, you won't know about me. The thing is . . . In the bus she wasn't sure what to say the thing was, and here she didn't have any better idea; she supposed she was hoping that Lynette would say something and they would go on from there.

Lynette said, Look, I'll have to ring you back, and put the phone down. Sorry, she said to Barbara. Barbara knew she meant, Sorry for being otherwise occupied, and also, Sorry, but who are you?

Barbara said, My name is Barbara . . . At that moment a girl came into the room. Barbara stood up, dropping her handbag from her lap. She put her hand over her mouth and stared at the girl. No sounds came, even muffled, from her mouth. Her eyes bulged. The girl looked at her with a frown.

Oh, said Barbara, pressing her hand to her chest, and slid to the floor in a faint.

She woke up with her head on a cushion and a rug over her. There were people standing around talking about a doctor. No, an ambulance, someone said. She sat up, feeling dizzy, but then it passed. She put her hand on the seat of a chair and stood up, holding on to its back. She looked at the worried faces regarding her. The girl had gone. Her handbag had been put on the table. She took it up.

Excuse me . . . excuse me. I'm sorry. I can't stay. No, no, she said, when people tried to stop her, begged her to sit down. But if it's your heart, someone said.

No. I need to walk. The air, that's what I need. Goodbye. Thank you so much.

What for? she wondered, as the young man walked with her to the door, let her out with questioning eyes and murmured words.

The air was cold and the walk downhill to Manuka was bracing. She sat in a cafe and drank a glass of red wine. She thought it would be the wrong thing but didn't care. She knew that girl couldn't be Chloe, even though she looked just as Chloe could have looked after the years passed. As though there had been some elaborate trick, and her daughter had been stolen away and brought up by someone else. But she'd seen Chloe in her coffin, pale, without breath, her lips and eyelids shadowed blue, had seen the coffin closed and slid into the flames. The trick wasn't in that past stealing but in this present sending of a double to make her mother believe she was here, alive. And maybe not a double, not really; if only she'd looked at this girl as herself she'd certainly have seen all sorts of ways in which she could not be Chloe. It was cruel of these people to play this trick on her, her heart had gone all sick and bruised again, any healing that had happened all undone.

Who were the people, the girl, the young man? Cecil's children? Lynette's? She knew nothing about them, he had told her nothing, she just knew the fact of his wife. Their affair was perfect and separate, not part of his family world at all. In its own iridescent bubble, like the ones Chloe had blown with detergent and a little ringed pipe. So beautiful. And popping so soon after they were made. You could not ever touch a bubble. They died as soon as blown.

She drank another glass of wine. Of course she knew this wasn't true, the plotting, the tricking, that there wasn't any ill intent on anybody's part. She should have stayed and said what she had gone to say. Yes, of course she should have done that. But she couldn't: even looking back and knowing she should have done it, she also knew it had been impossible.

She paid, and went and waited for the bus that would take her home. It was dark now. When it came there were quite a lot of people in it. She could see herself reflected in the bus's windows, herself and all the other passengers like dim ghosts in a rattling chariot. Home would be bright and warm. Solitary. She and Cecil had agreed, it was a series of occasions of mutual pleasure, not a love affair. But what you said wasn't always true. It was what you wanted, or thought you should want, not what was, not even what you truly desired. Not a love affair, maybe. But she had truly loved him, in their way, and she missed him.

Seeing his house, his wife, the forking brick-paved drive that he would have driven along every night, it threatened to rob her of her Cecil, to turn him into *their* William. She felt a choking in her chest, hot, bitter-flavoured. The light in the bus was darkly yellow. The ghosts all looked as though they had died of jaundice. She thought, this is the bus of the jealous dead, and I am one of them, and we are driving in limbo. On our way to hell, yes. At least that was a Cecil sort of thought, a fantasy thought, a quotation kind of thought; maybe she still had something of him.

On the seat by the baggage rack, side on to the others, sat Chloe. She'd managed to stop seeing her small lost daughter every-where, but now this Cecil girl had opened the door to an older, taller Chloe, a child still but promising adulthood. She stood up with the kind of whisking motion that Barbara recognised, and her pleated school skirt flared in a fan around her legs. She heaved a giant pack on to her back and got off into a dark suburb. The jaun-diced figures slipped and wavered in the wash of tears in Barbara's eyes. You weep for yourself, she told herself. You weep for your loss, of Chloe, of Cecil. I need to grieve, she argued. You need to find another lover, the hard voice said.

She jumped up. The bus was pulling away from the stop. Please, she said, I need to get off. Next stop, said the driver wearily, putting his foot down so the bus trundled heavily into the road. Couldn't you let me off, she began. He repeated, Next stop. She pressed the button, in case he pretended to think nobody wanted it, and got out. Sometimes bus stops are very far apart. When she got back there was no sign of the girl. She walked further along the street. There was a right of way, with a gloomy street lamp; she looked down it but could see nothing. She walked to the next cross street. It was deeply treed, and there was no sign of a figure in it. In the time it had taken Barbara to walk back, of course the girl would be well out of sight. She might have gone into any of these houses. This strange girl, who was not Chloe. Barbara walked along trying to look in the lighted windows but they had their curtains drawn against the cold night.

Buses weren't frequent at this hour. Anyway it was too cold to stand and wait. She walked home; it wasn't such a long way and she was fit.

The flat was bright, and despite its warmth it felt chilly. So bare, so spare as it was. As she had chosen. She stood at the window looking down at the street. The restaurants were busy. Cars double-parked at the video shop and people ran in, coming out with handfuls of DVDs. She felt a choking desire to live that kind of life, to be running into the video shop and coming out with movies to watch in a calm and banal manner, it would be so peaceful, so unhurtful. With friends, a partner, ordinary. She thought, the thing about adulterous lovers is they don't watch DVDs with you.

She could just walk down and borrow some. Get one of the old movies she sometimes watched. She couldn't imagine doing so now. She wondered if she would go down to the noodle house and order a bowl of laksa. The pork was good, or the vegetarian. You had to suppose the prawns would have been frozen. Was she hungry?

She hadn't taken off her coat or gloves. She called a taxi and watched until she saw it come, and went downstairs. The same young man opened the door at the Forest house and stood back for her to come in, smiling in a sweet way.

Are you William's son? she asked; he nodded, and she saw his father fleeting in the turn of his head. She almost put out her hand to touch his cheek, but stopped herself. Lynette was sitting with lists at the kitchen table, a glass of wine in front of her, some bread and some cheese on a plate. There was most of a camembert on the dark green platter, and bunches of purple grapes. There was another young woman in the room, not young like a child, standing by the fridge pouring out a glass of sparkling water.

I'm sorry, said Barbara, I shouldn't have run away in that ignominious . . . She stopped. She wondered if ignominious was the word she meant. Tears overflowed her eyes.

Do sit down, said Lynette, her voice wary but her words those of a good hostess. Have a glass of wine. And some cheese. Ferdie . . .

He was already getting one of the tall-stemmed glasses out of the cupboard.

Do you like red wine? said Lynette.

Yes. Thank you.

Ferdie poured it, and Barbara took several small sips. She was wondering if she could put the glass down and run from the room again. Lynette drank some wine too. She had already had a number of glasses and was feeling remote and calm, sitting in a comfortable small space of grief. Ferdie passed the plate of camembert to Barbara, who remembered that she'd had no dinner and cut a large wedge. The young woman said, Camembert. I must buy some hard cheese. Gruyere would be good. The doorbell rang.

Ferdie answered again. They heard a movement of voices in the hall, and then a large man came into the room. He was a rather beautiful elderly man, lean, his skin brown and his hair a white stubble across his head which gave him a salty look. Barbara thought of fishermen on Greek islands, looking like the gods their forebears had carved. The old gods, the fathers, the husbands, who still chased after young mortals. She'd never had such a thought about Cecil, though this man quite resembled him. Cecil had been a man of the world, not a fisher god.

He kissed Lynette. I was out for a walk, he said. I saw the light on, so I thought . . . I hope it's not too late?

Lynette shook her head. It's good to see you. She took his hand and held it.

Ferdie got another glass and offered wine. Would you have a

beer? said the man. He looked at Barbara. Jack Cecil, he said. Bill's brother. William's.

Oh, said Barbara. William's brother. I didn't even know he had a brother. The tears fell out of her eyes.

I live at the coast, he said. In Eden.

In Eden, she said. There's fishing there, isn't there?

Petals fell off one of the lilies in the singing cup. They landed on the table with a loud plop.

We should cut off the stamens, said Ferdie. Then we wouldn't get that yellow pollen staining everything.

The young woman said, I'm Aurora.

Hello, said Barbara.

Out for a walk, said Lynette.

From the motel down the road, said Jack. I drove up, the sarvo.

You should be staying here, said Lynette.

Oh, you've got enough on your plate. It's cheap, and handy. Just give us a shout when you want something.

Lynette took his hand again. Barbara ate the piece of cheese. Why doesn't Lynette say something? she wondered. Why doesn't she ask me who I am, what I'm doing here, what I want? She ticked the three questions off on her fingers, curled in her lap under the table. I don't know the answer to any of them, she said to herself.

Jack said, Did I tell you, I nearly drowned the night Bill died?

Yes, said Lynette. Of course William didn't exactly drown, he had a heart attack.

No, said Ferdie to Jack. What happened?

So Jack told the story of the storm and the engine failing and the sea anchor pulling out and the American game fishermen rescuing him. He even mentioned the man who had walked up the hill with him and told him the story of being swallowed by the whale and that people called him Jonah.

Did you believe him? asked Ferdie.

When he was telling me I did, said Jack. Afterwards I got a bit uneasy.

Quarantine Bay, said Lynette. Toxic silk. I suppose it killed people too.

I thought Bill might have come fishing with me, said Jack. Slowed down a bit in his old age.

He wasn't that old, said Lynette.

Old enough to slow down, said Jack.

Every time he said the name Bill, Barbara had to remember who he was. The idea of her William—well, of course he was her Cecil, even further removed from Bill—going fishing was so funny she gave a gulp of laughter. She hoped it sounded like a sob. She gulped again, just as she was swallowing a mouthful of wine. Jack reached out a heavy hand and smacked her on the back. Breathe, he said. A trickle of red wine ran out of the corner of her mouth. Ferdie passed her a napkin.

You're upset, said Jack. He finished his beer and stood up. Well, he said, I'd best be going. You'll be wanting to go to bed. Just thought I'd let you know I was here. Call on me, anything. I'd be glad to help.

I'll give you a ring, said Ferdie, keep you in the loop.

Ferdie's my PA, said Lynette, just what I've always wanted. Efficient, and beautiful.

What's a PA? asked Jack.

A kind of dogsbody, said Aurora.

Not at all, said Lynette. A personal assistant, a high-class private secretary person.

Oh, said Jack, a right-hand man. Just what you need, in these moments.

For a man of few words he says a lot, said Lynette when he'd gone.

You are angry, said Barbara, that Jack is alive and his brother is dead. She looked nervous, she hadn't meant to say it aloud.

Lynette looked at her out of heavy eyes.

Barbara said, You're wondering why I'm here.

Yes, said Lynette.

It's hard to tell you. That's why I'm failing.

You were William's mistress.

Did you know?

Lynette shrugged.

I wanted to say . . . I loved him. He loved me. You were his wife. That was different.

It always is.

So you knew . . . about me.

Oh, not you. Lynette sighed. I was his third wife. The love of his life, oh yes, he said that. But a third wife, she's an idiot if she has illusions. Being faithful wasn't William's thing. Well, I did have illusions. But when I saw you . . . She rubbed her fingers round the rim of her glass so it squealed. Do you want anything?

Barbara shook her head. Just honesty, I think. That I exist. He told me it was a game, I knew it was. But now, I'm bereft.

Yes, said Lynette.

I want to come to the funeral.

Sit in the front row, Lynette said.

Barbara shook her head.

You could have come. Anyone can come to a funeral.

Barbara put her empty glass on the table. She stood up. I think I'll go now. Could you ring a taxi? she asked Ferdie. I'm not sure I understand myself. Death . . . she paused. I know about death. Except you never do, of course. But I know it clears everything, you have to face it, and not hide.

It makes me tired, said Lynette.

Yes, said Barbara, it does that. She stood for about a minute with her head bent. William said we shouldn't lie.

Lynette laughed. He was a dab hand at lies. Lies of omission.

I'm not. Thank you, Barbara said, you have been good.

A good woman.

Yes. I'll wait outside for the taxi.

The camellias by the path were pale in the darkness, pale and luminous; moths would come to their glimmer. Would they, when there was no scent? Barbara hadn't done any gardening since Chloe died.

I'll wait with you, said Ferdie, and walked with her along the paved driveway to the gates, which were open still.

Do you ever shut them? she asked.

I don't know. I don't live here, you know, I live in England.

But you are William's son.

My mother was wife number two. He broke her heart.

Some men are good at that.

Aurora is the daughter of wife number one. I don't think he broke her heart.

The street was deserted. The houses were quiet behind their high dense hedges. Old plantings of pyracantha, frowned upon these days because birds eat the berries and drop them in the wild, where they become noxious weeds. Nobody thought of pulling these out, though. There were no people, no cars, the street lights seemed dim and muted in this secretive neighbourhood. The taxi came slowly round the corner; Ferdie stepped out and waved to it.

Goodnight, she said.

The young man bent forward and kissed her cheek. Go well, he said. He opened the car door, then closed it behind her. Barbara sank back into the seat. Lynette was right, about tiredness. She felt exhausted. She wanted to go to bed and sleep for a week. Sleep and never wake up? No, you always wake up.

FERDIE FINDS SATYRS

Cold, said Ferdie, waving his arms and stamping into the kitchen. Lynette was pouring more wine into her glass.

Aurora was saying, Can't decide whether she's cheeky or brave or stupid or a bitch.

Honesty, Lynette said. Her words were vehement, but her voice was without emotion. The most dishonest thing in the world, that kind of honesty. I'm sure your mother would agree.

Yes, said Ferdie, not knowing if she would or not.

Aurora said carefully, What kind of honesty is it, exactly?

Oh, the kind that goes around saying, Let us be honest with one another, let's never tell one another any lies, and maybe that's the case, maybe they don't actually lie through their teeth, whatever that means, but their lives are one big huge lie, they're living the lie but not telling you about it. And yes I know he'd say things were better like that, what you don't know can't hurt you, and I suppose I went along with that.

Not knowing, said Ferdie.

Yes, not knowing. Somehow choosing not to know. Or at least allowing myself not to. I knew he'd never leave me, I thought I did, that he loved the life we lived together, he loved me, he loved Erin, he would never walk away from that. If he had other recreations, well, no skin off my nose, I thought. He'd never leave me: that's a good joke, now he's gone and left the lot of us.

He didn't choose to, said Aurora. Given a choice, he'd still have been here with you.

If he hadn't been off fucking that woman, Lynette said in her calm voice, I think we can safely say he'd be here now. That's what kills people, you know, mad sex; did you take a good look at her? It's a wonder he didn't die on the job.

Ferdie held her hand. Lynette drank more wine.

Aurora said, But you had no idea of this woman, this Barbara.

Not a clue. Not the slightest. I'd have liked to keep it like that. Why did she have to come here, telling me?

It's the role of the mistress to know, the role of the wife not to know. I know, I've been there. Cezary's marriage was over, but he still had a wife. It's a kind of paradox, isn't it. A horrible thing. The mistress knows all about the other, has all sorts of evil imaginings, while the wife remains serene. Until of course she finds out.

So you reckon Barbara wanted me to know what she knew? So I'd be in the same boat as her? That's why she came here to destroy my past, my safety, my comfort. What a monstrous thing to do.

The right bitch role, said Aurora.

It does look like it, said Ferdie, wondering how to comfort her and not lie, or not exactly. But maybe she was looking for comfort for herself, he went on, and thinking that if you knew, it would help her. She wasn't trying to hurt you, she just didn't think of you, only of herself.

I think you fancy her, Ferdie; she's more your age than William's, that's for sure. But if that's the case, well, it's a pity. For me. I doubt it did her much good, either. Maybe she thought we'd become bosom buddies, having so much in common.

I don't think she thought much at all, really.

It's a game, William said to her. Life's always a game. Not often fun, though.

I don't think he thought his life with you was a game, Ferdie said. It was the serious thing.

You reckon he slept with her the way some men take up golf? I always wondered that he didn't take up golf.

Ferdie realised that this was a joke, and laughed gently.

Well, I didn't really, of course. I knew William wasn't the golfing type. And I suppose I did know he was the fucking type.

Lynette still spoke softly, not even emphasising her words, their bitterness in their meaning, not their iteration. Had you not known her, you would not perhaps have caught the sarcasm of her words. Ferdie had never heard her say 'fucking' before.

I'm so tired, she said. I've got to go to bed. She put her wine glass on the sink, and opened her arms to Ferdie and Aurora. My dears, she said.

Our lovely wicked stepmonster, said Ferdie. Lynette looked startled. Ferdie said, Not. Well, lovely. But otherwise, not.

They all laughed.

Ferdie said, I know it's probably not the time, but don't we have to start thinking about the funeral?

No, said Lynette, it's not the time, and no we don't have to start thinking. When the autopsy's done, that'll be plenty of time.

Oh yes, said Ferdie.

Funerals can happen very fast, said Lynette.

Ferdie decided he liked being PA to Lynette. It kept him busy, and required his intelligence, though it wasn't at all intellectual. It was straightforwardly useful, in a way that writing a PhD wasn't. He liked helping Lynette, and he'd always been fond of her.

Often he tried to think of Berenice. Berenice and her constellation of hair in the sky. It didn't really work. His talismanic image of her white body in its olive-green sheets had started slipping; he couldn't hold it. The wrong words attached themselves. They're Jimmy Choo you know, said her bare foot. Her mouth opened wide like a cat yawning, her small white teeth glistened, she meowed: Great Pan is dead. Perhaps he was, out here. Had never been alive. Perhaps that great groan that had reverberated around the ancient world had not reached the antipodes, had not needed to. But he didn't believe that. Oh, he didn't construct Sydney Long pictures of his native landscape, with satyrs stalking long-legged against sunset skies, under trees off a Royal Doulton painted plate. Pan in this country would be different, he wasn't sure how. One day he would think about it; for now it was one of those ideas that simmered away in the depths of his brain, not needing his attention until it was ready.

He could have emailed Berenice. He often had occasion to use Lynette's laptop, he could have sent her a message. But he didn't. He'd written a postcard, one he'd found in William's desk, an etching of a Picasso bull, with curling hair and delicate horns; his mild black eye might have had Europa in its sights. Wish you were here, he wrote. But I doubt you would. It had seemed quite witty until he posted it, but he shuddered when he remembered it. Crass, it had been.

Aurora got up early at Flavia's and worked on her computer; when he asked her what she did she said it would be nearly as boring for her to explain it as it would be for him to hear, and neither would understand it. When he said he didn't think that was true she said, You know how when you're learning a language at school they tell you, one day when you're really good you'll be able to think in it? Well, what I do is its own strange language, I can think in it but I can't translate it.

Yeah? he said.

Yeah.

She came round late in the morning, at the hour when Lynette had to have her coffee, and after that she wanted to go out for lunch. She was out of touch with Canberra restaurants, she wanted to catch up. Ferdie said he couldn't afford it. I'll pay, said Aurora. Lynette sent them down to Manuka to pick up some goodies to eat at home. They rode the bikes, it was exhilarating going down but rather a slog riding back.

He was having third and fourth and fifth thoughts about the postcard. It had seemed like a good idea at the time. Lynette had said, Use anything you need. Just make yourself at home. When he asked could he telephone Pepita in England she said, You don't need to ask, Ferdie. Just do whatever you think needs to be done. The postcard was one of a pile in the drawer. Now he imagined Berenice offended by the beefy qualities of the bull in the picture; he remembered it as quite essentially dumb, if friendly. Now he had a thought: he would send Berenice a postcard every day. Just little messages. If one seemed strange, it would be all mixed up in the messages of the others. He found one of the designs by Marion Mahony Griffin for Canberra, lovely linear shapes she'd painted gold silk, breast-shaped cupolas, arches, arcades charmingly reflected in a myriad pools. This is what the National Capital ought to look like, but doesn't, he wrote. This seemed a good cryptic solution to the problem of communicating.

He turned William's computer on, googled Berenice in southern skies. To see if she was visible. A lot of responses came up, but they were difficult to work out. The answer seemed to be yes, but only for more advanced and instrumental observers, that is, not to the naked eye. And only in autumn. Berenice's long amber hair was in the deep sky fields. Inaccessible to mortal eyes. Idly he wished he could talk to an astronomer.

He checked his emails via the internet, then thought he should take a look at William's. Maybe there was something that would need attention. He didn't know how it happened, what key he'd touched; suddenly he was in a slideshow of satyrs. They began as sculptures, bronze and finely carved, and metamorphosed into flesh, muscular and tanned. Interesting such flesh for mythical beasts. They paraded across the screen like giants, their goatish hairy thighs curling brown, white, black, walking on long downward-curving cloven hooves, displaying long upward-curving cloven erections. The noise of their march reverberated like drumbeats, the scene shimmered faintly in their echo. Nymphs appeared, buxom girls out of a Norman Lindsay etching, lying back and demonstrating their private parts. When the satyrs fell upon the nymphs Ferdie tried to get out of the slideshow but it wouldn't let him. It took him deeper and deeper into more orgiastic images. He knew the theory of such things, how they drew you in and you couldn't escape; trying to quit didn't work. It made him feel frantic. Aurora came in and he got her to help; she'd learned strategies to cope with such things, she said.

When they'd finally got rid of it she gave him a quizzical glance.

All your own work?

Not at all. Purest accident.

Yeah? All William's work, then?

I don't know. Maybe it was a trap for him, too.

Pornography waiting to pounce.

I hear it's proactive, said Ferdie. I was trying to call up his emails.

Maybe that was an email.

Do you think our father . . .?

Our father. What do we know of our father? He's still springing surprises from beyond the grave. Don't you think he gets more mysterious by the minute? That woman, that mistress . . . when we thought he was happily settled with Lynette. Getting it right after getting it wrong with our mothers. And Lynette so calm about her.

Not really calm, said Ferdie. That wasn't natural. I think she's in shock. He tried to repeat his earlier actions on the computer. I think I am, in shock I mean. And bloody computers, they're still pretty foreign bodies to me.

This time emails came up. Aurora scrolled through. Nothing that looks urgent, she said.

I don't think we need to say anything to Lynette about . . . the other, he said.

God, no.

It started off with marching satyrs, said Ferdie.

Satyrs. That's Pan, isn't it? Your field. Maybe he was trying to keep up with you.

Well, we'll never know, will we, said Ferdie with a kind of anger. William may have known nothing about it. Or it was straight-forward research gone wrong. Or he was an ardent pornographer.

Does it matter? said Aurora. There's William, we knew him and didn't know him. We love him, in our way. He's dead. I wish he wasn't. All the rest doesn't matter.

You don't mean that, said Ferdie. You want to know about him too.

I'm too clever to want things I know I can't have, said Aurora. She looked at him sideways. Most of the time.

Ferdie laughed. After a few seconds she did too. At least I've got a big sister now, he said.

You always did.

Ah yes, but it's not what you have, it's what you know you have.

Aurora turned and put her arms around Ferdie. He held her tight. He'd thought of her as a slender woman, but she was tight with muscle. The new woman, with her biceps and built-up shoulders, even in so tiny a package as Aurora.

I was thinking about Pan, said Ferdie. And those Sydney Long creatures . . .

What're they?

He painted all these satyrs. Black silhouettes against sunsets. Like art deco plates, with enlacings of eucalyptus boughs along the top edge. Playing Pan pipes.

As they do. Maybe you conjured them up. Typed in satyrs, or something.

Without noticing? Maybe. Maybe, as you say, William was researching satyrs and they were lying in wait.

Here we go again. I think it's Lynette's coffee time.

Lynette swirled the coffee in her cup. *This thing of darkness* . . . Ferdie, what's that? she said.

This thing of darkness I acknowledge mine . . .

And what's it about?

It's Prospero, talking about Caliban. *The Tempest.* You know how Caliban is a monster, always playing cruel tricks, trying to damage people. But when Prospero says this it suggests that Caliban is the bad side of his own self. A sort of alter ego, maybe.

It kind of popped into my head. I think I'm channelling William. The apt quotation is his thing, not mine. Except I'm not doing it very well. Only scraps.

Channelling's always imperfect. Getting stuff from the spirit world is like a mobile phone with bad reception.

Maybe I should go up on a mountain, said Lynette. It might come through loud and clear.

Ferdie started thinking of his mother. This thing of darkness . . . the light going out of her life with William, and any that was left absorbed by those black clothes. It made him sick to think of this. He was unpacking the dishwasher and the sickness made him clumsy. He dropped one of the tulip-shaped wine glasses; it smashed on the terracotta tiles of the kitchen floor. Lynette was making minestrone, she thought they needed some hearty food. She stopped and looked at the shards of glass. Ferdie stood appalled. I'm sorry, he said. I'm sorry. The beautiful glass. I bet it's a set and I've ruined it.

Lynette made a vague gesture with her hand that was holding a big cook's knife. I did that once, she said, making a chopping motion, when I was holding a knife like this, and chopped up a glass. Into fragments. She stood looking at these pieces in a kind of trance and then shook herself out of it. Doesn't matter, she said. What's a glass? Plenty more where that came from. A glass. In the context. The death of the glass.

Ferdie got the dustpan and brush and, using their glitter to find them, swept up the shards.

Put it in the bin, she said. Not the recycling, they don't seem to like drinking glasses.

This thing of darkness . . . she muttered, chopping the soup vegetables.

What made you think of it?

I don't know. That's why I reckon I'm channelling William. Darkness, of course, there's no surprise there.

We all go into the dark . . .

You're your father's son, Ferdie, no doubt.

Darkness be my friend . . .

What's that?

Dunno. Maybe William again.

I can see it could be good fun, popping out with other people's phrases. They're thinking for you.

Once they've got in there.

I think it's a song, said Lynette.

What?

Darkness be my friend. She made an attempt to hum a tune.

A bright little sparkle in a corner caught Ferdie's attention. A missed fragment of glass. He picked it up and a line of red dots ran along his finger. He hid it so Lynette wouldn't see. Of course his mother wasn't a thing of darkness. He knew people that were like black holes, who sucked all the energy out of a situation, or a relationship, but not his mother.

Ferdie rang Helen up. He was feeling bad about having left her. She'd pushed him to do it, insisted, but thinking about it now he could see that it wasn't what she wanted. He rang her up because he knew she wouldn't ring him. It was Lynette's phone and she didn't ring Lynette.

Ferdie! How lovely. How are you, dear?

Very well. Busy. There's a lot to do, with a death in the family. When are you coming down?

Ah, yes. I've been meaning to ring you. I've decided not to come. Yes, I know. But William wasn't my husband, better to leave things to Lynette. Nobody will worry if I'm not there.

Ferdie, through his shock, listened to her voice. It wasn't plaintive, or complaining, in fact it sounded unusually cheerful. It didn't sound as though she wasn't coming in order to punish someone.

I'm really quite busy here, Helen went on, and I'd rather not miss school if I can help it. She didn't say, considering that I will have already had several days off.

Ferdie thought he was probably quite pleased she wasn't coming. He could give his attention to Lynette. She'd always treated him as a child of the house, not particularly demanding of him but making him free of all the household had to offer, including her affection. Helen had never observed this; it seemed a good idea not to start now. On the other hand, why had she changed her mind? It didn't seem to be because of any painful reason. She hadn't sounded fragile or racked on the phone. He supposed he'd find out when he got back to Sydney.

William wasn't my husband, she'd said.

That was new.

LYNETTE HAS DINNER WITH JACK

Lynette said, I'm having dinner with Jack. I want to talk to him.

Sounds good, said Ferdie. Where will you go?

Oh, just his motel. I've ordered in some food. That way we won't be interrupted. She was packing a French market basket—available in the shop for a high price but that didn't seem to be a problem, people kept buying them—with a bottle of white wine in an insulating sleeve, two bottles of red, a six-pack of designer beer, two of the tulip glasses, some large linen napkins and some plates.

That should cover all eventualities, said Ferdie.

I think so, said Lynette.

And of course I'm driving you.

I thought you might, said Lynette. One way. I'll get a taxi back. Oh Ferdie, it's so good having you here. It's such a limbo time. You're a comfort.

I suppose when you've got a date for the funeral it'll be less of a limbo. Or anyway, a finite one.

Maybe, said Lynette. I'm not thinking about it. Remember?

I suppose by definition a limbo can't be finite, can it? Doesn't it just go on?

How would I know?

When they pulled up outside Jack's motel, Lynette glanced at it and rolled her eyes. He hasn't gone for glamour, she said.

Maybe it's comfortable.

I wouldn't lay any bets.

Lynette kissed him. Don't wait up, she said. She picked up the basket and went inside. In the lobby she avoided looking at herself in the mirror. She'd checked her appearance before she left home. She'd worked on it, wanting to look as pretty as possible, but not frivolous, not making much of the widow thing but not denying it either. Now, well, it had worked or it hadn't; she didn't want to know.

Jack seemed pleased to see her. He'd bought some wine too, a bottle of white, a New Zealand sauvignon blanc, which was thoughtful of him, she said.

The food should be here in half an hour, said Lynette. I thought we could have a drink first.

Maybe we should talk first. What was it in particular?

Oh, nothing in particular. Everything in general, you might say.

He looked so puzzled she laughed. She took his hand. Come and sit down.

Jack was being rather slow at drinking beer. This is a good sav blanc, she said.

She'd ordered a lot of oysters. They were small Sydney rock oysters from Batemans Bay; Jack said they were great.

Lynette served the hot food. She poured the wine, she tried to persuade Jack to take a little red. She helped him to special morsels, touching his hand lightly from time to time. She worked on getting him to do the talking, asking after his boat, the vegetable garden, the stranger from the belly of the whale. It wasn't very easy.

I'm not much of a talker, he said.

Saying that's a sign that you are.

Somehow, with Rosamund, there wasn't much need. And now, well, it's the blokes in the pub. They yap on but not much gets said. Not like Bill. He was the talker.

She wished he wouldn't mention William. She hadn't intended to talk about William and yet he seemed to keep coming up, as though Jack's mind was so full of him that talking about him was a kind of default mode, and he couldn't stop reverting to him.

Lynette sighed. You two were such good friends, she said. As boys, I mean. She knew that as adults they'd hardly seen one another. Though there were those yearly letters. She slid her fingers across the back of his hand.

He was a good brother to me. Jack picked up the hand she was stroking and rubbed his head. I remember once . . . we used to play on this old railway line. The Gully line, I think it was called. Never any trains on it. Built up on a sort of embankment. There were culverts under it, all full of prickles, lantana. You could push your way in but they were sort of scary. Because of the way they smelt, I think. Dead things. A lot of rubbish. You kept thinking you might find something useful but you never did. Bill had this game, you had to walk along the line in a kind of pattern, between the rails and the sleepers; I dunno, I wasn't any good at it, couldn't concentrate, kept forgetting the numbers, when it was the rail, when the sleeper. If you got it wrong you had to do a dare the other person made up. This day I was trying hard not to forfeit. Bill was ahead, he was a whizz at it, and then he suddenly starts yelling and waving his arms and jumps off the rails on to the embankment. I can't work out what he's doing, I stop to stare at him. Maybe he's trying to make me lose my step. He's running back. Then there's a whistle, one of those tooting steam whistles, and when I look around there's an engine coming. Bill's running along the embankment, shouting. I'm kind of stuck, you see. Like a possum in the headlights, I've thought since. Bill gets close enough to grab me and pull me out of the way. Nick of time. My foot hits some bit of the edge of the engine, but I didn't get run over. Thanks to Bill.

Lynette was thinking, all these different Williams. This is Jack's William. Jack's Bill. There's Helen's and Nerys's and his mother's, once, then Ferdie's, Aurora's, Erin's. Barbara's of course. There's mine, but not what I thought it was all these years. He tricked me. Fooled me. No lies. Ha.

It's another life, she said. Another person.

I've never forgotten it. He saved my life. I wouldn't have had one, without him.

You were obviously wrong about no trains using the line.

Never saw another one, before or since. It was an old engine, even for the time. The kind they called the old coffee pot, because it had a great big funnel in a sort of round triangle shape, a cone I suppose I mean, not that I've ever seen a coffee pot like that. There used to be one of those engines pulled coal wagons.

Maybe it was a ghost engine.

It caught my foot a fair enough whack. Had a ruddy great bruise on my ankle. Limped for days.

You were a dreamy child. Lynette remembered William saying this about Jack.

Yeah, that's what people said. I just thought that was the way people were.

Not hearing a train bearing down on you.

Trying to concentrate. Too much like hard work. There never were trains there, though.

Lynette had tried to persuade Jack to move on from beer to wine but he'd only had a sip. I'm not really a wine person, he said. Rosamund liked a glass of chardonnay occasionally. I kept one of those little casks in the fridge for her.

I am a woman who has lost her husband, Lynette thought. But now it appears I didn't in fact have that husband to lose. She looked at Jack's hands lying loosely on the table. They were clean, with short pink nails, brown, weathered, hands that did hard work in the soil and on the sea. She wanted them to hold hers. She wanted him to put his long strong arms around her and hold her tight. She wanted him to lead her over to the bed with its shiny brown nubbly cover and make love to her. She'd come here this night with these things in mind but didn't know how to make them happen. She'd thought that pouring him a glass of wine might warm him up, but he poured his own beer and not much of it. At home she could have lit the fire and sat beside him on the sofa, gradually slipping close. There wasn't a sofa here, just two plastic tub chairs on either side of the table that served as a writing desk. They were a bit low for dining, she felt as if her chin was resting on the table.

What do you think the most important thing in the world is? she asked. Jack looked nervous. She barely paused, because she did not expect or want him to answer. I think it is desire. William would have agreed with me. He was into desire. New, all the time.

I don't think it has to be new, all the time, said Jack. But what would I know?

Lynette leaned over and touched his hand, lightly. Of course you'd know. Tell me.

I don't think desire has to keep changing. It doesn't have to stop, or find different things. Fishing, he said, I've always wanted fishing.

And what about . . . people?

Rosamund, always. Still.

Me with William, too. It was a bit of a shock to find out it wasn't enough for him. I suppose I should have looked at the history, there was a message there. I suppose I thought I was the one would be different. Change the pattern. He moved on; I think I could, now.

Do you think?

Yes, she said, on a long sibilant breath.

Jack shrugged his shoulders. Well. What would I know, he said again.

You could find out.

She thought, I could say, *Let's go and lie on the bed and make love* and it might be a bit more obvious but not much.

Jack said, I wouldn't know how to start.

His glass was empty. She said, Shall I get you another beer?

I think I've had enough, thanks.

She poured herself another glass of red, stood up, stretched, said, These chairs are vilely uncomfortable, and went and draped herself along the bed.

Jack wrinkled his forehead. Do you want to talk . . . he paused, grimaced, well, about arrangements . . . things?

No, said Lynette.

I mean, I thought, the funeral . . .

No, said Lynette.

And there's the will, and so on. I suppose he did leave one.

William was a lawyer, of course he left a will. You mean, you think maybe it's like doctors' children being always sick?

What?

Professional men, neglecting their job when it's close to home. Doesn't seem like William.

Don't you want to know?

He'll have left things to me. To Erin.

He has other children. What about Ferdie and Aurora?

Jack! Are you trying to make me miserable?

No. I'm trying to help. Be the man of the family.

Yes, well, that's another thing.

She rolled on to one elbow and drank some wine. There'll be time for all that, wills, funerals, the rest of my life. I want another now. She drank some more of the wine, then lay down on the pillow. Her eyes closed.

Her mobile phone woke her up. It said, in a bored voice, *ring-ring, ring-ring, ring-ring*, over and over. Erin liked to try out different ring tones, which meant that Lynette was never sure it was her phone. Jack had been reading the paper, was looking up, mildly interested. Lynette answered. It was Ferdie, saying something about Nerys, and did she want him to come and get her.

No no, said Lynette, I'm okay. She shook her head, but that made it feel funny, not clear. She said, Did I fall asleep? in an indignant voice, as though it were Jack's fault.

For a bit. You didn't snore much.

You should have woken me.

I thought you needed a rest.

It looks like I'd better go. That was Ferdie. On about something.

I'll drive you, he said, and insisted.

She stuffed the dirty plates and glasses into the basket. Jack offered to wash them and bring them back tomorrow but she said the dishwasher at home would do it. She put in the wine bottles, the full and the half drunk. When she'd done that she stood and put her arm around Jack and gave him a hug. He hugged back, like a brother.

Kindness is no substitute for desire, she said.

Isn't it? I don't know, it might be. Might be better.

When he stopped his car in her driveway she turned and kissed him on the mouth. Like dates when she was a teenager, nervous and amateur and technically uncertain. Except then the boy did it first.

Look after yourself, said Jack. And no, he wouldn't come in, it was past his bedtime. But he carried the basket to the door for her.

NERYS FLIES SOUTH

Nerys sat on her balcony drinking orange and rosehip tea. The winter sun was warm in this sheltered place. She was looking at the sea. Watching it, you could say. Her partner Acacia did, she called this Nerys's sea watch. She teased her, saying that she was gauging whether it was coming closer. Well, everybody knew it was, there was evidence of that, the dune washed away, the sand disappeared, and the council wasn't going to do anything about it, not buttress the sand dunes, or wall the beach with rocks, or help people to deal with their houses gradually washing into the water. Her house was a series of pods on wheels, thanks to their architect, who had worked out what was happening to the fragile land's edge; they had enough land to move back, for a while anyway. Or they could just uplift and go. This afternoon the sea was blue, aggressively blue, excruciatingly blue. Blue was supposed to be a soothing colour but not in this sea it wasn't. The hard sparkle of the sun upon it could hurt the eyes, she always wore her sunglasses when she looked at it. Watched it. It was the colour of the lapis lazuli in the workshop. That was intense and richly dense too but in a comforting and restful way. No sparkle.

People change, of course. Once Nerys had thought that living this close to the ocean was a lifelong ambition realised. Now she was inclined to listen to Acacia when she said, We could live in a cool green rainforest, think how spiritual it would be. Nerys did think about it. Maybe not move the pods: this was a sea house, close to the elements, breezes, winds, storms. They could build a new house that belonged in the trees, not on wheels to move back from the relentless attack of the waves. Sell the pods, start again.

She found herself thinking of the Bhagwan, something she didn't often do, lately. She remembered him saying, I am guru to the rich, because they can be easily awakened. The poor are asleep. They are no good to me. As he drove round in his fleet of Rolls-Royces. That was in the early days, when she'd just become an Orange person, and it worried her because she knew she was poor. That wasn't the case now, thanks to the crystals. Not that she'd call herself rich, exactly, but money wasn't a problem. She thought of the possibilities of a house in the rainforest.

The Bhagwan would have liked it, provided it was luxurious enough. The Orange people: everyone thought they had died out. It was true that they didn't get about in orange robes any more. The crystals had been Ma Sheela's idea, and a very good one. Though the name, the Crystal Palace, had been all her own work. And the grounds, the tranquil pools and fountains, the grottoes, the statues, the secret themed gardens. All the different Buddhas, hidden among the plants. The Amethyst Cafe, with its gourmet meals and snacks and produce to take away, the obelisks, the labyrinth—not the kind you could get lost in, but paths you could trace to their centre of serenity. Lucky the business was no longer attached to her house, it would have been harder to move. The cleverness of the business owed a lot to her second husband, he'd been an accountant, and made sure it all worked financially. She'd learned a great deal from him, she was a natural, he said. And now the staff did the work, she mainly kept imagining it. Not to lose the vision which had begun it. Supervising, of course.

The light was taking on that furry quality of the late afternoon, when the lowering sun shines through the sea mist and the colours become pale and haunting. Chillier, too, but not yet time to go inside. This was what would be hard to leave, this subtle cloudy light which was like living in an oyster shell, all faint pearly iridescence. She said that about oyster shells to Acacia once, and Acacia had grinned and replied, The world is our oyster. Well, so it was, so it was.

Acacia would be home soon. This afternoon was her adult education class in how to have a fabulous funeral. People who have a lifestyle will want to have a deathstyle, her brochures said, and Acacia Solstice could help them to this. A lot of people came to the classes, she was a famous funeral celebrant. Nerys had met her when Acacia had organised the funeral of her second husband, his choice, he always had an eye for spiritual fashions.

It had taken a while, but they had got together. I knew we would, said Acacia, I just didn't want to rush it. Now Nerys did not want to think of ever being apart from Acacia. Tomorrow afternoon they would go to Canberra. Acacia had a funeral in the morning, a toddler who'd been run over in the driveway of her house by her father in his SUV. It would be a natural funeral, the child in a cardboard coffin which her cousins and all her little friends would spend some of the morning painting, and then it would be buried and a tree planted, no headstone, there would be coordinates that could be traced by GPS. There'd be a party in the field, not wailing and grief but a celebration of the child's life; no easy task in the circumstances, but Acacia had her ways of managing that.

She was a tall and stately woman with a cloud of white hair and she wore white garments, robes she called them, a bit Grecian, a bit Asian, flowing around and about her body, like a handmaiden of the earth goddess who welcomed the child into death. When Acacia's topaz eyes smiled upon you, you could believe she was the goddess herself. Her ceremonies were not ecumenical, but somehow you believed in Elysian Fields. Nerys would attend the funeral, she loved Acacia's ceremonies but did not go unless she had a reason. In this case she knew the family, the whole town did, and was distressed by the tragedy that had befallen them. They ran the aromatherapy shop, and were good citizens of the town. The mother did massages, she had magic fingers. The little girl who was called Willow had been known to everyone. Nerys knew Acacia was going to do her favourite reading from the Prophet, Kahlil Gibran, which always filled Nerys with such exultation she wanted to cry, and yet it was an exhortation to joy. Acacia said, Joy, tears; all life is one, you know that.

For what is it to die but to stand naked in the wind
    and to melt into the sun?
And what is it to cease breathing but to free the breath
    from its restless tides, that it may rise and expand and seek God
    unencumbered?
Only when you drink from the river of silence shall you indeed sing.
And when you have reached the mountain top, then you shall begin
    to climb.
And when the earth shall claim your limbs, then shall you truly dance.

She had already decided to have this at her own funeral. Acacia was big on planning your funeral well before you expected it to happen, so everyone knew where they were. A cardboard coffin, too; if—hopefully—Aurora had some children, they could decorate it. If not, maybe a shroud would be a good idea. The lightest possible footprint on the earth. And marked only by the coordinates recorded elsewhere. Much the best. She didn't think anybody would care to visit. Her own parents had a plaque in a crematorium garden, with a yellow rosebush, she knew though she had never seen it.

It was dark now. She shivered, and remembered to think that William was dead. A long time ago he had been her husband. There was a small pang of melancholy in that thought, not much sadness, as there hadn't been when she left him, all the excitement of becoming an Orange person carrying her far from any faint prickle of regret. All the important things of her life had been after William. Well, except Aurora. Briefly she'd wondered if Lynette would want Acacia to do the ceremony, but she decided she'd have her own ideas. Better not get involved. Except by going. She would do that.

She went inside and put together a meal for when Acacia came home. Pumpkin soup, Thai-style made with coconut milk; lettuce, avocado, tomatoes, a white bean salad with olives. Sourdough bread from the Amethyst Cafe.

Acacia when she came zinging in was hungry. Her adult education classes were a performance, they took it out of her. In her class was a local councillor; he reckoned there would be forced evacuations from seaside properties before too long, she said. What with global warming, rising sea levels, all that.

Nerys looked at her. I was thinking, she said. Time to do that tree-change. Move to the rainforest. Sell this while we can.

Acacia returned her look, smiled. Yes!

They hired a car at the airport in Canberra and drove to the Hyatt. Acacia intended to go straight to bed. A funeral always exhausted her, she gave so much, it is not easy to take a mass of grief-stricken people in the hands of one's will and carry them into celebration; all Acacia's energy had been used up. Then the plane trip, but first the drive to Coolangatta. And the plane needed a stop in Newcastle.

Acacia put her nightgown on and got into bed. Nerys made her a cup of soporific herbal tea. Now Acacia talked about the funeral. It was hard, she said. I knew it would be, but it was even harder. She stared through the steam from the cup. I found out that Willow was an IVF baby.

I didn't know that, said Nerys.

No. Nobody did. They'd been trying for years, and the IVF was long and slow too. They'd pretty well given up hope, then Willow was born. They talked to me about the joy of that. And I could see they were thinking that they'd killed her.

Well, I suppose they did.

You can't think like that, Nerys. Life and death aren't simple things. They are wondrous, beyond our understanding; we can only try to see them. We have to learn to accept. That's my job, to help.

Nerys held her hand tightly.

Acacia said, I thought they were spiritual people, their business and all, and so they are, but their spirituality has taken a beating. I needed a lot of energy to get a small flicker from it.

Nerys remembered how she used to think of Aurora, and what it would have been like to lose her. An only child. Your single hostage to fortune. She didn't think that now; maybe she had got into the habit of accepting Aurora's life. But she remembered the nightmare thought of it, all those years ago. Willow, the beloved child, and no more possible now.

You can't replace one child with another, said Acacia, as though she knew what Nerys was thinking. You have to see her as the gift of herself, and the importance of that gift isn't the length of time you have her but the strength of the love she brings.

It's hard.

Of course. Nobody's saying it's not. We can help by thinking of her, the little bright creature she was. Holding her in our minds, still.

Nerys wasn't tired, plane travel agitated her, she knew she couldn't sleep yet. She decided to pop up and see Lynette. If there were no lights in the house she wouldn't knock.

A young man opened the door. He was almost frowning. Hello, she said, I'm Nerys.

He smiled then. Ferdie, he said. Seeing her blankness, he said, Helen's my mother.

Oh yes, said Nerys. She reached up and kissed him; she liked beautiful boys. In a motherly way. You are your mother's son, she said to him.

Ferdie didn't know what this meant so he smiled a small smile. She meant slender and willowy but didn't say so. They went into the kitchen. Aurora was there. Nerys hugged her and patted her stomach; Aurora wriggled her shoulders, shaking off the hand, the thought. Don't go on, Mum, she said.

Ferdie offered white wine, Nerys asked for herbal tea. Ferdie couldn't find any, then he uncovered some rather old-looking peppermint at the back of the cupboard. I think the wine might be better, he said. Nerys shook her head.

I'm so sorry about William, she said. Such a loss . . .

Erin came in, in a rush, not paying attention. How's your French? she asked Ferdie.

Depends. He was phoning Lynette.

La Tuile à Loup. How would you translate it?

Say it again?

Erin wrote it on a piece of paper.

Oh yes. The Wolf Tile, I suppose. What's it about?

It's the name of a shop in Paris. Mum took me. It has a whole lot of painted ceramics. Pretty nice. That's one. She pointed to a bowl in yellow earthenware, thickly painted in brown and turquoise. I knew wolf. I need to know about wolves, I'm collecting them.

Slipware, said Nerys. You must be Erin. I've got something for you. She picked up her bag, sparkling with mirror embroidery, and took out a small package in a purple organza bag which had a strong perfume. Erin sniffed. It's patchouli, said Nerys. An ancient Indian scent. Don't worry, I'm Aurora's mum.

Hello.

Inside the organza bag was a big piece of quartz, much the shape of a heart. It was heavy, with a milky translucence. It filled Erin's hand.

It's quartz, said Nerys. One of the most important crystals. It brings the energy of the stars into the soul.

Oh, said Erin. Thank you. It's lovely.

Remember. The energy of the stars into the soul.

How will I know?

Ah, I think you'll know.

Erin said to Ferdie, What's it mean? The Wolf Tile?

Ferdie shook his head. I think I can translate it, but I don't know what it means.

I do, said Nerys. It comes from the high remote villages of country France. At certain times of the year, wintry times, the wind blows from a particular direction, and that causes a tile on the roof—I expect it's placed on purpose—to make a knocking sound, and that is a warning that the season of wolves is coming.

When the wind blows and the tile bangs, then you must beware of wolves.

Erin shivered. Aurora said, How do you know?

I've been to that shop too. They give you a slip of paper with the story written on it. It's a very posh shop in the Latin Quarter, a long way from wolves.

Listen, said Ferdie, the wind . . . Can you hear the tile knocking?

You don't get wolves here, said Erin.

Don't you? Are you sure?

Yes, said Aurora. We're all sure.

Dangerous, said Ferdie. Dangerous to dismiss them. When we were small, driving through the pine forest, we always kept a lookout for wolves.

The pine forest, said Nerys. The one near the dam? That's about as big as a backyard.

Room for wolves to lurk.

Nerys said, You have to look them clear in the eye. Then they can't hurt you.

Really? said Erin.

The thing about wolves, said Nerys, is they are much more endangered than we are. They might once have been a worry in the depths of the countryside in winter, but now, well, with our usual skill we've done a lot of work wiping them out.

My wolves are beautiful, said Erin. Fierce, of course.

And not very nearby, said Nerys.

There was one of those odd moments of silence, when nobody has anything to say. Nerys looked at the people in the room.

Aurora, and Ferdie, and Erin: One each, she said, he allowed each wife one child.

Do you think it was *allowed*? asked Ferdie.

It looks like it, wouldn't you say?

I thought it just happened.

William was good at control.

Lynette came into the house, looking distraught. At first she didn't see Nerys, she went to the fridge to get a glass of white wine. Good heavens, she said, but recovered and gave her a hug.

I'm sorry about William, said Nerys.

Yes. Yes.

I wanted to come to Canberra so I thought it would be a good chance. We're at the Hyatt. Acacia's with me.

How's Acacia? said Aurora.

Who's Acacia? said Lynette. She filled the wine glass too full. Oh shit. It's all shit, isn't it. I never thought that before. She bent her head and sucked up a draught of the wine.

Acacia's good on death and grief, said Nerys. Everybody needs help, even if they won't admit it. You don't look well at all, Lynette.

I'm not. I'm not well at all. I'm going to bed. Sorry, but I can't think of anything any more. And there isn't going to be a funeral. Lynette paused then walked carefully out of the room, her arms extended as if to support herself on the furniture on her way, except there was a glass in one hand, but though she wavered she got to the door safely and on her own. She stopped there, didn't turn round. You too, Erin sweetheart, she said, you should be in bed too. They heard her feet heavy on the stairs.

I brought her some crystals, said Nerys. She took up the mirror bag again and pulled out a turquoise organza pouch. She held up several long faceted stones on fine loops of chain. The light glittered in them, endless sparkles. Teardrop crystals, she said. They symbolise the end of tears and the beginning of joy and happiness. Feng shui. Channels the energy. Looks like she needs them.

Maybe we could hang them up, said Aurora, they could start working. In the window, perhaps. The end of tears and the beginning of happiness. We could all do with that.

Nerys gave her a sharp look. Good thinking, she said.

Keeping the wolves away, said Aurora.

What did she mean, no funeral? asked Ferdie.

No funeral, I suppose, said Nerys.

THE GARDEN IS FULL OF FOG

Ferdie slept with the bedroom curtains open, and woke the next morning to a dim grey light. He liked to wake early and not get up, to snuggle deep under the doona, the silky smoothness of the sheets. Egyptian cotton they were, 850 thread count, which meant they were very fine, you could hardly see the weave at all. They made him think of Berenice's olive-green satin sheets, their quite other slipperiness. He had never slept all night in those sheets, never woken in the morning to them. He somehow imagined them being difficult to sleep in, inclined to fall off, get lost, ruck up, but he didn't know.

Lying in bed like this he recollected once more Socrates and his remark that the unexamined life is not worth living. This was what he was doing, examining his life, not with rigorous thought processes but with wandering steps that found strange pathways and connections. Berenice was her satin sheets and her spread of red hair, she took him to Pegasus and the lost Jimmy Choos (he'd found out what they cost and felt sick) and the sinister oak forest and Pegasus's mistress, his gorgeous great-aunt Pepita.

William was her nephew. She'd never had children and now William was lost: father, nephew, husband. Trying to examine the death of William was hard work. You could summon up grief but other thoughts came. Wives. Children. Ferdie's mother, Helen as he had such difficulty calling her. Who didn't pay attention to sheets; hers had an airless synthetic harshness. Would his mother be happier if she worried more about sheets? How could worrying make you happier? But it could if it was about something quotidian like sheets and controllable and easy, something orderly and ancient and the domain of women who kept good houses, rather than huge and black and unassailable like a husband's betrayal. Nerys, Helen, Lynette, all betrayed. Lynette not finding out till after his death. Nerys, maybe not betrayed but betraying. Such a heavy word, betray, you could not use it lightly, it had to be heaved, and with a proper respect.

Nerys and William: maybe not betrayal but consent. And Barbara? Was she betrayed?

Ferdie wondered why the unexamined life is not worth living. Might not examining it wreck it? Might it not be better to go on heedlessly, simply living it? Being a lily of the field, being. Was that what Berenice did? He wasn't sure he admired her for it. Envied her, perhaps. Whereas he did admire Pepita, and she was an examiner, so it seemed to him.

He pushed the doona back and got out of bed. The room was warm. Lynette had the central heating set to come on well before anybody might think of getting up. When he looked out the window he saw a dim grey light pressed up against the glass, still, palpable, faintly luminous. Close to the house it was thin enough to see through, farther away it was opaque. At the bottom of the garden he could make out a figure, standing, not doing anything, watching, perhaps, though Ferdie couldn't tell whether it was the wall he was gazing at or the house. He was a shape, faceless. He was standing just where they were planning to plant the olive trees, and Ferdie thought that maybe it was the gardener come to do that, since the rest of them seemed to be failing. Day after day the olive trees were due to be planted, and never were.

He dragged his clothes on and ran downstairs, thinking he didn't need to do this, since Lynette must have organised it, but he hurried just the same. It took seconds to open the back door with its deadlock, and when he went along the path and across the lawn, through the uncanny silence of the fog, down to the place in the corner of the garden where the olives were to be planted, there was no one there. The trees, their roots wrapped in bulging sacks, stood about; forlorn was the word that came to mind.

He walked over to the gate that gave on to the side street; it was locked, as usual, nobody went in or out that way. He looked at the lawn. He could see his own footprints in its wetness, no others. He went round to the front of the house. The big gates still stood open. The man must have been checking up and slipped away in the time it took Ferdie to get down the stairs. Still, he felt annoyed. As if something was happening that he couldn't help. Unless, maybe, he had seen a shadow, a thickening of the fog; a trick of the light, as people sometimes said . . .

Aurora's car pulled into the driveway, turned aside and parked beside Lynette's.

You're early, he said, kissing her.

No I'm not, I'm late.

What's the time?

Ten o'clock.

What? Good grief. I thought it was about seven. What's happening? Nobody's about.

It's the fog.

I saw someone, down near the olives, but he's disappeared.

Maybe it was William.

A ghost, you mean?

A spirit, not wanting to leave its earthly places?

You don't think that, do you?

It's a thing to think.

Well, since he's apparently not going to get a funeral, maybe he's staying around.

I don't think Lynette meant that. She was upset.

They went into the kitchen and Ferdie set to making coffee. Erin came sleepily into the room. Too late, she said, I can't go to school today.

What's going on? he asked.

Erin shrugged. Mum didn't wake me up. Cool. I don't want to go to school, everyone is so nice to me.

Is she all right?

Mum? I don't know.

Maybe you could go and see? Wait a minute. Take her some coffee.

Erin pulled faces, but she went. She came back with the coffee. She's asleep. I didn't like to wake her.

Aurora went into the downstairs lavatory. She was gone a long time. When she came back she was crying. I think I was pregnant, she said. Ferdie went to put his arms around her but she pushed him away and squatted on the ground in a corner formed by the cupboards, pressing herself into the space, her sobs coming in hiccups. Erin began to cry too.

There was a ring at the doorbell. Nerys, with Acacia. Ferdie stared at the tall brown-skinned woman with the flare of white hair, the lean face lightly skeined with wrinkles. Nerys, looking small and round and smart and vivid in black jeans and boots and a poncho of crimson alpaca, introduced her. Acacia put her hands together in a prayerful point and bowed. The blessings of the goddess, she murmured. Nerys with a sketchy gesture repeated the action.

Aurora pressed her face further into the corner of the cupboards and went on sobbing. Nerys seemed to understand this; she sat beside her and stroked her arm. I don't like these high-tech interventions, she said. I don't think any good comes of them. Poor violated creature.

I think she should come and stay with us in the rainforest, said Acacia. In a healing environment. We'll work out the right natural therapies for her. She needs soothing and healing.

We don't live in the rainforest yet.

Soon, said Acacia.

Aurora slid down the cupboards until she was flat on the floor. She pressed her stomach down hard and her legs twitched. She held her face in her hands and began to moan; the moans and the movement of her legs made a grim rhythmic pattern, a pattern she was locked into and could not stop.

Ferdie was afraid of seeing red stains but she was wearing black trousers and there didn't seem to be any. He walked to the other end of the room and looked through the French windows at the dripping garden. The fog still thickened the light. It didn't swirl, it hung, in the bare branches of the elm, more thinly in the fruit trees edging the swimming pool fence, vaporous, breathless, waiting. For a moment he was in Pepita's garden in the misty winter, with its moistness and cold smells, and it was quite a different feel, but then with a small snap it was Canberra again and the leafless trees of his father's garden. My father's garden, he said to himself. He always thought of it as Lynette's garden.

Aurora began to wail. First it seemed to be meaningless sounds, and then words, in a series of crescendos. Dead. Dead. He's dead. Erin sat at the table, appalled. Nerys massaged Aurora's back. Acacia stood, stately, formidable, inscrutable. Ferdie thought, if Pepita were here, none of this would be happening.

He tried briskness. I shall make us all some coffee, he said. But the women had brought their own herbal tea. To release their psychic energy, said Acacia. Aurora should have some. Erin too.

She found a big flowered teapot and took down a pile of small porcelain bowls from a shelf. Aurora went on wailing the words out and rocking her legs so that the sound and the movement were a kind of lament, a physical keening that filled the room. Nerys knelt beside her, spread the poncho over her and rubbed her back in the same rhythm as her wailing. She needs to do this, she said. The sound suspended time, except for Acacia placidly making her tea, handing out the porcelain bowls. Nerys sat on the floor and sipped, her fingers holding gingerly to the rim of the cup. Erin stared at hers. Ferdie touched his and thought, far too hot. He went and sat beside Aurora and pulled her up into his arms, quickly and quite roughly sitting her up and turning her around to him. Blood was pouring down her face, mixing in with tears and snot. My god, he said. She lay in his arms with her eyes closed. What have you done? What is it?

I haven't done, she said, it's been done to me. Nerys grabbed a tea towel and mopped at her daughter's face. Ferdie saw a thin shard of glass sticking into her temple. Gently he plucked it out. He remembered the glass that had been broken on this kitchen floor, how hard it had been to sweep it all up. This bit must have lain unnoticed in the corner where the cupboards met.

Nerys looked at the sliver of glass and pressed at the wound with her tea towel. It's because it's on her temple, she said. Injuries to the temple always bleed a lot.

Should we clean it up? Use some antiseptic?

Erin, said Nerys. The child was staring at the steaming bowl of tea. Antiseptic? First aid? A look of terror crossed the girl's face.

Acacia opened cupboards and eventually found a basket with ti-tree oil, Dettol, plasters, cotton wool. She cleaned the wound and stuck a plaster over it. Aurora put her hand to her face and opened her eyes when she felt stickiness under her fingers. Nerys rinsed the tea towel in warm water, sponged her face, wiped her hands. Aurora lay back against Ferdie. He managed to stand up and pull her upright too and then with Nerys's help got her into Lynette's study, beside the kitchen, which had a daybed in it; they laid her down and covered her with a cashmere rug. Acacia brought the tea and tried to get her to drink some. Ferdie pulled the curtains against the grey fog light.

We're going to have a look at the gallery, said Nerys. We thought we might have some lunch there. I was going to say does anybody want to come. But . . .

Mm, said Ferdie, a nice thought. But I won't leave Aurora.

No, said Nerys. Well, we'll see you later.

He picked up his tea, which was cool now, and drank some. It was very herbal. He touched Erin's arm. Why don't you try a bit? She looked at him. I know, he said. Look. It's still pretty foggy. You know the best place to be? In bed. He put his arm around her and led her away. I think we're all really really tired. A good morning nap, that's what we need.

He wasn't sure of this at all. He knew he was out of his depth in all this sadness. And what about Lynette? Was she all right?

He looked out into the garden again. The distant fog was beginning to shred. He was in a house of sleeping women. All his family. Not his blood, that wasn't it, but his family. All belonging in his heart. He would stay awake and watch over them. William is gone and I am the man of the family, said Ferdie to himself, who had never thought in such terms before.

The end of tears and the beginning of joy. The crystals weren't working too well yet.

LYNETTE GETS UP LATE

Lynette had slept late because of the fog darkness. When she looked at her clock it was already impossibly late so she didn't try to get up. She was tired. She didn't want to. She thought of that: I don't want to. She thought what unfamiliar words they were to her. They weren't words that shaped her days. She thought of William. He was good at *I don't want to*. Just as he was at *I want to*. I am practising, Lynette said to herself. I don't want to get up. I want to stay in bed. I don't want to have a funeral. I don't want to run a shop.

That was a surprise. She hadn't known she thought that. She could sell the shop. Not be responsible for all that detail. Would she? Could she? She didn't know. But she did know that thinking it, lying warm under a many-feathered doona, was a wonderfully comfortable thought. That was William, of course, he sang a little song, *Life is a many-feathered doona*. With lots of vibrato. It was a joke but she didn't know how. There'd be some obscure reference.

She did not have to think of duty, not any more. Duty. Stern daughter of the voice of God, William used to say. When he was sitting doing something pleasant and had to get up and do something useful. Stern daughter of the voice of God. She used to laugh, as though it was funny. Once she said, What does it mean, actually?

It's Wordsworth, he said, distracted.

Yes, but what is it?

Oh, 'Ode to Duty', I think. A very long and almost impossible poem about duty. You know how Wordsworth can be sometimes. Prosing on. But I like the idea of its being not just the daughter but the *stern* daughter, and not of God but his voice.

But you don't believe in God, she said.

Ah, but I believe in the words, he replied.

William's duty: going from one pleasant thing to another. From one loving woman to another.

Ferdie, who was his father's son and once she'd loved him for that and now didn't any the less because of it, had said to Erin the other night, The unexamined life is not worth living, you know. Socrates said that, and I think it is still a good idea.

But since that woman had come there was altogether too much examining. Pointless examining, since it ran round and round and round. Coiling round her and William who was dead and couldn't explain anything, and had he not been wouldn't have anyway. *Never apologise, never explain* was a kind of mantra of his. Lynette would say, Oh, I'm so sorry, and mean it, but often it would be a frivolous thing she was sorry about, and William would say sternly, Never apologise, never explain. She'd asked him who said that, too, and he said he thought it was John Wayne in a movie, but it was just one of those things, everyone knew it. John Wayne, she said, astonished, and William said, Well, my dear, I am catholic in my tastes, and she had to think about that because she knew he wasn't at all religious, but she suspected there was more to it than that. But then she often couldn't follow his sayings. Not just the old-fashioned language, often the whole point escaped her. Not the not-apologising, of course; maybe being John Wayne it spoke her language. She wondered if he'd apologised to Helen, or explained. Neither would have worked, but she supposed at that scale of things he must have tried. Amazing how little thought she'd given to Helen, at the time. William had filled her mind, there wasn't room for anything else. They'd gone to the south of France for their honeymoon. He'd asked, and that's what she said she wanted. They'd gone to a stone house on the edge of an old village. The house had semi-cylindrical terracotta tiles, and William explained how this was a sign of the south; further north the roofs were covered in slate, or slices of stone, they crouched into the hillsides as though going back to the original earth they came from, he said. Trying to turn their backs to the bitter winds. Their house belonged to English people and was luxurious, with central heating and hot running water and a big downy bed. The other houses in the village were generally not like that but the locals didn't seem to hold the luxury against them. They hadn't had time to get sick of the English coming in and taking over then. William talked to them, and spent money in the small shops. People enjoyed telling him things.

The village was on a hill with a small ruined castle on top. Their house was on the edge of the village, so they looked over sloping rows of ancient olive trees. They sat on the terrace at the back (the front door opened on to the street) and drank pastis, which Lynette quite quickly learned to like, Tastes like liquorice, she said, and William talked about olive trees. Light lives in olive trees, he said. See how the blades of the leaves turn and shake silver. Shake: that's a Gerard Manley Hopkins word, but I don't know that he ever saw olives. That light—it's the light that Socrates saw, and Demeter and Persephone. And now we are seeing it too. Persephone, who ate just a few seeds of pomegranate and so had to stay part of the year in the underworld with her kidnapper, Hades. And so we have winter. Summer and the crops grow, winter they lie dormant, when Persephone is off in hell with Hades.

Lynette sat and listened to him. It was the image of their marriage: William talking, Lynette listening.

They're a long-term proposition, olives, he said. If you want to hurt your enemy, destroy his olives. It will take him many years to recover. A wheat crop is a year, but an olive is seven, and then you are barely starting.

Oh, he was a great imparter of information, was William. He loved telling people things. When she met Jack she guessed it was because William was pleased to have learned them, that he very easily might not have, that he had taken time and trouble to know things, not just getting his education at university but keeping it up, and he never lost his delight in his knowledge. Jack never had been interested in learning, had stayed the boy they'd both been once. Jack. No, don't go there. She didn't want Jack to be a disappointment.

In the foreground were the olive groves. In the distance the Mont St-Victoire. When they drove around, William sought out Cézanne paintings and got pleasure from looking at their mountain and remembering his. When we get a bob or two we'll buy a Cézanne of the Mont St-Victoire, William said, but of course they never did get that kind of money.

Lynette thought of all the lovemaking they did on that trip. Lovemaking, having sex, coition. A little coition before breakfast, William would say. A morning glory. Up and down the house, not just in bed. All through the day. Once on the terrace, after dinner, in a black velvet night, Lynette leaning on the stone wall and looking over the rows of invisible olives to where she knew the mountain to be, saying, We can't, someone will see us, and William, No, my Linnet, it's dark and they are all in bed, look, no lights, and she, Yes, they're in their bedrooms with the lights off watching us through the gap in the shutters; and all the time William sliding under her skirt, slipping down her knickers, doing it hardly moving, and her making no sound but a gasp at the end. Of course, that's what a honeymoon is; William murmuring *lune de miel* at the shopkeepers and the solid peasanty women smiling in complicity. *Lunes de miel*, funny to see it so literal, said William; honeymoons don't last. Ours will, said Lynette, we will never give this up.

They came home, and bought their house, renovated it, extended it, Erin was born, and no more sex up and down the house at all hours. Satisfactorily often and happily in bed, so she thought, but now she wondered, looking back, if that had been enough for William. She'd thought it to be growing up, growing into a relationship, but maybe ought to have read more warning into her position as the third Mrs Cecil. Not that she even now was supposing he had plans to make Barbara the fourth. But then the thought came: she hadn't been thinking of marrying him when she began fucking him on the boardroom kitchen floor. Maybe he was getting round to marrying Barbara. She'd thought he was happy, that they both were, that life was good, fruitful and flourishing (as she wrote on Christmas cards her wishes for friends' new years), that there was even a kind of perfection in the pattern of her days.

In those advice-to-the-lovelorn columns it always said that a spouse straying was the fault of both parties in the couple. Had it been Helen's, as well as William's? Had it been Lynette's fault that William had sought out Barbara (or been sought out by her)? If she'd maintained that sex up and down the house would he not have done it? It seemed a kind of frenzied mad thing for a wife to be doing to keep her husband amused, but maybe that was what William needed. The thought that he might have been on his way to marrying Barbara suddenly made her think, lucky he died, spared us all that mess. A wicked thought, but satisfying.

In that honeymoon village was a small hardware and kitchen shop. It sold Laguiole knives, and two-handled rocking choppers, saucepans, gratin dishes, brown earthenware pots and white Pillivuyt porcelain. The shelves seemed sparse and dusty and the old lady who kept it spent most of her time in the kitchen at the back, but it was surprising what could be found there. Lynette bought some curious things to take home for her catering business. That was when she had the idea of opening her Batterie de Cuisine, as a good thing to do when she got tired of the catering. Which she did quite soon, when she realised what her working hours could do to her evenings with William. But then she had Erin and everything went on hold for a while. William said his wife didn't need to work, and she was happy with that, until Erin went to kindergarten. Then Janice was keen, so the two of them started the shop. Angus and Janice broke up, so Janice had more time. But it was mainly Lynette's, her planning over the years when Erin was a baby; Janice went along. Maybe Janice would buy her out, run the shop for herself. Lynette couldn't see it. But then, she said to herself, how good am I at understanding people? But Janice did depend on her, worked best when she did what Lynette planned. Perhaps Janice could get another partner.

Am I really going to get rid of the shop? she asked herself. Who knows. But I am not having a funeral. The firmness of that thought comforted her, and she turned over and slept the deep sleep that had eluded her all the nights since William died.

When she woke it was dim outside, not still but again. She had slept solidly through the lifting of the fog and the brief cold shining of the sun. Now it was twilight. The house seemed not so much quiet as muted. She went downstairs: nobody in the kitchen. She looked in her study; there was Aurora, asleep under the rug. She found Ferdie in William's study, sitting at the laptop. He looked furtive, she thought, closed the lid when he saw her. Something made her go over and lift it back up again. She saw creatures with enormous penises pointing to the sky. They had hairy haunches with cloven hooves and neat little horns on their curly-bearded heads. The screen flipped over into pictures of women impaled on these giant penises, frolicking in the air.

I can't get rid of them, said Ferdie. I think they're gone, then they come back. Each time it seems worse than the last.

But where do they come from? Lynette was staring at scenes of orgies.

I don't know. They just came. Maybe I touched something, I can't tell.

William, said Lynette.

I don't know, I don't understand.

Things like that don't just turn up. They have to be got in the first place.

I do know that pornography sites draw you in, deeper and deeper, you can't get out.

Only when you've made the first move. They don't reach out and get you. Oh, it's all shit, all shit. That's all it is.

No, said Ferdie, only bits are shit. Remember the bits that aren't. William loved you. You have to hang on to that. I knew it. You knew it. He knew it.

Yes, but look at this. The screen kept jumping into yet more orgiastic scenes, which had nothing to do with satyrs and nymphs, though it might have been huge fat rolling Bacchanalian women doing things with bananas. Ferdie found himself thinking helplessly and madly that surely bananas were anachronistic in these scenes.

He didn't need this, Lynette said, and suddenly with a violent hand swept the little laptop off the desk. It flew through the air and landed on the head of one of those bronze replica statues of Hermes that people used to buy in Pompeii and stand on their hearths.

It didn't explode, or fizz into sparks, or anything like that, but it did crack apart and the screen went grey. Lynette stood looking at it, her hand over her mouth, her eyes like a guilty child's. On the head of Hermes. How did I do it? My aim is never so accurate.

When she turned to Ferdie she smiled. Guiltily at first. He smiled too. Then in a moment they were both laughing, leaning over, clutching themselves, gasping. They'd stop, look at one another, start again. Gales, paroxysms, weeping furies of laughter. Till they were too weak to do anything but flop back in chairs.

Well, said Lynette. Drastic situations need drastic actions. Am I still channelling William? Anyway, that's got rid of them.

And the laptop?

Well? I've got one, Erin's got one. We don't need it.

I suppose it's a clean break, said Ferdie. I didn't mean you to see that. I was looking to see if there was anything that mattered.

We'll never know. And it will never matter. Except we'll know that your father and my husband used to look at pretty nasty pornography.

Maybe. It's sad if he did. But maybe it wasn't anything to do with him. We did wonder, said Ferdie, if maybe William knew I was doing my thesis on Pan and was looking him up.

He did like to know about things, you know that. And by accident got into this.

You're a sweet boy, Ferdie.

Lynette scrabbled together the pieces of computer and put them in the wastepaper basket, a kind of tall square box of tooled Florentine leather. I quite hate this room, she said. She squeezed her lips in a tight line. I'm going to turn it into a study for Erin. Get rid of all this gentleman's den crap. Erin, she said. Is she back from school?

She didn't go. She's in bed, asleep. I think.

Lynette felt sick. She'd forgotten about Erin. All that examining, of honeymoons and new babies and fruitful lives, of marriages with not enough sex for greedy husbands, and she hadn't once thought of Erin today.

She's okay. I reckon she needed to sleep.

And what about Aurora?

She said something about a dead baby.

What? Lynette thought, a day in bed and the world goes mad. Though parts of it have been mad for a long time. Me sleeping didn't have anything to do with William and pornography. Clay feet, she thought. Clay dick, more like. I can't begin to understand it, she thought, but women never can, it's a cliché that women can't understand men's capacity for betrayal.

She went back upstairs. Erin was sleeping beautifully, lightly, on her side, her lips slightly parted. Lynette couldn't bring herself to wake her. Ferdie's right, she thought. Wise boy. She went back down. Aurora was creeping groggily into the kitchen. She yawned. I thought I heard a joke. Insane laughing. What's the time? she asked, looking at the station clock on the wall. That late. I need a drink, now I'm not pregnant any more.

Lynette got one of the bottles of sauvignon blanc out of the fridge, and two of the tall-stemmed glasses.

Aurora said, Got any vodka? A good slug. A double or even a triple.

Lynette made a long drink with lime and soda and a lot of ice. What's all this about? she said.

Aurora took a luxurious gulp. The baby's dead, she said.

I didn't even know . . .

Nobody did. Not me either. I was hoping I might be. I was putting off doing the test. The longer the safer, I thought.

So how . . .?

Blood. A bloody great smear of blood.

I see. Yes.

The thing is, it was the last egg. The last of my eggs and Cezary's sperm. They tried to do a few but only a couple took and then only one was viable. They can tell, you know. Now I'll have to start all over again from scratch. She drank more vodka. She sighed. Maybe it's all too hard.

Ferdie came into the room carrying the Florentine wastepaper basket. Aurora's eyes goggled when she saw its contents.

The pornographic laptop is no more, intoned Ferdie.

Aurora began to laugh, and that made her hiccup, and then she sobbed. I hate men who need pornography, she said.

Do you hate William? asked Ferdie.

Yes! In that way I do. How could he do that to us?

I suppose we should all live our lives as though we were going to die in a minute, said Ferdie. Keep them in perfect order. No secrets. Or else all safely hidden forever.

Lynette shuddered. Nobody could be that perfect.

JANICE GOES OUT FOR LUNCH

Janice had got into the habit of having lunch with Angus every few months. She'd gone from wanting to kill him to being quite happy to talk to him. This was the idea of the amicable divorce, and though she hadn't given up saying evil things about his behaviour she wanted to stay on civil terms. There were the children, for one thing. And then she liked to keep an eye on how matters were going with him. She enjoyed wondering if the new wife were causing trouble. Once she wanted to kill her too; now she looked on with only faintly malicious amusement.

And then there was the gossip, which Angus was good at. On this occasion she was finding out the story of Barbara. She knew that Lynette didn't know anything about Barbara. In their brief encounter she'd perceived her as a demon who had stolen William away. She didn't think of her as anything but a vast dark cloudy shape which had destroyed her happiness. And now was stopping her grieving for her husband as a loved wife should. That was what she said to Janice, telling her in all its vividness about William's betrayal with this Barbara person.

Janice began by making barbed remarks about women getting their hooks into other people's husbands.

What? said Angus. I knew she was a client of his.

She was having an affair with him, you mean.

Well, he didn't tell me about that. I knew why she was seeing him.

He told her about the little girl being killed on a school excursion, the possibility of suing, the breakdown of the marriage, and the firm, William, handling the divorce.

Oh, said Janice. The account of the child's death upset her. Oh, she said, and paid that attention that mothers do to the deaths of other women's children, the horror, the fear, the recognition that there can be no worse thing, and then the demeaning gratitude that it hasn't happened to them.

Oh, she said again, and was silent. Well, I suppose she didn't much care what she did after that.

Nothing to lose, you reckon.

You can't condone it, but you can understand it. What? Oh, just an ordinary old affair. Sleeping with him on a regular basis. But very contained, it seems. No suggestion of breaking up a marriage. Of course that's what they all say at the beginning. And Lynette's very upset. She takes it as a sure sign that he didn't love her.

But that's silly . . .

Yes, but she's in a state anyway. Perhaps she'll see things more clearly when she feels better. The woman says they weren't supposed to be in love but that now she realises that she did love him.

Why didn't she stay away and shut up?

You could say that. I think she wanted to be part of his death somehow. Belong there. Not thinking what it would do to his wife.

Angus sighed, and touched Janice's hand across the table. Sometimes she thought that he regretted the ending of their marriage, would like still to be with her. But she knew he would never say.

William, he said. I wouldn't have thought he'd have done such a thing. With a wife like Lynette.

Janice raised her eyebrows. She is the third Mrs Cecil, she said. It is clear that William liked women, and he liked change.

What about you? said Angus. Did he ever crack on to you?

Only at parties.

What?

You remember those parties. William used to range round sort of feeling you up but you knew it was just the party . . .

Did you?

Of course. And I was a happily married woman who believed in being faithful to her marriage vows.

And, she said to herself, had the kind of husband who didn't notice what was going on under his nose and who I thought would always be faithful too.

Angus clapped his hands slowly, very softly.

Well, I was, said Janice. I can say it. She smiled. I don't care any more, she said.

She remembered a certain party, when she was wearing a loose but clinging silvery-grey dress with very high-heeled green platform-soled crocodile-skin (fake to be sure) sandals; for a moment she mourned the absence of such fuck-me shoes in her life these days. She'd been sitting on a big cushion on the floor, and William had come and sat slightly behind her. She was talking to someone and didn't pay much attention to him. He put his hand in the small of her back, an affectionate gesture, you could say. And suddenly, she didn't know how he'd done it, but it wasn't the first time, he had undone her bra, she knew it when her breasts tumbled, that was the first she'd felt of it. She ignored him, folding her arms across her chest to hold herself in place, and then after a bit going to the loo and doing it up. It was a party trick of his, a great skill, he thought, and Janice did wonder how he did it, since she didn't find it that easy to undo her own bra, and certainly couldn't with one hand. William never did anything more, he smiled dreamily, innocently, and apparently took no notice of the confusion he had caused.

She smiled herself now, a gentle thoughtful smile, not so much for William's sleight of hand as for that past time and the people they were, young, and heedless. Mainly young. Compared with now. At times since she had wondered, what if something had come of this interest of William's? He had made it clear that he fancied her. She was the one not interested. She felt her smile becoming sad, as she thought, now he is dead. That carry-on at parties: these days young women would say it was sexual harassment, but William was so charming, so comically wicked about it, nobody seemed to think that.

That party: it had been because William had just got his partnership, and he had bought a lot of different brands of French champagne (a tautology, he kept saying, if it was champagne it had to be French) and went steadily around filling glasses, saying, Come on, finish that, this is a different one. So she'd swallow down the last bit and he'd give her the next. There's a viva at the end of the evening, he said, I shall quiz you on their different properties. Of course he didn't. She remembered how sick she'd been afterwards. Angus had to stop the car in the pine forest and she'd opened the door and vomited.

Angus saw the smile. I reckon he succeeded, he said.

Oh Angus, don't be silly. What's it got to do with anything now? I was remembering how nice it was to be young. Well, a good bit younger. She looked at him. You think he had a go with Sarah? She likes older men.

Janice! You're making him out the most frightful old lech.

Not me. It's you that's doing that.

Suggesting that Sarah . . . He snorted. Meaning to convey speechlessness, she thought.

Suggesting that I . . .

Angus looked at her strangely. Janice wondered if he was jealous. In some mad retrospective irrelevant fashion. Maybe . . . maybe, during those years when she was a good wife, she ought to have made him jealous. Things might have been different. She might have still been married to him.

Not a good thought. She was happy the way she was. A woman with a career, a lover, soon a grandchild. All passion spent. Ugly passion, not the good kind, there was still plenty of that. It doesn't get better than this, she murmured.

What? said Angus.

Pardon? Oh . . . She realised she'd said the words aloud. Poor William, she muttered vaguely.

Poor everybody else, it sounds like.

He's the one that's dead.

Leaving a number of clients in the lurch.

Angus! Surely someone else can do them.

Of course. But it's messy.

That's death for you.

Angus looked uncomfortable.

Leaving lots of loved ones in the lurch too, said Janice. That's messier. Well, she said. How's Archie? How old is he now? Though she knew.

Fifteen months. Very cute. Terrible sleeper. Sarah thinks it's his active brain. Won't let him relax.

Janice thought Angus would have liked this child to be a girl. He already had two boys, Richard and Antony. She'd have liked a girl, once, but the two boys were a great pair. She didn't regret them. It was her policy not to regret, but here it was no effort. Richard lived in Geneva and was about to have a baby. It would be a little girl, Jasmine.

Janice said to Angus, I think it spoils the fun, knowing what sex the baby is going to be.

Richard had said, Mum, its sex is known, and if it's known I want to know it. That's how it is these days.

Angus said, It's the modern way. He and Sarah had known about Archie, but they pretended they didn't.

He told Janice that Sarah was going back to uni. She was going to do a Master of Business Studies, she thought it would help her in her career as a lawyer, when she went back to it. Janice pulled a face. Sounds hard work, she said. Dull.

She won't find it so.

They were silent for a moment. They weren't drinking wine, Angus in the middle of a working day, Janice because she was going out for dinner with Maurice and didn't want to eat or drink too much for lunch. They sipped fizzy water.

Will you mind being a grandmother? he asked.

Mind? I'm thrilled.

Janice was going to go to Geneva to see Jasmine as soon as she was born. Maurice would come after a bit and they would go to Venice, and Provence, and Paris and London. All by train. But she didn't say that. She said, And Sarah will be a step-granny. She kept all malice out of her voice. Sarah was younger than Richard.

I don't suppose that will worry her. Just another baby.

Just another baby! I don't think so.

They were silent again. Janice said, Heard from Antony lately?

Not so's you'd notice. Is he still with that . . . bloke?

You could hear in Angus's voice that he had rejected a number of words before coming up with bloke.

Marcel? Oh yes. They're very much an item, you know.

Do I? I know he buggered off to New York with him. Well, went off, I should say.

It's not a slight thing, you know. They're really in love. Yes, Angus, that's the word for it. And Marcel knows the theatre scene very well, he's helping him enormously.

Angus shrugged his handsomely suited shoulders. You'd feel happier if it was a more, a more professional relationship.

I don't see why. Marcel knows the scene, who better to help him? He's really got Antony's interests at heart. And emotional involvement won't do any harm, here.

How do you know all this?

I ring him up. Best way to stay in touch.

Expensive.

If he came for a visit I'd feed him, open bottles of wine; this is a lot cheaper. And I can easily afford it, it's not even extravagant.

Well, what's actually happening?

He's got some sort of stage-managing thing. Off-Broadway.

Doesn't sound very grand.

Well, of course it isn't *solid*, like the law and MBAs and stuff. But it's his lifelong desire. And you have to start somewhere. Beginnings are always humble.

Janice had a round-the-world ticket. When she'd seen Richard and the new baby and done the European travelling she was going to see Antony and Marcel. Antony had already told her about the marvellous loft in TriBeCa that he and Marcel were doing up. Plenty of room to stay, provided they didn't mind being in the thick of things. Maurice said, Perhaps a hotel would be easier. She didn't say anything of this to Angus either.

Well, time will tell, I suppose, said Angus.

It usually does, said Janice. You should go and visit him, she said, still without malice in her voice.

Are you kidding? MBAs don't come cheap, you know. And the rest of it. I thought he might come out here.

I think he's got to concentrate on his career.

I suppose.

They ordered coffees. The little cafe was emptying. It was mainly a place for lunch hours. There were some Manuka lunching ladies drinking tea, and grandparents with a toddler slurping up a babycino.

Does Archie like babycino?

Oh yes, he's quite keen. We don't come here though, they do marshmallows. He doesn't have sugar. Angus was spooning the last of the froth out of his cup. He said, And what about you, Jan . . . Janice? How are things with you?

Oh, I'm fine. No problems. A bit unsettling, this business with William, so sudden and all. I thought he was fit and healthy.

Yes, you never know. I thought he looked after himself.

Angus was William's age.

Of course, he said, he liked to live well.

Don't we all?

Some of us are a bit more . . . austere than others.

Austerity, said Janice. She thought of Sarah. There'd be the austerity. She was bone thin, back to the gym straight after the baby's birth. Not austere where clothes were concerned, or possessions; plenty of extravagance there. Austerity wasn't one of Angus's words. It hadn't been one to use when Janice was around. Not opulence or greed, but not austerity.

How's the shop going? asked Angus. The Battery Hen.

Flourishing.

Making any money yet?

Janice smiled. Retiring to the tax haven of our choice any minute. Seriously, she said, with a faint note of anger in her voice, I know you don't want to hear it, but it's a good living. Brilliant, even.

I do want to hear it, said Angus. I'm very happy for you.

Janice laughed.

Outside the cafe the sun had gone from the square, leaving it grey and chilly despite the shiny green of the grass. There were several gas heaters on the terrace; it was probably warm, but not inviting. Nobody was sitting there.

Oh well, said Angus. Stern duty calls.

As ever, said Janice.

She imagined both of them thinking, no, not always.

They kissed with gentle pecks on both cheeks. Ciao, said Angus. Go well.

Yes, said Janice. She felt she did go quite well, after seeing Angus.

Janice called in to visit Lynette, keen to tell her about Barbara.

You mean I have to feel sorry for her, said Lynette. No, I don't want to know.

But you want to understand, said Janice. You can sort of see why she did what she did. Imagine losing a child like that. Janice shuddered.

I don't want to, said Lynette. I've got my grief and it's keeping me very busy, thank you very much.

She went to William to see about suing, and he did her divorce for her.

All of which makes his conduct even more reprehensible. Taking advantage of someone in such a precarious emotional state.

I suppose he thought he was comforting her.

I don't think he thought of her at all. He was only interested in a bit of pleasant fucking.

Janice sighed. She'd called in on her way home to get dressed for dinner with Maurice.

I had lunch with Angus, she said.

Was it nice?

You know.

I expect he's been quietly terrified by William's death.

He's not going to let on.

Lynette said, I've had William cremated. It's done.

What! You did mean it . . .

Didn't you believe me? Yes, his body was released, so I went ahead. I'll put a notice in Saturday's paper.

You'll have a service? A ceremony of some sort?

I don't think so.

There didn't seem to be anything more to say. Or rather, Janice couldn't think how to say it. Lynette offered wine, but she declined. I have to be going, she said.

Lynette said, The shop's going well, isn't it.

Wonderfully well.

It's a good business proposition.

Oh yes.

Janice wondered why Lynette was mentioning this, now. Not for long. She started thinking about wearing her Easton Pearson jacket out to dinner; it was new, and she was thrilled with it as well as slightly shocked by how much it cost. She had to work out what to wear with it.

AURORA DRINKS VODKA

Aurora rang up Cezary to tell him about the lost baby. She dialled his mobile over and over and listened to his voice saying he couldn't take her call at the moment and please leave a message. The words *lost baby* echoed in her head as though it were a small live creature she had mislaid somewhere. That she should get a move on and try to find before it was too late. She hadn't said anything to Flavia about being pregnant, partly because she didn't say much to Flavia anyway, being at work on her computer in the morning and mostly not there in the evening. Partly because she had been exhausted by events at Lynette's. And a lot because Flavia was still so sad about the loss of her own baby. Aurora telephoned her now to say she wouldn't be back that night. Too much vodka. She'd gone back to the daybed in Lynette's study and the cashmere throw. She thought she could spend the rest of her life there, waiting for Cezary to ring.

Finally Cezary rang back. Oh my poor Bunnie, he said, oh love, oh I am so sad. For you and for me, and our sweet little atom. Shall I come down? Or no, you should come home. Oh my poor Bunnie. I shall come down and bring you home.

Oh Honey. She was soothed by his honey-rich Polish voice. This was why she had started calling him Honey, and why with the logic of rhyme he called her Bunnie. She liked being Bunnie, it didn't need living up to as Aurora did.

Then his voice firmed up. Aurora, he said, tell me exactly what happened.

So she did. She told him about the blood.

Doesn't sound much, he said. Of course I'm not an obstetrician. Sounds like just a smear. Maybe . . . well, we won't get our hopes up. Have you got a pregnancy test? Could be an idea to have a look . . .

So she did, and it was positive. She rang Cezary again.

Sounds as though you just had a bit of a show.

But oh, oh Cezary . . . Her voice was a wail.

What?

When I thought I wasn't pregnant I had some vodka.

Is that all? That doesn't matter.

But it was a whole lot of vodka.

My mother had a pregnancy book that said it was quite all right to drink alcohol when you were pregnant, so long as it wasn't so much that you fell over. Did you fall over?

No . . .

There. But seriously, this no-drink thing, a good thing of course, is pretty new. A little drink never seemed to hurt women in the past. Takes more than that to cause foetal alcohol syndrome. And of course you aren't going to keep it up. Your one-off won't be a problem.

Oh Honey, I can't believe it's going to be all right.

Don't be too hopeful. But I think you should be a bit. Dear Bunnie.

Come down soon, Honey.

I will. As soon as I can see my way clear. And in the meantime, don't you do anything. You hear? Rest. Calm. Let everything settle back to normal. And rest, real rest: feet up, doing nothing.

She was glad she hadn't told Flavia. She wished she hadn't collapsed in front of the family. She'd tell Ferdie, Ferdie could explain.

He came in, carrying a large glass of white wine. Dinner in a minute, he said. Lynette's amazing minestrone and bread and cheese. You can feast on brie.

Well, the thing is, Ferdie, I can't, after all. Cezary got me to do a pregnancy test. It seems I still am.

That's marvellous. Fantastic. Oh, I'm so glad.

Unless it's not true. I'm not quite game to believe it.

I think you can believe it, just allowing a tiny margin of error, in the corner of your brain.

You're a good help, Ferdie. Anyway. Back to no brie or wine or vodka, definitely no vodka. And . . . can I get you to tell Lynette? I'm embarrassed, after that performance.

Okay. Ferdie picked up the wine. Minestrone's all right, isn't it?

LYNETTE WEEPS

Next morning Lynette said, Ferdie, would you be a love and ring up all the people and ask them to come round? End of the afternoon, early evening? We'll have a glass of wine.

All the people?

Oh, you know. All the gatherers. Jack, Nerys. That Acacia person. Aurora. Janice. You know.

What if they can't come?

Tell them they have to. I'm asking them. It's all I'm asking. Put a few bottles in the friggo. Some beer, for Jack.

They did come. Nobody even demurred. They sat round the kitchen table. Ferdie had put out the tall-stemmed glasses. There were a lot of them. The wine was a riesling from the Clare Valley. He'd remembered to get some organic apple juice for Nerys and Acacia, and Erin. Lynette peered at the bottle. Free-range apple juice, she said. I wonder how they stop it wandering off.

Ferdie had set several cheeses and some biscuits on a platter and this gave people something to do. Aurora refused wine, took instead a glass of juice with a secret smile. Nerys looked at Acacia.

Is this a party? Erin whispered to Ferdie.

That's a good question. No, I don't think you'd say it was. I think your mother has something to tell us.

It occurred to him that he hadn't phoned Barbara. He assumed that was the right thing; he didn't think Lynette wanted Barbara here, and she certainly didn't seem to be missing her.

Lynette was drinking wine, and Ferdie thought, when I remember this time, it will be Lynette with her nose in a wine glass, serious, drinking. As though she would find wisdom in a wine glass. Not, so you'd notice, drunk. He supposed she'd slow down, soon.

The exhibition was good, said Nerys. But I must say I don't much admire your gallery. Too big. The Brisbane one is much friendlier, much more accessible.

Too many words, said Acacia. Always telling you what to think. Why can't you just look at the art?

Ferdie thought how in the time he'd been here he hadn't considered going to the gallery. Just sent its postcards to Berenice. He had read a book he'd found in the study, about William Robinson, and been delighted to discover his idiosyncratic view, of landscapes and chook pens and goats. Some of the paintings made him remember going on a picnic with Lynette when he was quite young, out to one of the river crossings, and he had twirled round and round until he'd fallen over, giddy, and looked up at the white branches of the trees above him and the clouds in the sky whirling round as though they were the visible expression of the earth moving. Robinson's pictures gave him the same excited, slightly queasy feeling in his tummy that he could recall after all these years.

The one he sent to Berenice had almost abstract patterns of corrugated iron, enfolding noble-looking goats and the comical figures of Robinson and his wife minding them. He wrote on it, I think this is great art and it's great fun too. He realised he didn't actually know what Berenice thought about any kind of art.

This is very nice wine, said Lynette. You forget, all that sauvignon blanc, how nice riesling is.

Yes, said Janice, but we aren't here to praise the wine, are we.

Lordy, said Lynette. She drank some more wine and looked round the table. William's family, she said. His three children. Two of his three wives. His brother. No mistresses. Who knows where or how to find them? We might have had to hire the convention centre.

Janice put her hand on Lynette's and shook it slightly.

Yes, well, said Lynette. I've asked you here to make an official announcement. There will be no funeral. I know I've already said that, but possibly people did not believe me. No funeral. William is already cremated. His ashes are in a box in the cupboard.

You'll have some sort of ceremony, though, said Janice. A service. A commemoration. A wake.

No. Not unless this is it.

But all William's friends, his colleagues, his acquaintances. They'll want to pay their respects. William loved a party.

They can raise a glass in the privacy of their own homes.

This is very dangerous for you, said Acacia in her low and rather thrilling voice. Death offers so many gifts.

Lynette lowered her eyelids. Loss? Betrayal? Sorrow?

Yes, all those things. But a chance to grow through those things, and celebrate the great narrative that is life.

Mine's been snipped off.

No it hasn't. William has ceased, on this plane. But you have not. Life's richest experiences are available to you. The joy of grief. The gift of sorrow, which without love you could never know.

It's like a weird pattern. Threads of words all plaited together. A pretty pattern, maybe, but no meaning at all.

Beauty is a comfort, said Acacia. William was part of your life, of your being, you deny him at your peril.

Deny him.

Yes, said Acacia. You deny him. You say you will have no ceremony, and for why? To punish him. But you cannot punish the dead. You can only punish yourself. And that is not a good thing to do.

Lynette burst into tears. She sobbed in stormy gusts of noise and damp. She lost her breath in hiccups. Ferdie put his arms round her and stroked her neck. Aurora got a packet of tissues and mopped her face. Janice poured more wine.

I haven't done that before, said Lynette.

So much anger, said Acacia. Of course it's easy to understand. But you must put it away. Anger is natural, but like many natural things it is a poison. It is poisoning you.

I loved William. I believed he loved me. Having him die was the worst thing. But then it wasn't. It was his betrayal, and that was so much worse than anything.

Betrayal. I am not sure it is a useful word. I think William loved you. He was not a monogamous man, that appears to be the case, but I think his love was true. He died, and you were secure in his love. You have to hang on to that.

He turned it all to shit. It's all shit.

Acacia shook her head. Erin in her turn burst into tears. Don't say that, Mummy. He's my daddy. I loved him. He loved me.

Sweetheart, said Lynette, clutching tight hold of her, I know, I know, that's the true thing and we'll never not know that.

The true thing, said Erin.

Lynette and Erin held one another and cried for a long time. Everyone else simply sat and waited while they did it. Ferdie wondered what people were thinking. For himself he thought he was sitting there not thinking, staring at the long table with its silver singing cup of lilies that Aurora had already replaced once. He wondered what people had sung, to win the cup.

This is necessary, said Acacia. I do not think it has happened before. Weeping clarifies. Washes away and clarifies.

Lynette stopped crying, then Erin. They still held one another, with little sobs from time to time.

Until William is laid to rest you will have no rest either.

You mean he'll haunt us, said Aurora, whose eyes were full of tears too.

Haunting. Haunting has its meanings.

Jack said, I can't see William as a ghost.

Aurora said, You might have the gift.

All people have rites of death, said Acacia in a musing voice. It may be sky platforms for vultures to pick the bones clean, or funeral fires, or burning ships put out to sea. Shrouds, coffins, mausoleums, wrapping the bodies and putting them in the ground, or exposure to the elements: earth, air, fire, water. Fire is what you have chosen for William. But you need a ceremony as well.

Why don't I take care of it? said Jack. We could go out beyond Ben Boyd's tower, you know, around the edge of Twofold Bay, and cast his ashes into the sea. Bill was keen on the sea. Say a few words. Then come back to the pub and have a glass. Do it late one morning. Anyone who wants can come.

Yes, Mummy, said Erin.

Who's going to say the words? said Lynette.

I'll say them, said Jack. Ferdie can help me get them into shape.

Lynette stared at him. You'd do that? A public ceremony, and talk, and things?

Yes. Yes, I would. Bill's my brother. We need to say farewell.

Farewell, thought Ferdie, moved by Jack's choice of words. He is a good man, he thought. Could you have said that of William? He wasn't a bad man. He was charming, witty, good company, but he wasn't a good man. Would I want that for my epitaph? he wondered. Emulate Saint Augustine: make me a good man but let me have a go at being witty clever fun first. Why should goodness not go with those things? He couldn't think of a reason, only that when he thought of Jack as a good man he knew William wasn't. Not in that way. Jack had fallen in love with Rosamund, years ago.

Not only was he faithful to her in life, he was faithful in death, Ferdie knew, there'd be no one else. Rosamund was past having her heart broken, not like Lynette, who'd had hers broken by a dead man, but still Jack paid attention. But then you could say that wasn't virtue so much as nature. Jack was that kind of person. The faithfulness before and after death was a symptom. I suppose it really comes down to a kind of selfishness, thought Ferdie; you know William always put himself first. But then doesn't everyone, in their own way? It's just that for some people, putting themselves first means considering other people. It was what Jack needed, being faithful, whereas William didn't; it wasn't anything to do with the people he loved.

And what about Berenice?

Too hard.

Lynette had been silent for moments, and so had everyone else, watching her. Okay, you do it, Jack.

Jack and Ferdie wrote a notice to put in the paper. Ceremony of farewell for William Cecil. Meet at Ben Boyd's tower.

Will people know where it is?

Oh yes. Great big landmark. See it for miles. Ask any local. Boyd built it for a lighthouse. But he only wanted to light it when it suited him. So the government wouldn't let him. A lighthouse has to be all the time, you see, or not at all.

Right, said Ferdie. So you can't have your own private lighthouse.

We'll just hang on to this notice for a bit, said Lynette. Until we know the date.

Ferdie rang up his mother. You know how you aren't coming down for the funeral, he said. Well, there isn't going to be one. Lynette's had him cremated already.

What, said Helen, no funeral? Isn't that . . . outrageous?

Yes, well, people think so. But they've persuaded her to have a ceremony. At Ben Boyd's tower. Cast the ashes into the sea. Jack's organising it.

Good old Jack.

That's what I thought. But anyway—I don't suppose you want to come to that?

Oh Ferdie. There was a pause. No, I think not. I'd made up my mind. I don't want to change it.

No, of course. How are you?

Oh, well. Really well. Busy.

Oh good. Busy's good, isn't it?

Better than being bored.

I reckon. Not much chance of that around here.

I suppose not.

Nerys and Acacia are here.

Nerys and—who's Acacia?

She does funerals. A funeral celebrant. Kind of new age, I suppose. Ferdie knew that for his mother this would be an entirely pejorative remark. Nice, though. Some good ideas.

Yes, I see.

She and Nerys are an item.

Really? I didn't think Nerys . . .

Lots of gossip to tell you when I see you. Shouldn't be long now.

Well, that will be nice.

Bye, Ma.

Bye, dear.

Damn. He was supposed to say Helen.

BARBARA DRINKS THE LAST OF THE WINE

Barbara found the satin nightgown in a crumple at the back of the wardrobe. She rinsed it out—no more fabulously expensive dry-cleaning—and ironed it while it was still damp. It had lost some of its gleaming ivory richness, and even after ironing was still faintly creased and crazed like the skin of an old woman. She hung it on a coathanger and thought what hard work it was. Would a woman seeking glamour in the heyday of this gown have been prepared for the work it took, or would such a person have had a lady's maid? It was a garment out of a film; film stars didn't do their own ironing. The idea of ironing kept running through her mind. Like so much work it was ephemeral. Teach a class and something of it might remain in one mind or several and be important. Ironing, vacuuming, washing up: they were keeping disorder at bay, and how interesting was that? Bring on disorder. She looked round the apartment; she'd done it well. Disorder somehow didn't happen in it. Not like the old cluttered house in Reid, full of beloved objects. People.

She had bought a bunch of grapes at the fruit shop, perfect oval green globes taut with juice. The label had said 'Product of USA' and normally she would not have bought them, but this time it had not seemed to matter. The refusal of her small purchasing power, one bunch of grapes, how could it make a difference? They were already here, in the country, had used up whatever time, trouble, fuel was necessary to get them here. And she needed grapes. She washed them and placed them on one of her white plates, and put that on her grandmother's cedar table.

She made herself a strong vodka and tonic and drank it down like medicine. Then she had a bath, long and slow and scented, with tealight candles all around, and anointed herself with the unguents of Tuscan nuns. She put on the satin nightgown; it might have gone a bit limp but still felt silky against her limbs. There were three bottles of sauvignon blanc left from a dozen that Cecil had sent her. She got one out of the fridge and poured some into a tall glass. She read the label: New Zealand, from Martinborough. She remembered Cecil saying, Martinborough, not Marlborough, notice. An altogether different terroir. More rare, more distinguished.

I see, she said, expecting that she would.

North Island, just outside Wellington. Over the hills, the Rimutakas, great steep sweeping roads. A group of winemakers carefully choosing the perfect place, no accident. Making their wine with great subtlety.

It had been good, having Cecil tell her things.

She ate one of the American green grapes and took some sips of the wine. It was very fine, and elegant, and delicate, which was a nice thing at this moment. She sat at the yellow table, taking slow sips, tasting. The double-storey window seemed very high, very wide. She could see an expanse of indigo sky, strangely lit. No stars, but an underbelly of cloud. The day was nearly done.

The yellow honey surface of the table had a smooth and waxy feel. She imagined her grandmother polishing it, rubbing in lavender-scented beeswax. She pressed her nose to it, but no trace of any odour remained. The word evanescent came into her mind. Everything is, of course. The table lasts longer than the grandmother, but one day it will be gone too. It will have a history before its final decay, but no one can guess what it will be. Certainly its family runs out here, no child or grandchild to pay attention to its bloom. Chloe could have grown up to care for it, but maybe not. People often cannot be bothered with that kind of labour. But she'd have liked the story of the grandmother from whom it came. Barbara believed that.

She went upstairs to her bedroom, gathering up the slippery folds of the nightgown so she wouldn't trip. If she fell down the stairs and hurt herself, how long would it be before someone came? It might be weeks, months. People would ring, she would float into consciousness to hear the phone's useless trill but would be able to do nothing. Pain would come in waves, and hunger. I suppose I would die of hunger, she thought. People living alone died and nobody knew. How sad that thought was. She held carefully to the rail. Not a good idea, to die of hunger.

In the bedroom she got packets and jars of pills out of a drawer. She'd been collecting them, afraid of insomnia, doling them out only when she was desperate. Her GP understood her fear of not sleeping, and gave her a script when she asked for it.

She paused to look out the window. There was the woolly-headed man walking across the car park, holding Chloe's hand. So slender she was, so tall now, such grace in her limbs, she walked with her back straight like a dancer, her steps full of energy. Why were they walking away, why weren't they coming to see her, going down the lane at the side, ringing the bell at the front gate, speaking into the intercom? Chloe's voice sweet and light, full of music, as it had always been. They went across the car park to a big black four-wheel drive, and as the girl turned to get into the car the light from a street lamp fell on her face. Of course she'd known that it wasn't Chloe. Of course. But the way her stomach fell into twisting griping spasms belied that knowledge. She took some large mouthfuls of the wine. She'd have to go downstairs and get more. Making a carry bag of the skirt of the nightgown, gathering it up and holding it in one hand so she could transport the packets and bottles of pills, holding the wine glass in the same hand so the other was free to hold the rail, mindful of not stumbling and falling down and lying in slow waves of pain over weeks, a month even. She felt the terror in each step, of falling and injuring herself.

She put more wine in her glass and sat again at the yellow table. She ate another grape. They behaved in a perfectly grape-like fashion, sitting taut on the tongue then bursting with a certain sweetness, but there wasn't much flavour. Maybe it had all leached away, in the time it had taken for them to get from there to here. Pale green clouds of grape flavour, floating over the Pacific Ocean. Would they have come by plane? Surely a boat would be too slow. Bunches of grapes, loaded into the belly of a cargo plane. It seemed improbable.

She emptied the bottles of tiny coral-coloured pills on to the table. Then she popped the others out of their foil packets. There seemed a lot. She pushed them with her fingers in a pile to the side then slid them one at a time to form letters, the letters spelling out a name. Capital C, H, L, O, E. It didn't take long, and didn't take all the pills. She didn't think of spelling out another name. She thickened up the letters of the one she already had.

She needed another bottle of wine. The elegant Martinborough sauvignon blanc was just wine now, delicious, but no longer insisting on its suavity, its elegance. She swallowed the C. The pills were small, enamelled, easily sliding down with a good mouthful of wine. She stood up and walked over to the window. It seemed very large, tall, towering. Across the road the restaurants had their names written in neon light, long swooping words that she couldn't read, they seemed to have blobbed together as though dissolved in coloured water. She saw Chloe sitting in the window of the bistro wearing a lemon-yellow jumper, but when she squinted her eyes to see better, the glass of the window squinted maliciously back and the girl's face wobbled out of view.

She went back to the yellow table and looked at the remaining letters. After a while thinking about it she swallowed down the E. Another period of time passed. She looked at the H, the L, the O. They didn't seem to make any sense. She sat with her head resting on one hand, using the other to hold the glass and pick up the pills, carefully, carefully does it. She bunched the L into her fist and swallowed it, and after a bit did the same with the H. The O remained, very round. O, she said. She felt tired. There wasn't much wine in the bottle, she poured it into her glass and went over to the sofa. She drank some and lay down. It was very comfortable. A bit cold. She'd turned the heating up but lying down in a flimsy nightie she felt chilly. There was a soft wool throw folded on one of the sofa arms, or was it on a chair, she couldn't seem to reach. It was very comfortable on the sofa. The room was turning but quite gently, horizontal, safe. The sofa held her. She thought, I cannot come to a bad end here, and a small laugh caught in her throat.

She was right about the likelihood of nobody finding her fallen to the bottom of the stairs, washed in waves of pain, slowly starving. It would have been a long time. But she did not have to find this out. She was comfortable on the sofa, safe, nothing hurting, the world turning, herself going to sleep and then not waking up. Not knowing that, or how cold she became, or how many weeks it was before people came and found her.

LYNETTE VISITS THE SHOP

When it came to the point, Jack didn't want any help with his words for William. He was my brother, I'll do it, he said to Ferdie. You should do some of your own, though. That's a usual thing.

So we'll have a number of speeches?

It's the usual thing.

Jack tried to get Lynette to set a date for the ceremony.

Not yet a bit, she said. I want to get things sorted out first.

Ferdie would have liked to say, What things?, but could not be so rude. He and Jack caught one another's glance over Lynette's head.

She said, I've got to sort out the shop.

Isn't Janice looking after it?

Can't do that forever. And she's going overseas.

Jack said, I think I have to get back. You can let me know when you want to come down. I'll do my words at home— that'll work better.

Oh Jack. Do you have to go?

I better, he said. Can't leave the chooks any longer. Well, another day.

Ferdie said, I have to go too. I'm feeling worried about all the work I'm not doing.

Oh Ferdie, said Lynette. Oh, now I feel bad. Why don't I set you up in the study, with my computer?

I've got to get back to London, he said. I can't really do anything here. The gods are only dead if you believe them so. I'm worried about believing.

Oh dear, said Lynette. It was clear she had no idea what he meant, but then he wasn't sure himself.

Jack said, The gods are only dead if we stop worshipping them, and looked surprised. So did Ferdie.

Lynette wasn't worried, she'd made her mild protest and was accepting their departure.

You'll miss the casting of the ashes, said Jack.

I'll have to, said Ferdie. But I'll write some words, if you like.

That would be good, said Jack.

Ferdie could see that they were all accepting departures. Nerys and Acacia came to say goodbye. Acacia had a funeral to prepare. They said they'd like to come to Eden for the ceremony, but Ferdie thought they probably wouldn't.

I'll let you know when it's going to happen, said Lynette.

Yes please, they said.

They could see that Lynette was taking her time over working out the next stages. When you think, said Ferdie, William was such a control freak. Death must be hard for control freaks.

Lynette laughed. Watch out, I'll assume the mantle.

Go for it, said Aurora.

Jack shook Ferdie's hand and invited him to come fishing, one day.

One day, said Ferdie. Yes, I'd like that. Won't be soon, but one day. He meant it.

Cezary came down to take Aurora back. She went to the airport to meet him. Ferdie had imagined he would be big and fair, but he was small and dark with a lean face, he spoke lively English in a rich deep voice with a faint accent. Ferdie put out a lunch of bread and cheese, salad and grapes; Lynette fetched the tall glasses and a bottle of riesling. Cezary wouldn't have any because of driving; he announced that they would leave immediately after lunch. He sat beside Aurora and hovered over her, his brow furrowed. She called him Honey. She ate no cheese and drank no wine. Ferdie savoured the dry honey taste of the riesling, knowing that his days of wine with lunch would soon be over.

He asked Cezary about his dream book. Ah, he said, it goes slowly. Since I noticed many patients report strange dreams after they have been for a while on the heart-lung machine I have been collecting them. It is patient work. Patient, he smiled. And I am not sure about the interpretation of these dreams.

You're going to write about what they mean?

Yes. Dreams are dreams, however bizarre. It is what they are telling that matters.

That sounds quite difficult, said Ferdie.

But you know this, I think, that the things that are hard are the things that are worth doing. Look at you yourself.

When Lynette was out of earshot, Aurora muttered to Ferdie, Has she found out about the will? I don't mean I want to know what's in it, just whether she knows.

Whether he had one or not?

Ferdie! He was a lawyer!

Just the kind of person to die intestate.

Oh, there was one, said Lynette, coming back in. Just what you'd expect. Perfect William. No surprises. Except perhaps in the final worth of the estate.

They looked at her, but she was pouring wine, and clearly wasn't going to say any more.

On television they have the family solicitor reading the will, said Aurora. Usually to gasps of horror.

I wouldn't worry about that, said Lynette. Small legacies all round. You'll hear soon enough.

After lunch, Aurora hugged Ferdie. Stay in touch, she said. Email me, I'll write back. She suddenly looked contrite. I'm ditching you, aren't I? Or shall I take you back to Sydney, now?

I'll be all right, he said. He liked the idea of the bus, its solitude.

No, said Lynette. He can't go yet.

I have to, soon.

Come to the shop with me, said Lynette, then you can go.

The pavement outside was still stained from the vandalising of the cumquats. Inside there were a few sale bins, from the work Lynette and Janice had been doing on the day of William's death, but generally it was its elaborately ordered self, with its arcane and expensive objects seductively displayed.

Aren't they beautiful, said Ferdie. I don't even know what most of them are for. But they are beautiful.

They're a kind of pinnacle of ancient generations of arts and trades. Skills and techniques and ancient knowledge.

Is that what people buy them for?

Are you suggesting it's just because they're cute and decorative?

It's something of a mystery to me.

Of course they're cute and decorative, and I'm sure that's all some people think. But they're useful, said Lynette. I use them. I have in the past.

A young woman in jeans and white shirt and navy-blue butcher's apron came up to them. Can I do anything, Mrs Cecil? she asked.

No, Hannah, I'm just looking, said Lynette, and laughed. You know, she said to Ferdie, I had decided I was going to sell the shop. Get rid of everything.

Yeah? You'd do that?

Well, I was going to. But now I look at it, I'm thinking I won't. It's too nice.

Yes. And I think you'd make yourself very unhappy.

Will the shop make me happy? But no, not the question. It does work. I know how to do it. It keeps me off the streets.

She peered at a shelf. Mind you, it is nice, but if I don't pay some attention it might not be soon. I think I'd better do that. Leave William in the cupboard till the spring, and work on this place. And after that, take Erin on a buying trip. She might as well start learning the business, even if she doesn't want it. Will you mind not being here for the throwing ceremony?

Ferdie said, I saw a photograph, in a gallery in London. Of a man's ashes being thrown into a river. As they fell they assembled themselves into his shape. They were a kind of pale dust, they shimmered, and the photograph caught them forming the shape of a man. The photographer's father, it was, the ashes were.

His ghost, said Lynette, floating above the river. I'll get someone to take a photo of William's ashes, in case that happens. She shivered. Before he's dashed to pieces on the rocks. Do you believe in ghosts, Ferdie?

Only as figments of the imagination.

She took his hand, and stared around at the shelves.

It is full of images of order, said Ferdie. Same with same, like with like, in all this mad variety. It's a taxonomy, and taxonomies are wonderful things. You are lucky.

On the counter were free postcards. People could use them as gift cards when they bought presents, or just take them away. Ferdie picked one with rows of wooden spoons and whisks making patterns. He addressed it to Berenice, and wrote, My stepmother's shop. It is full of beautiful taxonomies.

They walked out of the shop, Lynette calling over her shoulder, Thanks Hannah, I'll be in tomorrow morning, we'll get to work on that sale we advertised. She went on, I'm glad you came, Ferdie, it's been good having you here, you've helped.

Never got the olives planted.

Oh, I'll get a man in for that. It's what I've always done. I'll be surprised at how little has changed. No, you've been lovely. She gave him a little hug around his waist. Shall I come and see you in London?

Yes please.

I thought it might be the end of the family, but it won't be, will it.

Not if we don't let it.

Not that William ever did much towards holding it together. No, you'd have to say his line was more breaking up.

So, nothing will change. You will still be the one holding us together. I'm thinking, he said, Erin and I have ties of blood, and Aurora and I, but there are ties of family, what were once chosen ties, and they come to be binding. You're not my blood, but you are my family.

A stepmonster, said Lynette.

You know not that.

Let's have a cup of coffee. She turned into the cafe they were passing, which was also a bakery. It had a glass cabinet full of tarts. Lemon, custard, apple, passionfruit, mandarin, grapes in a reddish juice, gooseberry. Rows and rows of them, as big as small saucers. Other rows, of eclairs, and those cakes like plump little nuns with round heads called réligieuses, and small brioches.

Would you like a tart, Ferdie? she asked. It's like France, isn't it, you can look at all this stuff and feast your eyes, you don't need to eat it. But I think today we will. Yes.

He chose one mandarin, and one of the grapey ones. The woman next to him asked for her apple tart to be heated up.

I'm afraid we don't do that, madame, said the waitress.

What, said the woman, I never heard of that. Just stick it in the microwave.

We don't have a microwave.

Lynette bought one to take home to Erin. Passionfruit. I have to watch that she keeps eating, she said.

I don't know, Ferdie, she said. I won't sell the shop yet, I'll get it in really good order. But I might after that. I might not have the energy.

Sell it and go and live in the south of France.

Everybody's dream idea. I don't think so.

You're young . . .

Don't tell me I'll get married again.

Ferdie grinned. Okay. I'm not saying it. But who knows. The world is full of things to do.

The next morning Ferdie made coffee and grabbed Lynette before she started drinking wine. I've been thinking, he said.

Oh yes?

Yes. One of those long nights where you think and don't sleep.

Lynette turned her head and looked at him sidelong.

Yes. And you can't do this, you know. You do know, don't you.

Of course I can. I've started doing what I want, not what I ought. So I can.

Yes, said Ferdie, but not yet a bit. I think we have to have that ceremony for William now.

Lynette folded her arms on the table and rested her head on them. She sighed, not noisily. He used to call me Linnet, you know. I used to like that. Though, I suppose, not much lately. Nobody ever will, now.

But he used to, that's the thing. You can remember that, it's lovely. Especially if you do the right thing now. You have always been a woman who behaves well.

Married to a man who always behaved badly.

Not always. And we loved him. He liked to be loved.

It's all too hard, Ferdie.

No it's not. We can do it.

We?

It's your moment for delegation.

It's too late. Everyone's gone.

Going. We can catch them, maybe, but if not it doesn't matter.

Okay. Fix it. We'll go down to Eden on Friday and do it on Saturday.

Then it'll be done, and you'll feel a lot happier.

It'll probably be vile weather with a howling gale and the ashes'll blow back all over us and get stuck in our hair and eyelashes and teeth.

We'll shut our eyes and mouths, at least. Ferdie laughed. It'll be a lovely still winter's day, brilliantly sunny, you'll see.

Oh, so you control the weather now, do you?

Do you want me to put a notice in the paper?

Do we have to? Couldn't we just tell people?

That's hard work. Anyway, putting a notice in the paper is telling people.

I'll leave it to you, said Lynette.

Jack called in to say goodbye again. He said, Good. It's the right thing. People could stay with me, well, Lynette, but I think she'd prefer the Seahorse Inn. Built in 1840-something, by the same Ben Boyd as the tower. Bit of a crook, he seems to have been. On a grand scale. Took people's money as investments and lost it.

I think Lynette might like somewhere a bit newer, bit more luxurious.

Oh, it's new and luxurious now. All done up, hardly a sign of the original. I'll ring up if you like. What about you, would you like to stay with me?

Yes please, said Ferdie.

She's doing the right thing, said Jack.

Yes. Except I dunno what William's got to do with Eden.

The sea, said Jack. His boyhood was by the sea.

PEPITA GOES TO DINNER

It was a morning in late summer, the leaves on the great trees round the village green a little dusty, their green dark and worn. There was no change of colour yet and no sign of a break in the hot weather. At ten o'clock the manicurist came, as she did every week, a sweet girl, and good at what she did. She seemed about fifteen, but wasn't. She cleaned off last week's varnish, filed her nails in the shape she had learned Pepita liked, soaked them in some scented soapy water, dried them in a soft towel and rubbed her hands with cream. They were small hands, with shapely long fingers, the veins and tendons showing and the skin age-spotted, but elegant even so. Sometimes the girl, who was called Vivienne, chatted to her about her life in the village, an artless little runnel of conversation that Pepita listened to in a slightly dozy fashion. She knew the girl thought she was a sleepy old lady, and that suited Pepita. Listening was quite comforting but there was nothing she wanted to say to her.

Vivienne began painting the nails, base coat, several coats of polish, the finishing varnish. You have lovely nails, the girl said. So large and oval and smooth.

The colour was a kind of dusky pink that would match her silk taffeta cocktail dress. Pepita said, I like this ashes of roses colour, it's very pleasing.

Ashes of roses, said the girl. The label says Phantôme de Fleur. She pronounced all the words as though they were English.

Ashes, ghosts—they're much the same thing.

The girl left her with her hands resting on a small pillow, waiting for the varnish to dry and harden.

The finishing coat is very quick-drying, said Vivienne. But best be on the safe side. I'll let myself out.

She said these things every week. She liked saying them, and Pepita found herself soothed by them. Vivienne was a nice child, pleasant looking; nothing remarkable about her features but her skin was lovely, fine-textured, very white and clear, with a faint natural rose about her cheeks, and dark lashes that fluttered as she concentrated on her work. Pepita once asked her about the make-up she used, and Vivienne blushed a bit and said, None really, just moisturiser, and Pepita said, Very wise. To herself she said, it is youth that looks like that. When she gets older she will be a woman with skin still lovely, but it will not have that bloom of youth, that downy smoothness, that luminous freshness. Each of those phrases had a melancholy absence. She sighed faintly to herself. It was a long time since she'd possessed any such things, and when she had she'd not known it.

She sat with her hands on the small pillow long after the varnish had dried. She probably doesn't know it either, she said to herself. Next time I'll tell her, so she can enjoy it before it fades.

After a while the lawyer came. This was not a weekly habit, though not uncommon, and it was not a social call. Pepita took out a small cedarwood chest and they discussed certain papers. Notes were made, documents signed. There, she said, it is all in order, is it not?

Perfectly, said the lawyer. It is of a textbook orderliness.

After he went she sat for a while longer, looking out the window at the greenness of the trees. The village was very pretty at this season. Village was what it called itself, though a colder glance might have said suburb. She felt beautifully calm, watching the green, the pond, the little school beside the church; she could not see beyond and did not need to think about what might be there.

She ate a peach and a banana and after this lunch went to bed with a book and had a long sleep. Her nap she called it. Then she had a scented bath and put on the ashes of roses dress. Its silk taffeta rustled mysteriously. She put on some Joy by Patou. All the men who bought her perfume knew this was what she wore. She had been wearing it for almost as long as it was old. It was invented in the Great Depression, a scent wonderfully glamorous and extravagant, to cheer people up. Apparently people buy perfume, and lipstick, in times of public financial stress. She had read that there were twenty-eight dozen roses and a thousand jasmine flowers in every ounce. She loved the smell of it, late in the evening. Ashes of roses. Phantom of roses. Deep, precious, complicated. So many flowers perishing to make it. But not perishing, preserved.

Tonight she was dining with Andrew. That happened about once a year. He would come and collect her in a car. Andrew expected to be chancellor when the current party lost power. She had taught him to speak as if born to rule, with just a faint tinge of a vernacular, to add sincerity. A long way from the newsagency in a Manchester suburb where he had grown up.

They went to a restaurant on the river which had two Michelin stars. I expect you are worried it might be vulgar, he said in the car, but I don't think it is. No molecular gastronomy, and none of this head-to-tail eating-the-pig business either. Just nice modern interesting food.

They sat in a kind of conservatory and watched the late summer light on the river, the way it thickened perceptibly into twilight. Just out of sight was a weir, you could hear the gentle falling of the water over it, a slight, restless, never-changing sound. They began with champagne, as always—The '96 Pol Roger is drinking very well at the moment, Andrew said—and went on to a decent burgundy. They raised their glasses in a toast. The ashes of roses dress was neither new nor fashionable, but it was beguiling, slipping prettily to one side over her smooth round shoulder, and she smiled at him over her glass. Her eyes sparkled.

Well, Andrew, she said, this is lovely, as always. Now, tell me, how are you?

So he did, his wife, his two daughters, at present at school, in London, maybe boarding school soon, if they could bear to part with them.

Ah, yes.

Such advantages, for them. None that I can see, for us.

That is the nature of children, she said, that the parents sacrifice themselves. Oh my, how sententious I am.

Wise, as always. He patted her hand. He knew that what she was looking forward to was gossip. Once she'd said to him, You know, my dear, there are certain things in life that are absolutely trivial and absolutely essential, like scented tea in Rockingham cups—they were drinking it as she spoke. Like gossip. He was surprised. He'd imagined her upright and somehow beyond such things. Gossip is the story of our lives, she said. It is the way a society works out how it is to behave. Our manners, our morals, our mores.

After that he always liked to have a choice piece of gossip for her. Tonight it was the death of a cabinet minister whose nickname was Porky. Not because he was particularly fat, but because he was infamous for his pork barrelling. He was always drawn in political cartoons as a very fat pig.

They say, said Andrew, that he died on the job. The cardinal's death, he murmured.

Ah, said Pepita. That kind of job.

It's not in the papers, he said. Yet.

But it will be. Without doubt.

With a wife standing by.

Grieving widow.

So it goes, said Andrew.

I suppose she knows.

She is in the country. But yes, she must.

Pepita looked pensive. Indeed. So it goes, she said.

Now, said Andrew, the lady . . .

She is known?

Some people think so. Cynthia Somerton, the novelist.

Nineteenth-century bodice-ripping melodrama.

Exactly. Apparently the name is a pseudonym. She's the daughter of a duke. So she's Lady Cynthia.

Is she? I wonder. Surely the title goes with her real name; she couldn't use it with the pseudonym.

No . . . said Andrew. Except, maybe, in her skin she is a lady, whatever name she uses.

Ah, who knows. Whatever happened to etiquette these days. Pepita made a delicate flying-away motion with her hand. The grandmother's ring, too big for her now, slid off her finger and flew across the room, flashing and glittering, landing with a chink. Like a comet, said Pepita.

A waiter saw it as it flashed and where it fell. He picked it up and brought it to her on a silver tray. I must be more careful, she said. It was my grandmother's; I mustn't lose it. Not now. Cynthia Somerton—I haven't read any, have you?

God no. She's not young—he showed remarkably good taste for once, said Andrew, neatly saving himself from what might have been a faux pas. And of course he's no youth. Still, what a way to go.

Good, or bad? asked Pepita in a demure voice.

Andrew gave a snort of laughter.

Nice for him, I suppose. Hell for everyone else.

Poor old Porky. It will be part of his story forever, said Andrew. He will never escape his death.

Younger than he might have expected, too. He wasn't sixty.

A child, said Pepita. You know, I often find those words of Macbeth's coming into my head. *Nothing in his life became him like the leaving it.*

Oh yes?

Yes. It suggests a noble death, it seems an admirable thing. But he's talking about the thane of Cawdor, who was a traitor, and executed for it. A death well met, but is that much, in the circumstances?

Maybe it is, if the life was so ignoble. A bad life, redeemed in death. Whereas poor old Porky, a generally good life made farcical.

I expect cardinals managed better, keeping secrets. Though people knew, otherwise they wouldn't have given it the name.

Andrew said, Would it be less a sniggery topic if the lady had stayed at the scene, called a doctor, acted with dignity?

Interesting question. Imagine if it had been his wife whose embrace he died in. Would that have made a difference?

You never hear of that. I suppose it's not scandalous, dying in bed with your wife, people keep it quiet, out of respect. And of course in such a case I don't imagine it's a cardinal's death.

No, it has to be adulterous.

Pepita refused pudding, but drank a small cup of black coffee.

How can you do that? asked Andrew. Doesn't it keep you awake all night?

No, said Pepita.

He was finishing the burgundy. She had not drunk her share of it, but had had enough. That was the way of it, enjoy your small portion and let the man have the lion's share. Roaring and shaking his golden mane. Of course not literally. Not when she'd trained them.

She'd never been involved in a cardinal's death. But then she'd avoided a lot of messy things. Marriage. Children. Circumspection, she'd been good at it. Regrets she'd never allowed.

The river was dark now. Only the rustling of the weir kept its memory alive. The sound came softly through the French windows.

Perhaps, a cognac?

Pepita was about to say, Thank you, no, then she thought, why not. That would be delightful, she said.

The moon suddenly slid up over the trees on the opposite bank. There was suddenly white blanching light and inky shadows.

The cognac comes in small tulip glasses. Pepita takes a small sniff, the fumes rush up her nose, down her throat, hit her stomach. I had forgotten. She gives a little laugh. Who would have thought you could forget the smell of cognac. She takes a sip, there's the same rush down to her stomach.

A very good digestif, said Andrew.

Pepita smiled, but to herself rather than Andrew. She was seeing her life through all the decades, herself a small woman, holding a glass, sipping, sipping, sipping. And the sparkling of her eyes over the rim of the glass, at the man who paid, who was thanked in the charm of her company. She put the glass on the table and let her lids slide down, then raised her head so she could see the river. There is the moon walking on water, she said.

The moon followed them all the way home, playfully nipping from side to side of the car, carrying the inky shadows and pallid light with it. So many moons. How many moons have I seen? she wondered. Not all that many really, thirteen a year multiplied by ninety; ninety will do. How old was I when I first recognised the moon? That was many moons ago, as primitive people used to say in novels. Andrew beside her was quiet, too; maybe he was thinking of how to oust the current lot from power. Probably not. She pulled her pashmina more closely round her neck. It was warm in the car, but in her bones there was a chill.

She thanked Andrew in her pretty manner when he helped her out of the car, took her arm up the path to her door and unlocked it for her. The golden light of a lamp lit up the hall. He would not come in. *À bientôt*, he said, and kissed her hand.

She heard the car drive off into the moonlit silence. She was tired, not like her. But first. She took off her grandmother's ring, watched its half-hoop of diamonds catch the light and flash it brilliantly back. A girl's best friend: no, they weren't. But nice. She put the ring in its small plum-coloured box, the velvet worn threadbare, clicked it shut and put the box in a thick brown envelope on which she had written in her beautiful hand: For Ferdie, for his love. She put it in the box with the lawyer's papers and went to bed. So cold she was, so cold. The electric blanket was on but it didn't seem to help. She rested her foot against her calf, it was as cold as stone on a frosty morning. Perhaps I am

271

turning into my own marble monument, she thought, feeling herself sinking into sleep. It did cross her mind that perhaps she was sleeping herself to death, but she lost consciousness before she could examine it.

TO EDEN

Lynette drove down on Friday, dropping Ferdie off at Jack's and going on to the Seahorse Inn with Erin. They had a room upstairs at the front, looking over the sea, a suite in fact. It was evident that the main business of the place was weddings. There were photograph albums artlessly strewn everywhere, the staircase had a Hollywood glamour curve, and under it was a table set with silver, glassware, linen, and white-dressed chairs with organza ribbons tied round their bosoms. In the photographs, brides peeped coyly out from behind palm trees or turned plump shoulders at stained-glass doors or glided down the gilded stairs. Erin was fascinated. I could get married here, she said. It's very commercial, said Lynette. It's a business, that's what it is. Very cold-blooded.

They went down to the bar and sat in the window looking out at the sunlight shining on the roofs of Eden across the bay, shining on the boats; watching as it was all lost as the sun slid away. A mist blew in from the water, up the slope of the shore, and the low sun shone through it so that it was thick and dusky. As the sun disappeared, Eden was lost in the distant dimness. The folded-down umbrellas on the terrace flapped like vultures.

They went out to walk across the terrace and the lawn to the edge of the bay, where the little waves rolled in, but the wind was cold and the melancholy creak of the umbrellas too gloomy. The faint pink light over Eden wasn't cheering. They went in, and ate dinner in the bistro. Oysters are off, said the waitress, the rains and winds have stirred up the mud in the lakes and they can't be harvested. I think oysters were William's favourite food, said Lynette. It would have been nice to eat them and think of him.

Back in their suite Erin couldn't make the television work. They asked the receptionist who had turned into the barmaid but she couldn't fix it. I think it's just generally bad reception, she said. Bad reception, said Lynette.

An early night, said Lynette. Did you bring a book? She looked out over the water, it was pitch dark with occasional twinkles of light; nothing that meant anything.

They sat in a bow window to eat breakfast. The bay was a bowl full of glitter from the slanting sun. I can't look at it, said Erin, it's too bright. Jack and Ferdie came and Ferdie drove them all in Lynette's car to Ben Boyd's tower. They had to park the car and put money into an envelope since it was a national park, and walk some distance to the tower. There were dying melaleucas falling about the track, and living ones making a gothic arch above it. These were wind-sculpted into bright green cushion shapes. Erin read a lot of information off panels along the track. It's very pedagogic, said Ferdie.

The tower's made of Pyrmont sandstone, Erin told them. Very beautiful it was, pink and greenish colours, walls more than a metre thick. Skilfully made. It was meant to be a lighthouse, she read, but Ben Boyd wanted it only for his ships, and you can't have that. A lighthouse has to work all the time, otherwise it's too dangerous. So he used it as a tower to look out for whales.

I wonder how many people he ruined in pursuit of his grandiose schemes, said Ferdie. Crook that he was.

They were walking along a fine wooden boardwalk. Beside it was a big piece of flat rock carved out in squares. For the whale spotters, said Erin, they amused themselves playing draughts and stuff. Ferdie looked at the old scored lines, imagined bored men filling in time. Under this still sun. The wind hadn't got up, you could hear the distant sea splashing against the cliffs, they were held in a space of silence within the shell of the sound of the sea. He looked at Lynette; she was frowning, he imagined her thinking, this isn't William's place. Erin had been carrying the box of ashes but it had got too heavy and she passed it on to Ferdie.

They came out on to a fenced lookout. The sea was not close, if they threw ashes from there they'd fall on to the sloping cliff. Jack went off on a path to the side and found a rock edge dropping sharply down to the water, very level till it fell away, pointing to oblivion. The red rocks were jumbled below it, the sea smashed against them, flaring up in jets of foam. Lynette took the lid off the box. The ashes were white and chalky, with odd shards of bone. Gingerly she put in her hand and took some, cast them over the cliff. They fell down into the sea. Erin next. Be careful, said her mother, don't throw yourself in. Jack put his arms round her. They all threw in handfuls and then Lynette took the box and upended it, the ashes shimmered down into the sea. Goodbye, my daddy, said Erin. Goodbye, William, said the others. What about our speeches? said Jack.

Go ahead, said Lynette, and Jack took out a piece of paper and read his words. Mainly that William was a son, a brother, a husband, a father, that he loved and was loved. Then Ferdie spoke some sentences remembering his father's Citroëns and driving to Sydney, the story about Lake George. The sun shone down on this sheltered cliff top, very warm, ticking with its quiet life.

So much for people coming, said Lynette. The notice in the paper didn't bring anybody at all. I said it wouldn't.

But we have paid due ceremony, said Ferdie, that is what matters.

It is best with just us, Mummy, said Erin.

They went back to the whale lookout and sat on a bench there for a little while, in the shell of the silence inside the sound of the sea.

It is peaceful, said Erin.

They looked across the bay at the little settlements, along at the bottle shape of the wood-chip factory. There were no boats at its wharf. When they were driving in, the empty timber trucks had gone screaming past, bucketing all over the road, making Ferdie pull aside nervously.

Do you want to have a look at the old whaling station? he asked.

No, said Lynette. We're not tourists.

When they got back to the Seahorse Inn they went to the restaurant for lunch. Lynette ordered a bottle of white wine.

Do you want to go back this afternoon? said Ferdie. Lynette looked at him. I could drive, he said, I'm happy to do that.

Thanks, said Lynette. She drank most of the bottle, Jack had a light beer, Ferdie half a glass. In the car going back she said, before she closed her eyes and went to sleep, It was a good idea, Ferdie. It's done now. I know I grizzle, but I am grateful.

My daddy's in the sea, said Erin. Now he can go round and round the world forever.

FERDIE TAKES THE BUS

Ferdie took the bus to Sydney from the Jolimont Centre. Once he had despised this trip: only the elderly and the poor and the very young took the bus. But now he liked it, it was easy and quick and you saw a different landscape from a high bus than a low car. You could see over the bridges to the rivers deep in their gorges, observe the tidy rows of olives, see untouched wild country beside neat field patterns, complicated and ancient-seeming. You could contemplate. Take the bus and contemplate. This trip he was tired, and dozed, falling into a troubled sleep as his head bumped against the window pane. And he dreamt.

It was one of those dreams in which you know you are dreaming. Not the sort where you can control what happens, use your will to change things, but the sort where you are mildly aware of yourself observing this phenomenon, unable to do anything about it. It was a dream of Berenice, of her bed covered with its silvery green sheets and her white body lying on it. It was a kind of cliché by now, but none the worse for that. She was almost face down, so he could see the curve of her bottom. The colours were strange, their essential nature washed from them, so they were darker or paler than themselves, her skin like a black and white photograph, the sheets more silver than green, her hair a dark crimson tangle round her head.

He was saying to himself that this was a good dream to be having, that he should be grateful for this gift of Berenice naked and so poignantly there. Then he became aware of another figure coming into the scene, walking slowly from the right-hand side, a man, also naked. He recognised his father from the particular flaring curve of his thighs, and the way his hair grew in slight side-burns on his cheeks; he remembered saying once that William's hair was never quite fashionable, either too much sideburn or too little; William liked to say that he prided himself on his consistency. What he did not recognise was the enormous erection, the penis pointing upwards in a tense curve.

The man climbed on to the bed and knelt over the Berenice figure, bent down and plunged between the buttocks, began to move. Ferdie wanted to look away but he couldn't, it was a dream and he was obliged to be observing it. He groaned, and must have given a twitch in his own body, because his head bumped hard against the window and he woke up. The girl next to him, who'd spent the trip till now on her phone texting, Ferdie admiring the speed of her thumbs, gave him an odd look. He coughed, making a groan-like sound at the same time, wondering why he was bothered about what this girl thought. He looked out of the window at lines of olive trees that swept away as the bus sped past.

The dream disturbed him. Staring at that swiftly passing land-scape, trying to remark to himself on the things he saw, he felt its powerful presence in his mind as something that had actually happened, that he had seen. He felt angry with William; Berenice was *his* lover. How typical of his father, to see something that belonged to someone else and simply walk in and take it. Belonged wasn't the right word, but it would do for now. She certainly did not belong to William. All his life William had done that, had picked whatever he desired. He had to tell himself that this wasn't fair, William hadn't done this, it was his dream, Ferdie's dream, it must be what he was thinking, and why was he thinking this, what did it say about his own fears? Did it mean he thought he wasn't the man his father was, able to come and take what he wanted? Masterful, even brutal? Ferdie had never had that thought, but maybe he should have. Whatever it meant, the dream was about Ferdie, not William. What about Berenice? Not her, either.

All the way up the highway he felt ignoble, like a person who had spied on someone else's intimate moment, he felt grubby and weighted down by what he had seen, and no matter how often he said to himself, it was a dream, you fool, it was your subconscious banging about, he could not rid himself of the sense that he'd done something wrong.

He took out his book, he'd brought *The Golden Bough*, thinking he'd have a look at some things. The girl next to him put her phone away and said, The key to all the mythologies, hey.

He thought he must have misheard. Pardon, he said. Why did you say that? He looked at her. She had a plait of long straight hair hanging over her shoulder, and brown eyes. She was quite pretty in a plain sort of way. He wondered if he was inventing her.

I always think that's the book that Casaubon wanted to write.

And failed.

Oh. She shook her head. That hypocrite Casaubon. All ego and image. Pretending he was doing the work, not even admitting to himself that it wasn't happening. In his terms he's rotting in hell.

I sometimes wonder if I'm a Casaubon, said Ferdie.

What? I don't think so. If you can think that you aren't. She laughed in a rather rude way. She got a book out of her bag. *Daniel Deronda*. On the back cover he saw the familiar portrait of George Eliot gazing out from her heavy loops of hair. This girl could probably fasten her hair like that. She had a pad of yellow post-it stickers and wrote copious notes with a fine felt pen and stuck them on as she read. She was right, he thought. He wasn't a Casaubon. He ought to have known himself well enough to know that. The thought was so comforting that he didn't try to talk to her again. That was enough. He wasn't a hypocrite. He'd know and would admit to himself if he couldn't do it. He closed his eyes and smiled.

When the bus arrived in Sydney the girl stood on the pavement waiting for her luggage, which seemed to be right at the back. He suddenly said, Can I have your phone number? She looked at him, not unfriendly exactly, but not very keen. Oh, she said, I shall be in England next week. So shall I, he said, delight in his voice. She still gazed at him, then pulled the fine felt pen from her pocket and wrote an email address on the back of his hand. She shrugged on a vast backpack and walked off briskly, giving him a small wave as she went. He watched her, still delighted.

He couldn't see Helen. But actually he was looking straight at her. His eyes slid past her without registering and he stood waiting, thinking she must be late. He looked up and down the sandstone cloister of the railway station, wondering which direction she would be coming from. The arches were worn and nubbly, the keystones heavily marked. The traffic growled and hooted, the sun shone and there was a smell of salt in the wind, with car exhaust as well, and a gritty chill. The air was noisy and palpable, different from the stillness of Canberra, though he knew he would be used to it soon. People hurried past in that anxious way of city walkers, expecting no charm or pleasure, simply wanting to get somewhere else. It wasn't until she waved and called, staying near her car which was parked in a dangerously illegal spot, that he realised that this young woman was his mother. He was speechless, and greeted her with a hug and a kiss and got into the car without saying anything.

When he began with a tentative Ma, she said, Hang on a bit, dear, I can't negotiate city traffic and talk at the same time. That's the definition of a supermodel, isn't it? Can't walk and talk at the same time. Oy, watch it, she said to the car in front, which had changed lanes with a tricky sideways glide that made her brake drastically. So he took in the fact that she was wearing a soft and shapely jumper with close-fitting jeans in silence. On her feet were pretty little flat shoes. Ferdie thought, in astonishment, this is the woman William married. He didn't remember ever seeing her before.

When they got to the house she sent him to his room with his luggage. On his pillow was an envelope addressed to him. In it was a postcard from Berenice. A picture of the Arnolfini wedding. A tit for tat, he supposed. He wasn't familiar with her writing. It was easy to read.

Dear Ferdie, I want to tell you straightaway. I am getting married. Probably next spring. He is in IT too. He works in France. I know you will wish me well. XXBerenice.

She drew circles over her letter i's. He looked at the painting. He'd always thought it very beautiful. Green was Berenice's chosen colour. The woman didn't look at all like her. He remembered enough of what she looked like to be sure of that. He felt hollow, but calm as well. This is clarity, he said to himself. This sorts things.

In fact it wasn't just clarity, it was lightness, and it was certainty. Berenice turned into a woman who worked in a campus computer shop, who hardly cared for picnics and didn't like reading. She stopped being a constellation in the heavens, an arty photograph on decoloured sheets. It was like being expelled from Eden: the world was all before him, where to choose. Entirely a good thing, really. Exciting. He didn't think he was just telling himself this, trying to convince.

When he went back to Helen she was sitting on the sofa with an opened bottle of riesling.

I decided I wasn't ready to join the angels yet, she said.

What?

The marble creatures in the cemetery. Remember I said I've always had this fancy that they walk the streets and if they want to they can make you follow, you have to join them. You can't refuse.

I remember you said it. I wasn't sure you believed it.

Ah, well, probably not. But it's a thought I've often had, that I would have to go with them. But I've decided to give it up.

Ferdie was uneasy. Were you really worried?

Helen looked at him, wrinkling her eyes. Lynette told me once that I looked like an angel on a tombstone, she said, carved in black basalt. Did she mean I was obdurate, I suppose. Hard. Things don't have to be literal to be powerful images, Ferdie. You know that. I've seen—well, apprehended—those angels walking the streets round here; they don't make you feel good.

Figments, said Ferdie.

Well, anyway, I don't look like one any more.

Too young to be an angel, too much of a girl.

Her eyes sparkled. Ferdie smiled. He'd often tried to have what he would have called a real conversation with his mother but she always slipped and slid away. Superficial things were okay, she spoke in her serious and formal way about them, and listening you could think they mattered to her, but Ferdie knew they didn't. She just liked the safety of the superficial. Whereas this conversation seemed quite trivial, but he knew it wasn't.

Now he thought she might be ready to talk to him he settled back with his glass of riesling, attentive. She was saying, and he could tell with what difficulty, Shallow. It's a pretty word, isn't it. Shallow water. Shallow rivers. Shallow pools. But then, when you get to people, or their responses, no, not attractive at all. Nobody would want to be described as shallow. I remember— and here she laughed—I remember a review of a book of poems by a man who used to go diving off the Barrier Reef, taking a waterproof pen and paper (I didn't know you could get such things!) and actually writing the poems underwater. The heading on the review was: 'The reports of his depth have been greatly exaggerated'. The whole piece went on like that, cruel but very funny.

Were the poems any good?

Well, apparently not. The poet I recall was considered promising in his youth, I even bought one of his books, but it seems he has not fulfilled that early promise. Helen sighed. Well, she said, what's new.

Ferdie looked at her, in the new rose-pink cashmere jumper that brought colour to her face and perhaps light to her eyes, the firm jeans that neatly fitted her slender figure. There was a cyclamen in a dark blue pot on the coffee table, thickly covered in flowers the same colour as the jumper. The flowers, the glasses with their round bowls half full of straw-coloured wine were beautiful to look at, like a painting. They were an illumination in the dark room, that made his heart lift and feel joyful. He smoothed his fingers around the dark blue ceramic pot.

I came for a death, he said, my father's death. I don't know what I hoped for. Some meaning, I suppose.

Oh, we always want meaning. We want to find meaning. I'm thinking, meaning is what we make for ourselves. Do you know that T.S. Eliot poem, 'Journey of the Magi'?

The silken girls bringing sherbet. And the old white horse galloping away across the paddock. That's death, isn't it.

The pale horse. I often think of those travellers wondering about being brought all this way, and was it for birth, or death? That they'd thought the two were different, but that this birth was so hard and bitter it was like death. And I was thinking of it working in the opposite direction, that we have come all this way for death but that it is birth we may be finding.

Are you channelling William? asked Ferdie, and then wished he hadn't.

Helen was frowning. I think I can manage to quote the odd poem for myself, she said. I do read too, you know.

Yes, I know, Ma. It's just it seems to keep happening since William died. Lynette's been doing it, and it's not one of her habits. Helen looked gloomy. A birth . . . you mean Aurora, the baby?

Well, of course there's always birth to counter death. But that's very literal. She paused, her eyes looked sideways at him. Hard, she said. I mean, well, me.

Ferdie felt like crying. Instead he gave her a hug. The rose-coloured cashmere was very soft over her slender bones. She smelt of that elemental dry lavender he'd found in the bathroom cupboard, that he found disturbing.

It shouldn't have taken William's death to do it, she said. But maybe that was only one of the things. She thought of Ruth, or Nellie, looking for her shilling.

The Eliot poem ends with the old man looking forward to another death, said Ferdie, doubt in his voice.

Possibly. But maybe another death/birth. She made the slash with her finger. They are hard to tell apart. But no angels, remember, said Helen. I've got other plans.

Ferdie looked at her. She smiled, and told him.

She was going to Italy to do a course in teaching English as a second language. Then she would get a job doing that somewhere in Europe. It might be Slovenia, or Romania. That would be an adventure.

I got a flyer in the letterbox, she said. Azure blue, like the sky, very romantic. And I thought, why not?

When?

In a couple of months. I have to give notice at school.

You can come and see me, he said.

Would you like me to?

Of course. It'll be a squeeze, but so good. We'll do wonderful things. You can meet Pepita.

Not Berenice. Somehow he hadn't pictured introducing Helen to Berenice. Was that Helen's fault, or Berenice's? Or quite likely his own. But of course, now, she might be a friend, perhaps . . . But somehow he couldn't imagine her being a friend. He looked at Helen gently smiling, and realised he was taking her new appearance for granted, and that he would be proud to walk around London with this handsome woman.

I like your new clothes, he said.

Isn't this pink a great colour. I feel good in it.

After the widow's weeds.

She blushed, and frowned, and laughed a bit. And now I'm a real widow I've given them up. Oh yes, I know that's not true, that Lynette's the widow. But somehow I'm free now.

Of yourself, said Ferdie. He was liking this new daring way of speaking to his mother, without self-censoring or bowdlerising.

He was my father, he said. I came for his death. But I expected grief. And there's not. Just sadness. Maybe I wanted a birth too.

Sadness is good, said Helen. I think sadness is nourishing. Ferdie . . . maybe it's my fault. Maybe I kept you away from your father.

He considered. But you didn't, did you. Remember those car trips to Sydney. And all that time staying with him.

I reckon staying with him was staying with Lynette, really.

You're right, I suppose, said Ferdie. But you didn't keep me away. I was there for his taking.

But sadness, you know, I think that's enough. Respect, remembering, taking thought—it includes all of them.

Mm, said Ferdie. I expect I wanted revelation.

His mother sighed. Don't we all.

You found it.

From an old woman under a bush.

Ferdie looked at her.

I think it was a kind of epiphany. Always hard to explain epiphanies, they seem so unlikely. Helen poured out more wine. I think there's a time in your life when you're ready to do something, change or something, and you get sort of nudged; something you'd not even usually notice speaks to you.

Yes, he said, I see . . . hoping he would.

And it's most often not where you expect to find it.

You're lucky, he said. I need to get back and find some epiphanies of my own. I'm getting very anxious about not getting any work done.

You can think on the plane, said Helen.

A fine thought. I always find it's more like suspended animation.

I wondered if we might walk down to the pub for dinner, she said, it's fish and chips night, they do good flathead tails. They've fixed up the old upstairs dining room and now it's got views over the water. Not that that's much help at night, unless there's a moon. My shout, she said. I looked in the bank and I'm really not short of money. Shillings aren't a problem.

Careful, said Ferdie. We'll have you recklessly spending.

Oh, I think old habits die too hard.

Ferdie wasn't so sure. There was a new phone on the table. Helen blushed a bit. It's a clever thing, I'm getting the hang of it, she said.

Ferdie said, Can I send an email?

Do you know how?

I think so, said Ferdie, reading the address off the back of his hand. Hardly stopping to recall that in all the days he had been at Lynette's he hadn't wanted to write to Berenice, but now, this woman with the backpack, he couldn't wait. He typed her address: dot@dot.com. Funny. Maybe her name was Dorothea? That would be a bit much. He put his own address in the message, his big computer at home in England, explaining that this was his mother's phone, that he would be here for a day or two. Please tell me your name, he said.

They put on their coats to walk down to the pub. The streets had a winter emptiness. No stone angels whisking about. Helen put her arm through his and walked swiftly, easily, as though she were enjoying the journey. There was a moon, rising big and yellow out of the sea. Ferdie did think of William, but with a kind of finality, that he was really dead and not there any more and that his remembering would become more and more vague. Perhaps for some people the recollection of him might be grateful, for others anger, perhaps, or disappointment; some would smile, with tenderness, or grief, but he did not imagine any more weeping. There were a lot of people who would feel something, and perhaps the alternative to that could be a few people feeling a great deal, but that wasn't how it was, you couldn't choose, William's life had done that. Some small number of his family had stood on the headland by Ben Boyd's tower and watched his ashes shake down into the sea, to become part of the shredding of the water on the rocks below. Melancholy, the moment had been, but no one had wanted to cast herself into the water and join his mortal remains.

Look, said Helen, the path of the moon on the water. We should watch it while we can.

ACKNOWLEDGEMENTS

The epigraph is from Stéphane Mellarmé, *Divagations*, from a small piece called 'Long Ago, in the Margins of a Copy of Baudelaire'. Translated by Barbara Johnson, published by the Belknap Press of Harvard University Press, Cambridge, Massachusetts.

'This story begins by water' is the opening line of a story, *The Division of Love*, by Margaret Barbalet, in a collection of the same name (Penguin Books).